D1564271

Court Duel

Also by Sherwood Smith

WREN TO THE RESCUE
WREN'S QUEST
WREN'S WAR

CROWN DUEL

Court Duel

SHERWOOD SMITH

Book II of the Crown & Court Duet

HARCOURT BRACE & COMPANY
San Diego   New York   London

Requests for permission to make copies of any part of the work should be
mailed to: Permissions Department, Harcourt Brace & Company,
6277 Sea Harbor Drive, Orlando, Florida 32887-6777.

Library of Congress Cataloging-in-Publication Data
Smith, Sherwood.
Court duel / Sherwood Smith.
p.   cm.—(Crown & court duet; bk. 2)
Sequel to: Crown duel.
Summary: Brought to court by a mysterious letter, teenage Countess
Meliara finds herself the subject of all sorts of courtly intrigues
and attentions, including those of the deposed king's sister and an
ardent, secret suitor.
ISBN 0-15-201609-0
[1. Fantasy.]   I. Title.   II. Series: Smith, Sherwood.   Crown and
court duet; bk. 2.
PZ7.S65933Co   1998
[Fic]—dc21   97-23879

Text set in Janson Text
Designed by Ivan Holmes
First edition
F E D C B A
Printed in the United States of America

*As before, my special thanks to
my writing group, the Foam Riders,
and to Kathleen Dalton-Woodbury,
for reading this in draft*

*Again, this story is dedicated
with affection and gratitude to
Valerie Smith*

Court Duel

PROLOGUE

THE SCRIBES IN THE HERALDRY GUILD WRITE THE history of Remalna. What I am doing here is telling my own history: how I, Meliara Astiar, who grew up running wild with the village girls and scarcely knew how to read, managed to find myself swept up in the affairs of kings.

Who will read my history? I try to imagine my great-great-great-granddaughter finding this book some wintry day—because in summer, of course, she will be rambling barefoot through the mountains, just like I did. Harder to imagine are people in other lands far from Remalna, and in future times, reading my story.

You might ask why I wrote this, when we have court scribes whose job it is to record important events. One thing I have learned while reading histories is that though the best scribes will faithfully report *what* people did at crucial moments, they often can only guess at *why*.

The scribes will begin, for example, with the fact that I was the second child born to the Count and Countess of Tlanth, a county high in the northwest mountains of Remalna. My brother, Branaric, was the elder.

Even in our remote part of the kingdom, the people struggled under King Galdran Merindar's heavy taxes and became restless under his increasingly unfair laws. My father paid most of those taxes himself to spare our people, and thus we Astiars, in our old, crumbling castle, were not much better off than the poorest of our villagers.

Our mother was killed when Branaric and I were young. We were certain it was done by the order of the King, but we did not know why. It was enough to make our father—until then a recluse—work hard to overthrow an increasingly bad government. On his deathbed ten years later, he made Branaric and me swear a vow to free the country from the wicked King. Branaric and I shared the family title, as Count and Countess of Tlanth, and shared the work of governing our county and preparing for the revolt.

Soon after Father's death we discovered the latest, and worst, of King Galdran's acts: He was going to betray our Covenant with the mysterious and magical Hill Folk in order to harvest and sell the fabulous colorwood trees, which grow nowhere else in the world. The forests have been home to the Hill Folk since long before humans settled in Remalna. The Covenant made with the Hill Folk centuries before our time guaranteed that so long as we left the forests—common trees as well as our fabulous colorwoods—uncut, they would give us magical Fire Sticks each fall, which burned warmly until at least midsummer.

So, untrained and ill prepared, Branaric and I commenced our revolt.

It was a disaster.

Oh, we were successful enough at first, when the huge army the King sent against us was led by his cowardly, bullying cousin Baron Debegri. But when the Marquis of Shevraeth—son of the Prince and Princess of Renselaeus—replaced Debegri, we lost ground steadily. I stumbled into a steel trap our side had set out in a desperate attempt to slow up Shevraeth's army, was caught, and was taken by the Marquis to the capital, where the King condemned me to death without permitting me to speak a word in my defense.

2

But I escaped—with help—and limped my way back toward home, chased by two armies. Both Branaric and I nearly got killed before we found out that some of King Galdran's Court aristocrats—led by the Marquis of Shevraeth—had actually been working to get rid of the King without launching civil war.

King Galdran and Baron Debegri forced us into a final battle, in which they were killed. After that Branaric rode with the Marquis and his allies to the royal palace Athanarel in Remalna-city, the capital, and I retreated home. As a reward for our aid, Shevraeth—who was favored to become the new king—turned over Galdran's personal fortune to Branaric and me.

That much, I know, is in the records.

What the scribes don't tell, because they don't know, is exactly how—and why—I subsequently got mixed up again in royal affairs.

It began with a letter from the Marquise of Merindar—sister of the late King Galdran.

ONE

I STOOD AT MY WINDOW, AN OLD BUT COMFORTABLE blanket wrapped about me. The warmth of the low midwinter sun through the new paned glass was pleasant as I read again the letter that had arrived that day.

> *Esteemed Countess Meliara:*
>
> *I have had the pleasure of meeting, and entertaining, your estimable brother, Count Branaric. At every meeting he speaks often and fondly of his sister, who, he claims, was the driving spirit behind the extraordinary events of last year.*
>
> *He also promised that you will come join us at Court, but half a year has passed, and we still await you. Perhaps the prospect of life at the Palace Athanarel does not appeal to you?*
>
> *There are those who agree with this sentiment. I am one myself. I leave soon for my home in Merindar, where I desire only to lead a quiet life. It is with this prospect in mind that I have taken up my pen; I would like, very much, to meet you. At Merindar there would be time, and seclusion, to permit leisurely discourse on subjects which have concerned us both—especially now, when the country has the greatest need of guidance.*
>
> *Come to Merindar. We can promise you the most pleasant diversions.*

I await, with anticipation, your response—or your most welcome presence.

And it was signed in a graceful, flourishing hand, *Arthal Merindar*.

A letter from a Merindar. I had brought about her brother's defeat. Did she really want friendship? I scanned it for perhaps the tenth time. There had to be a hidden message.

When I came to the end, I looked up and gazed out my window. The world below the castle lay white and smooth and glistening. We'd had six months of peace. Though the letter seemed friendly enough, I felt a sense of foreboding, as if my peace was as fragile as the snowflakes outside.

"Looking down the south road again, Meliara?"

The voice startled me. I turned and saw my oldest friend, Oria, peering in around the door tapestry. Though I was the countess and she the servant, we had grown up together, scampering barefoot every summer through the mountains, sleeping out under the stars, and dancing to the music of the mysterious Hill Folk. Until last winter, I'd only had Oria's cast-off clothing to wear; now I had a couple of remade gowns, but I still wore the old clothes to work in.

She smiled a little as she lifted the tapestry the rest of the way and stepped in. "I tapped. Three times."

"I was *not* looking at the road. Why should I look at the road? I was just thinking—and enjoying the sunshine."

"Won't last." Oria joined me at the window. "A whole week of mild weather? That usually means three weeks of blizzard on the way."

"Let it come," I said, waving a hand. I was just as glad to get off the subject of roads as I was to talk about all the new comforts the castle afforded. "We have windows, and heat vents, and cushions. We could last out a year of blizzards."

Oria nodded, but—typically—reverted right back to her subject. "If you weren't looking down the road, then it's the first time in weeks."

5

"Weeks? Huh!" I scoffed.

She just shrugged a little. "Missing your brother?"

"Yes," I admitted. "I'll be glad when the roads clear—Branaric did promise to come home." Then I looked at her. "Do you miss him?"

Oria laughed, tossing her curly black hair over her shoulder. "I know I risk sounding like an old woman rather than someone who is one year past her Flower Day, but my fancy for him was nothing more than a girl's dream. I much prefer my own flirts now." She pointed at me. "That's what you need, Mel, some flirts."

I too had passed my Flower Day, which meant I was of marriageable age, but I felt sometimes as if I were ten years younger than Oria. She had lots of flirts and seemed to enjoy them all. I'd never had one—and I didn't want one. "Who has the time? I'm much too busy with Tlanth. Speaking of busy, what make you of this?" I held out the letter.

Oria took it and frowned slightly as she read. When she reached the end, she said, "It seems straightforward enough, except… Merindar. Isn't she some relation to the old king?"

"Sister," I said. "The Marquise of Merindar."

"Isn't she a princess?"

"While they ruled, the Merindars only gave the title 'prince' or 'princess' to their chosen heir. She carries the family title, which predates their years on the throne."

Oria nodded, pursing her lips. "So what does this mean?"

"That's what I'm trying to figure out. I did help bring about the downfall of her brother. I think a nasty letter threatening vengeance, awful as it would be to get, would be more understandable than this."

Oria smiled. "Seems honest enough. She wants to meet you."

"But why? And why now? And what's this about 'guidance'?"

Oria looked back at the letter, her dark brows slightly furrowed, then whistled softly. "I missed that, first time through. What do you think she's hinting at, that she thinks the new king ought not to be king?"

"That is the second thing I've been wondering about," I said. "If she'd make a good ruler, then she ought to be supported..."

"Well, would she?"

"I don't know anything about her."

Oria handed the letter back, and she gave me a crooked grin. "Do you want to support her bid for the crown, or do you just want to see the Marquis of Shevraeth defeated?"

"That's the third thing on my mind," I said. "I have to admit that part of me—the part that still rankles at my defeat last year—wants him to be a bad king. But that's not being fair to the country. If he's good, then he should be king. This concerns all the people of Remalna, their safety and well-being, and not just the feelings of one sour countess."

"Who can you ask, then?"

"I don't know. The people who would know her best are all at Court, and I wouldn't trust any of *them* as far as I could throw this castle."

Oria grinned again, then looked out the window at the sunlit snowy expanse.

Materially, our lives had changed drastically since the desperate days of our revolt against Galdran Merindar. We were wealthy now, and my brother seemed to have been adopted by the very courtiers whom we had grown up regarding as our enemies. While he had lingered in the capital for half a year, I had spent much of my time initiating vast repairs to our castle and the village surrounding it. The rest of my time was spent in banishing the ignorance I had grown up with.

"How about writing to your brother?" Oria asked at last.

"Bran is good, and kind, and as honest as the stars are old," I said, "but the more I read, the more I realize that he has no political sense at all. He takes people as he finds them. I don't think he'd have the first notion about what makes a good or bad ruler."

Oria nodded slowly. "In fact, I suspect he would not even like being asked." She gave me a straight look. "There is one person you could ask, and that is the Marquis of Shevraeth."

"Ask the putative next king to evaluate his rival? Not even I would do that," I said with a grimace. "No."

"Then you could go to Court and evaluate them yourself," she stated. "Why not? Everything is finished here, or nearly. We have peace in the county, and as for the house, you made me steward. Will you trust me to carry your plans forward?"

"Of course I will," I said impatiently. "But that's not the issue. I won't go to Court. I don't want to . . ."

"Don't want to what?" Oria persisted.

I sighed. "Don't want to relive the old humiliations."

"What humiliations?" she asked, her eyes narrowed as she studied me. "Mel, the whole country thinks you a heroine for facing down Galdran."

"Not everyone," I muttered.

Oria crossed her arms. "Which brings us right back," she said, "to that Marquis."

I sighed again. "If I never see him again, I will be content—"

"You'll not," Oria said firmly.

I shook my head and looked out sightlessly at the snow, my mind instead reliving memories of the year before. I could just picture how he must have described our encounters—always in that drawling voice, with his courtier's wit—for the edification of the sophisticates at Court. How much laughter had every noble in the kingdom enjoyed at the expense of the barefoot, ignorant Countess Meliara Astiar of Tlanth?

"Lady Meliara?" There was a tap outside the door, and Oria's mother, Julen, lifted the tapestry. Oria and I both stared in surprise at the three long sticks she carried so carefully.

"More Fire Sticks?" I asked. "In midwinter?"

"Just found them outside the gate." Julen laid them down, looked from one of us to the other, and went out.

Oria grinned at me. "Maybe they're a present. You did save the Covenant last year, and the Hill Folk know it."

"*I* didn't do it," I muttered. "All I did was make mistakes."

Oria crossed her arms. "Not mistakes. Misunderstandings. Those, at least, can be fixed. Which is all the more reason to go to Court—"

"And what?" I asked sharply. "Get myself into trouble again?"

Oria stood silently, and suddenly I was aware of the social gulf between us, and I knew she was as well. It happened like that sometimes. We'd be working side by side, cleaning or scraping or carrying, and then a liveried equerry would dash up the road with a letter, and suddenly I was the countess and she the servant who waited respectfully for me to read my letter and discuss it or not as I saw fit.

"I'm sorry," I said immediately, stuffing the Marquise's letter into the pocket of my faded, worn old gown. "You know how I feel about Court, even if Bran has changed his mind."

"I promise not to jaw on about it again, but let me say it this once. You need to make your peace," Oria said quietly. "You left your brother and the Marquis without so much as a by-your-leave, and I think it's gnawing at you. Because you keep watching that road."

I felt my temper flare, but I didn't say anything because I knew she was right. Or half right. And I wasn't angry with *her*.

I tried my best to dismiss my anger and force myself to smile. "Perhaps you may be right, and I'll write to Bran by and by. But here, listen to this!" And I picked up the book I'd been reading before the letter came. "This is one of the ones I got just before the snows closed the roads: 'And in several places throughout the world there are caves with ancient paintings and Iyon Daiyin glyphs.'" I looked up from the book. "Doesn't that make you want to jump on the back of the nearest horse and ride and ride until you find these places?"

Oria shuddered. "Not me. I like it fine right here at home."

"Use your imagination!" I read on. "'Some of the caves depict constellations never seen in our skies—'" I stopped when we heard the pealing of bells. Not the melodic pattern of the time changes,

9

but the clang of warning bells at the guardhouse just down the road.

"Someone's coming!" I exclaimed.

Oria nodded, brows arched above her fine, dark eyes. "And the Hill Folk saw them." She pointed at the Fire Sticks.

" 'Them?' " I repeated, then glanced at the Fire Sticks and nodded. "Means a crowd, true enough."

Julen reappeared then, and tapped at the door. "Countess, I believe we have company on the road."

She looked in, and I said, "I hadn't expected anyone." Then my heart thumped, and I added, "It could be the fine weather has melted the snows down-mountain—d'you think it might be Branaric at last? I don't see how it could be anyone else!"

"Branaric needs three Fire Sticks?" Oria asked.

"Maybe he's brought lots of servants?" I suggested doubtfully. "Perhaps his half year at Court has given him elaborate tastes, ones that only a lot of servants can see to. Or he's hired artisans from the capital to help forward our work on the castle. I hope it's artisans," I added.

"Either way, we'll be wanted to find space for these newcomers," Julen said to her daughter. She picked up the Fire Sticks again and looked over her shoulder at me. "You ought to put on one of those gowns of your mother's that we remade, my lady."

"For my brother?" I laughed, pulling my blanket closer about me as we slipped out of my room. "I don't need to impress him, even if he has gotten used to Court ways!"

Julen whisked herself out.

Oria paused in the doorway. "What about your letter?"

"I guess I will have to ask Bran," I said, feeling that neck-tightening sense of foreboding again. "But later. When I find the right time."

She ducked her head in a nod, then disappeared.

I pulled the letter from my pocket, crammed it into a carved box near my bed, and ran out of the room.

The flags were chilly on my feet, but I decided against going back in for shoes. If it really was Bran, I wanted to be in the court-yard to see his face when he discovered the improvements to the castle.

The prospect of Bran's arrival, which we had all anticipated so long, made me slow my steps just a little, to look at the familiar work as if it were new: windows, modernized fireplaces, and best of all, the furnishings. My prizes were the antique plainwood tables from overseas, some with inlaid patterns, some with scrollwork and thin lines of gilding; all of it—to my eyes, anyway—beautiful. Half the rooms had new rugs from faraway Letarj, where the weavers know how to fashion with clear colors the shapes of birds and flow-ers, and to make the rugs marvelously soft to the feet.

As I trod down the main stairway, I looked with pleasure at the smooth tiles that had replaced the worn, uneven stones. They made the area look lighter and larger, though I hadn't changed anything in the walls. The round window at the front of the hall had stained glass in it now, a wonderful pattern that scattered colored light across the big stairway when the sun was just right.

Oria reappeared as I crossed the hall to the front door.

"I wish the tapestries were done," I said, giving one last glance around. "Those bare walls."

Oria nodded. "True, but who will notice, with the new tiles, and these pretty trees?"

I thanked her, feeling a little guilty. I had stolen the idea of the potted trees from the Renselaeus palace—where I had been taken briefly during the latter part of the war—but how would they ever know? I comforted myself with this thought and turned my atten-tion to the others, who were all gathering to welcome Bran.

Oria, Julen, and I had designed a handsome new livery, and both women wore their new gowns. Little Calaub was proud of his new-sewn stablehand livery, which marked him out to his friends in the village for his exalted future as the Astiar Master of Horse.

Village? *Town,* I thought, distracted, as the sound of pounding horse hooves preceded Bran's arrival. Many of the artisans I'd hired

11

had elected to remain, for everyone in the village had decided to improve their homes. We suddenly had lots of business for any who wanted it, and money—at last—to pay for it all.

The rattle up the new-paved road—our first project during summer—grew louder, and to our surprise, not one but four coaches arrived, the first one a grand affair with our device boldly painted on its side. Outriders clattered in, their magnificent horses kicking up the powdery snow, and for a time all was chaos as the stablehands ran to see to the animals and lead them to our new barn.

"Four coaches?" Julen said to me, frowning. "We've room for the one. Two, if they shift things around and squeeze up tightly."

"The last two will have to go to the old garrison barn," I said. "Leastwise it has a new roof."

Out of the first carriage stepped Bran, his hair loose and shining under a rakish plumed hat. He was dressed in a magnificent tunic and glossy high blackweave riding boots, with a lined cloak slung over one shoulder. He grinned at me—then he turned and, with a gesture of practiced grace that made me blink, handed out a lady.

A lady? I gawked in dismay at the impressive hat and muffling cloak that spanned a broad skirt, and looked down at myself, in an old skirt Oria had discarded, a worn tunic that I hadn't bothered to change after my sword lesson that morning, and my bare feet. Then I noticed that Julen and Oria had vanished. I stood there all alone.

In fine style Bran escorted the mysterious lady to the new slate steps leading to the big double doors where I stood, but then he dropped her arm and bounded up, grabbing me in a big hug and swinging me around. "Sister!" He gave me a resounding kiss and set me down. "Place looks wonderful!"

"You *could* have let me know you were bringing a guest," I whispered.

"And spoil a good surprise?" he asked, indicating the lady, who was still standing on the first step. "We have plenty of room, and

as you'd told me in your letter the place isn't such a rattrap anymore, I thought why not make the trip fun and bring 'em?"

" 'Them?' " I repeated faintly, but by then I already had my
answer, for the outriders had resolved into a lot of liveried servants
who were busy unloading coaches and helping stablehands.
Through the midst of them strolled a tall, elegant man in a heel-
length black cloak. I looked at the familiar gray eyes, the long yellow hair—it was the Marquis of Shevraeth.

TWO

"YES," BRAN SAID CARELESSLY, INDICATING HIS TWO guests. "Nimiar—and Danric there, whom you already know." He frowned. "Life, sister, why are there trees in here? Aren't there enough of 'em outside?"

I gritted my teeth on a really nasty retort, my face burning with embarrassment.

The lady spoke for the first time. "But Branaric, you liked them well enough at my home, and I think it a very pretty new fashion indeed." She turned to me, and I got a swift impression of wide-set brown eyes, a dimpled smile, and a profusion of brown curly hair beneath the elaborate hat. "I am Nimiar Argaliar," she said, holding out a daintily gloved hand.

Trying desperately to force my face into a semblance of friendly welcome, I stuck my own hand out, rather stiffly. She grasped it in a warm grip for a moment as I said, "Welcome. I hope...you'll enjoy it here."

"Do you have a welcome for me?" Shevraeth said with a faint smile as he came leisurely up the steps and inside.

"Certainly," I said in a voice so determinedly polite it sounded false even to my own ears. "Come into the parlor—*all* of you— and I'll see to refreshment. It must have been a long trip."

"Slow," Bran said, looking around. "Roads are still bad down-mountain, but not up here anymore. You have been busy, haven't you, Mel? All I remember in this hallway is the mildew and the broken stone floor. And the parlor! What was the cost of this mosaic ceiling? Not that it matters, but it's as fine as anything in Athanarel."

I'd been proud of the parlor, over which I had spent a great deal of time. The ceiling had inlaid tiles in the same summer-sky blue that comprised the main color of the rugs and cushions and the tapestry on the wall opposite the newly glassed windows. Now I sneaked a look at the Marquis, dreading an expression of amusement or disdain. But his attention seemed to be reserved for the lady as he led her to the scattering of cushions before the fireplace, where she knelt down with a graceful sweeping of her skirts. Bran went over and opened the fire vents.

"If I'd known of your arrival, it would have been warm in here."

Bran looked over his shoulder in surprise. "Well, where d'you spend your days? Not still in the kitchens?"

"In the kitchens and the library and wherever else I'm needed," I said; and though I tried to sound cheery, it came out sounding resentful. "I'll be back after I see about food and drink."

Feeling very much like I was making a cowardly retreat, I ran down the long halls to the kitchen, cursing my bad luck as I went. There I found Julen, Oria, the new cook, and his assistant all standing in a knot talking at once. As soon as I appeared, the conversation stopped.

Julen and Oria turned to face me—Oria on the verge of laughter.

"The lady can have the new rose room, and the lord the corner suite next to your brother. But they've got an army of servants with them, Countess," Julen said heavily. Whenever she called me Countess, it was a sure sign she was deeply disturbed over something. "Where'll we house *them*? There's no space in our wing, not till we finish the walls."

"And who's to wait on whom?" Oria asked as she carefully brought my mother's good silver trays out from the wall-shelves behind the new-woven coverings. "Glad we've kept these polished," she added.

"I'd say find out how many of those fancy palace servants are kitchen trained, and draft 'em. And then see if some of the people from that new inn will come up, for extra wages. *Bran* can unpocket the extra pay," I said darkly, "if he's going to make a habit of disappearing for half a year and reappearing with armies of retainers. As for housing, well, the garrison does have a new roof, so they can all sleep there. We've got those new Fire Sticks to warm 'em up with."

"What about meals for your guests?" Oria said, her eyes wide.

I'd told Oria last summer that she could become steward of the house. While I'd been ordering books on trade, and world history, and governments, she had been doing research on how the great houses were currently run; and it was she who had hired Demnan, the new cook. We'd eaten well over the winter, thanks to his genius.

I looked at Oria. "This is it. No longer just us, no longer practice, it's time to dig out all your plans for running a fine house for a noble family. Bran and his two Court guests will need something now after their long journey, and I have no idea what's proper to offer Court people."

"Well, I do," Oria said, whirling around, hands on hips, her face flushed with pleasure. "We'll make you proud, I promise."

I sighed. "Then . . . I guess I'd better go back."

As I ran to the parlor, pausing only to ditch my blanket in an empty room, I steeled myself to be polite and pleasant no matter how much my exasperating brother inadvertently provoked me— but when I pushed aside the tapestry at the door, they weren't there.

And why should they be? This was Branaric's home, too.

A low murmur of voices, and a light, musical, feminine laugh drew me to the library. *At least this room is nothing to be ashamed of,* I thought, trying to steady my racing heart. I walked in, reassuring myself with the sight of the new furnishings and, on the wall, my framed map of the world, the unknown scribe's exquisitely exact use of color to represent mountains, plains, forests, lakes, and cities making it a work of art.

And on the shelves, the beginnings of a library any family might be proud of. Just last winter the room had been bare, the shelves empty. Ten years it had been so, ever since the night my father found out my mother had been killed; and in a terrible rage, he'd stalked in and burned every book there, from ancient to new. I now had nearly fifty books, all handsomely bound.

My head was high as I crossed the room to the groupings of recliner cushions, each with its lamp, that I'd had arranged about the fireplace. Of course this room was warm, for it had a Fire Stick, since I was so often in it.

Bran and his two guests looked up as I approached, and I realized that they had somehow gotten rid of their hats, cloaks, and gloves. *To one of their servants?* I should have seen to it, I realized, but I dismissed the thought. Too late—and it wasn't as if I'd known they were coming.

Lady Nimiar smiled, and Bran gave me his reckless grin. "Here y'are at last, Mel," he said. "We have something warm to drink on the way?"

"Soon. Also had to arrange housing for all those people you brought."

"Some of 'em are mine. Ours," he corrected hastily.

"Good, because we plan to put them all to work. The servants' wing is all still open to the sky. We're having it expanded. Had you ever *seen* the tiny rooms, and half of them with no fire vents? Anyway, the first snows came so early and so fierce we had to abandon the construction."

"They can go to the garrison," Bran said. "We saw it on the way in. Looks nice and snug. Where'd you get all these new books?"

"Bookseller in the capital. I'm trying to duplicate what Papa

17

destroyed, though nothing will restore the family histories that no one had ever copied."

"Most of 'em were dull as three snoring bears, burn me if they weren't!" he said, making a warding motion with one hand.

I wished I'd had the chance to decide for myself, but there was no purpose in arguing over what couldn't be fixed, so I just shook my head.

Right then Julen came in, her face solemn and closed as she bore the fine silver tray loaded with spiced hot wine and what I recognized as the apple tart we would have had after dinner, now all cut into dainty pieces and served with dollops of whipped cream on the gold-and-blue edged porcelain plates that were our last delivery before the roads were closed. She set those down and went out.

Bran looked at me. "We serving ourselves?"

"Until we get some people from the inn," I said.

Bran sighed, getting up. "You were right, Nee. I ought to have written ahead. Thought the surprise would be more fun!" He moved to the table and poured out four glasses of wine.

Lady Nimiar also rose. She was short—just a little taller than I—and had a wonderful figure that was round in all the right places. I tried not to think how I compared, with my skinny frame, and instead looked at her gown, which was a fawn color, over a rich dark brown underdress. Tiny green leaves had been embroidered along the neck, the laced-up bodice, and the hems of sleeves and skirt. I felt shabbier than ever—and studiously ignored the other guest—as I watched her pick up two wineglasses, turn, and come toward me without her train twisting round her feet or tripping her. She handed one glass to me, and Bran carried one to Shevraeth.

I tried to think of some sort of politeness to speak out, but then Bran held up his glass and said, "To my sister! Everything you've done is better than I thought possible. Though," he lowered his glass and blinked at me, "why are you dressed like that? The servants look better! Why haven't you bought new duds?"

18

"What's the use?" I said, feeling my face burn again. "There's still so much work to be done, and how can I do it in a fancy gown? And who's to be impressed? The servants?"

Lady Nimiar raised her glass. "To the end of winter."

Everyone drank, and Bran tried again. "To Mel, and what she's done for my house!"

"Our house," I said under my breath.

"Our house," he repeated in a sugary tone that I'd never heard before, but he didn't look at me. His eyes were on the lady, who smiled.

I must have been gaping, because Shevraeth lifted his glass. "My dear Branaric," he drawled in his most courtly manner, "never tell me you failed to inform your sister of your approaching change in status."

Bran's silly grin altered to the same kind of gape I'd probably been displaying a moment before. "What? Sure I did! Wrote a long letter, all about it—" He smacked his head.

"A letter which is still sitting on your desk?" Shevraeth murmured.

"Life! It must be! Curse it, went right out of my head."

I said, trying to keep my voice polite, "What is this news?"

Bran reached to take the lady's hand—probably for protection, I thought narrowly—as he said, "Nimiar and I are going to be married midsummer eve, and she's adopting into our family. You've got to come back to Athanarel to be there, Mel."

"I'll talk to you *later*." I tried my very hardest to smile at the lady. "Welcome to the family. Such as it is. Lady Nimiar."

"Please," she said, coming forward to take both my hands. "Call me Nee." Her eyes were merry, and there was no shadow of malice in her smile, but I remembered the horrible laughter that day in Athanarel's throne room, when I was brought as a prisoner before the terrible King Galdran. And I remembered how unreadable these Court-trained people were supposed to be—expressing only what they chose to—and I looked back at her somewhat

19

helplessly. "We'll soon enough be sisters, and though some families like to observe the formalities of titles, I never did. Or I wouldn't have picked someone like Branaric to marry," she added in a low voice, with a little laugh and a look that invited me to share her humor.

I tried to get my clumsy tongue to stir and finally managed to say, "Would you like a tour through the house, then?"

Instantly moving to Lady Nimiar's side, Bran said, "I can show you, for in truth, I'd like a squint at all the changes myself."

She smiled up at him. "Why don't you gentlemen drink your wine and warm up? I'd rather Meliara show me about."

"But I—"

Shevraeth took Bran's shoulder and thrust him onto a cushion. "Sit."

Bran laughed. "Oh, aye, let the females get to know one another."

Nimiar merely smiled.

So I led her all through the finished parts of the castle, tumbling over my words as I tried to explain what I'd done and why. When I let her get a word in, she made pleasant comments and asked easy questions. By the time we were nearly done, though I didn't know her any better, I had relaxed a little, for I could see that she was exerting herself to set me at ease. I reflected a little grimly on how maintaining an unexceptionable flow of conversation was an art— one that neither Bran nor I had.

We ended up downstairs in the summer parlor, whose great glassed doors would in a few months look out on a fine garden but now gave onto a slushy pathway lined by barren trees and rose-bushes. Still sitting where it had for nearly three decades was my mother's harp.

As soon as Nimiar saw the instrument, she gave a gasp and pressed her fingertips to her mouth. " 'Tis a Mandarel," she murmured reverently, her face flushed with excitement. "Do you play it?"

I shook my head. "Was my mother's. I used to dance to the music she made. Do you play?"

"Not as well as this instrument deserves. And I haven't practiced for ages. That's a drawback of a life at Court. One gets bound up in the endless social rounds and forgets other things. May I try it sometime?"

"It's yours," I said. "This is going to be your home, too, and for my part, I think musical instruments ought to be played and not sit silent."

She caught my hand and kissed it, and I flushed with embarrassment.

And just then the two men came in, both wearing their cloaks again, and Bran carrying Nimiar's over his arm. "There you are. Found Mama's harp?"

"Yes, and Meliara says I may play it whenever I like."

Bran grinned at me. "A good notion, that. Only let's have it moved upstairs where it's warm, shall we?"

Nimiar turned at once to see how I liked this idea, and I spread my hands. "If you wish," I said.

Bran nodded. "Now, Mel, go get something warm on, and we'll take a turn in the garden and see what's toward outside."

"You don't need me for that," I said. "I think I'll go make sure things are working smoothly." And before anyone could say anything, I batted aside the door tapestry and fled.

THREE

As soon as I reached my room I took out the Marquise's letter and reread it, even though by then I knew it word for word. It seemed impossible that Branaric's arrival on the same day—with Shevraeth—was a coincidence.

I sighed. Now I could not ask my brother outright about this letter. He was as tactless as he was honest. I could easily imagine him blurting it out over dinner. *He* might find it diverting, though I didn't think Shevraeth would, for the same reason I couldn't ask him his opinion of Arthal Merindar: because the last time we had discussed the possible replacement for Galdran Merindar, I had told him flatly I'd rather see my brother crowned than another lying courtier.

Remembering that conversation—in Shevraeth's father's palace, with his father listening—I winced. It wasn't just Bran who lacked tact.

Oria is probably right, I thought glumly, *there are too many misunderstandings between the Marquis and me.* The problem with gathering my courage and broaching the subject was the very fact of the kingship. If I hadn't been able to resolve those misunderstandings before Galdran's death, when Shevraeth was just the Marquis, it seemed impossible to do it now when he was about to take the crown. My motives might be mistaken and he'd think me one of those fawning courtiers at the royal palace. Ugh!

So I asked Oria to tell them I was sick. I holed up in my room with a book and did my best to shove them all out of my mind—as well as the mysterious Marquise of Merindar.

At sundown the next day there came a cough outside my room. Before I could speak, the tapestry swung aside as if swatted by an impatient hand, and there was Bran. "Hah!" he exclaimed, fists on his hips. "I knew it! Reading, and not sick at all. Burn it, Mel, they're our guests."

"They are your guests, and you can entertain them," I retorted.

"You don't like Nee?" He looked upset.

I sighed. "She seems as nice as any Court lady could possibly be, but how can she think I'm anything but an idiot? As for that Shevraeth, you brought him. He's yours to entertain. I don't need him laughing at me for my old clothes and lack of courtly finesse."

"He isn't going to laugh at you, Mel," Bran said, running his fingers through his hair. "Life! We didn't come all the way up here to talk to ourselves. Nee's going to play the harp before supper. She spent all afternoon retuning the thing. If you don't come, after all I said about how you like music, she'll get hurt—think you don't want her here. As for your clothes, you must have *something* nice."

I remembered my two remade dresses. "All right," I said grumpily. "I'll change and be right down."

He kissed the top of my head and left.

I opened my wardrobe, eyeing the two gowns. Most of my mother's things had been ruined when the weather got into her rooms. But we'd saved these, and Hrani the weaver had reworked them to fit me. One was a plain gown Mama had used for gardening, its fabric sturdy enough to have lasted. The other had taken some patient restitching, but I really loved it. The color was a soft gray blue, with tiny iridescent mois gems sewn over the tight

23

sleeves and edging the square neck. It gathered at a high waist, opening onto a deep-blue skirt with gold birds embroidered on it. I had a vague memory of her having worn it, and I liked the idea of having something of hers for myself.

Besides, I thought it looked nice on me. She'd been a little taller, but otherwise our builds were much alike. I put the gown on, combed out my hair and rebraided it, and wrapped it up in its accustomed coronet.

Then I went down to the upper parlor that they seemed to have adopted. I could hear random notes from the harp, a shivery pleasant sound that plucked at old and beloved memories, just as wearing the gown did.

I slipped through the door tapestry, and three faces turned toward me.

And my dear brother snorted. "Mel! Where are your wits gone begging? Why d'you have to wear an old gown thirty years out-of-date when you can have anything you want?"

I turned right around and started to leave, but Nimiar rose and sped to my side, her small hand grasping my gem-encircled wrist. "This is a lovely dress, and if it's old, what's the odds? A lady has the right to be comfortable in her own home."

Bran rubbed his chin. "Don't tell me you ever looked like *that*?"

"Oh, Branaric. Take Lord Vidanric up to dinner. I'll play afterward. The harp isn't ready yet."

"But—"

"Please," she said.

Shevraeth's lips were twitching. He jerked his chin toward the doorway and my brother followed, protesting all the way.

My eyes stung. I stood like a stone statue as Nimiar sighed then said, "Your brother is a dear, and I do love him for the way he never fears to tell the truth. But he really doesn't understand some things, does he?"

"No," I squeaked. My voice seemed to come from someone else.

Nimiar ran her fingers along the harp strings and cocked her

24

head, listening to the sounds they produced. "No one," she said, "—well, no ordinary person—sits down to a harp and plays perfectly. It takes time and training."

I nodded stupidly.

She dropped her hands. "When Branaric came to Athanarel, he knew nothing of etiquette or Court custom. Arrived wearing cast-off war gear belonging to Lord Vidanric, his arm in a dirty sling, his nose red from a juicy cold. There are those at Court who would have chewed him like jackals with a bone, except he freely admitted to being a rustic. Thought it a very good joke. Then he'd been brought by the Marquis, who is a leader of fashion, and Savona took to him instantly. The Duke of Savona is another leader. And..." She hesitated. "And certain women who also lead fashion liked him. Added was the fact that you Astiars have become something of heroes, and it became a fad to teach him. His blunt speech was a refreshing change, and he doesn't care at all what people think of him. But you do, don't you?" She peered into my face. "You care—terribly."

I bit my lip.

She touched my wrist. "Let us make a pact. If you will come to Athanarel and dance at my wedding, I will undertake to teach you everything you need to know about Court life. And I'll help you select a wardrobe—and no one need ever know."

I swallowed, then took a deep, unsteady breath.

"What is it?" She looked unhappy. "Do you mistrust me?"

I shook my head so hard my coronet came loose, and a loop settled over one eye. "*They* would know," I whispered, waving a hand.

"They? Your servants? Oh. You mean Branaric and Lord Vidanric?"

I nodded. "They'll surely want to know my reasons. Since I didn't come to Court before." I thought of that letter hidden in my room and wondered if its arrival and Shevraeth's on the same day had some sinister political meaning.

She smiled. "Don't worry about Bran. All he wants, you must

see, is to show you off at Athanarel. He knew you were refurbishing this castle, and I rather think he assumed you were—somehow—learning everything he was learning and obtaining a fashionable wardrobe as well. And every time he talks of you it's always to say how much more clever you are than he is. I really think he expected to bring us here and find you waiting as gowned and jeweled as my cousin Tamara."

I winced. "That sounds, in truth, like Branaric."

"And as for Vidanric, well, you're safe there. I've never met anyone as closemouthed, when he wants to be. He won't ask your reasons. What?"

"I said, 'Hah.' "

"What is it, do you mislike him?" Again she was studying me, her fingers playing with the pretty fan hanging at her waist.

"Yes. No. Not mislike, but more . . . mistrust. Not what he'll do, but what he might say," I babbled. "Oh, never mind. It's all foolishness. Suffice it to say I feel better when we're at opposite ends of the country, but I'll settle for opposite ends of the castle."

Her eyes widened. If she hadn't been a lady, I would have said she was on the verge of whistling. "Well, here's a knot. But—there's nothing for it." She closed the fan with a snap, then ran her hands over the harp.

"Why should it matter?" I asked, after a long moment. "If I don't want to be around Shevraeth, I mean."

She plucked a string and bent down to twist the key, then plucked it again, her head cocked, though I have a feeling she wasn't listening. Finally she said, "Of course you probably know he's likely to be the new king. His parents are in Athanarel now, his father making his first appearance in many years, and he came armed with a Letter of Regard from Aranu Crown in Erev-li-Erval. It seems that in her eyes the Renselaeus family has the best claim to the kingdom of Remalna."

Half a year ago I would have been puzzled by this, but my subsequent reading gave me an inkling of what protracted and ticklish diplomacy must have gone on beneath the surface of events to have produced such a result. "Well. So the Merindars no longer have a legal claim. If they mean to pursue one." I added hastily, "*Meant* to pursue one."

She gave a little nod. "Precisely. As it transpires, the Prince and Princess of Renselaeus do not want to rule. They're merely there to oversee what their son has accomplished and, I think, to establish a sense of order and authority. It is very hard to gainsay either of them, especially the Prince," she added with a smile.

When I nodded, she looked surprised. "You have met him, then?"

"Yes. Briefly."

"Would that be when you made the alliance? You know how bad Bran is at telling stories. A random sentence or two, then he scratches his head and claims he can't remember any more. And the Renselaeuses don't talk about the war at all."

This news surprised and amazed me. A portion of the tightness inside me eased, just a little.

"To resume—and we'd better hurry, or they'll be down here clamoring for our company before their supper goes cold—Lord Vidanric has been working very hard ever since the end of the war. Too hard, some say. He came to Athanarel sick and has been ill off and on since then, for he seldom sleeps. He's either in the saddle, or else his lamps are burning half the night in his wing of the Residence. He's here on his mother's orders, to rest. He and your brother have become fast friends, I think because Branaric, in his own way, is so very undemanding. He wants no favors or powers. He just likes to enjoy his days. This seems to be what Vidanric needs just now."

"Do you think he'll make a good king?" I asked.

Again she seemed surprised. "Yes," she said. "But then I've known him all my life."

As if that explains everything, I thought. Then I realized that to her it did. He was a good prospect for a king because he was her friend, and because they were both courtiers, raised the same way.

And then I wondered just who—if anyone—at Court was willing to speak not for themselves, but for the people, to find out who really would be the best ruler?

A discreet tap outside the door brought our attention round. Calden, the server from the inn, parted the tapestry and said, "Count Branaric sent me to find out if you're coming?"

"In just a moment, thanks," I said.

"Will you agree to my pact, then?" Nimiar asked.

I opened my mouth to ask why they couldn't just marry here, but I knew that was the coward's way out. I did not wish to get involved in any more wars, but that didn't mean I ought not do what I could to ensure that the next reign would be what Papa had wished for when he commenced planning his revolt.

And the best way to find out, I realized as I looked into Nimiar's face, would not be by asking questions of third parties, but by going to the capital and finding out on my own.

So I squashed down my reluctance and said, "If you can teach me not to make a fool of myself at that Court, I'll gladly come to see you marry Bran."

"You will like Court life, I promise," she said, smiling sweetly as we went out of the parlor.

I took care to walk behind her so she could not see my face.

For the next several weeks Nee and I spent nearly all our days together as she tried to remake me into a Court lady. Most of the time it was fun, a little like what I imagined playacting to be, as we stood side by side facing a mirror and practiced walking and sitting and curtsying. Nee seemed to enjoy teaching me. The more we talked, the less opaque I found her. Beneath the automatic smiling mask of Court, she was a quiet, restful person who liked comfort and pleasant conversation.

In between lessons she talked about her friends at Court: what they liked, or said, or how they entertained. Pleasant, easy talk, meant to show all her friends in the best light; she did not, I realized, like politics or gossip. She never once mentioned the Marquise of Merindar.

In my turn I told her my history, bits at a time, but only if she asked. And ask she did. She listened soberly, wincing from time to time; one cold, blustery day I recounted how I had ended up in Baron Debegri's dungeon, and my narrow escape therefrom.

At the end of that story she shuddered and asked, "How could you have lived through that and still be sane?"

"Am I sane?" I joked. "There are some who might argue." Her reaction secretly cheered me, exactly like a ten-year-old who has managed to horrify her friends. *It isn't much of a claim to fame, but it's all I have*, I thought later as I stared down at the third fan I'd broken, and when—again—I'd forgotten which curtsy to make to which person under which circumstances.

The one thing I couldn't talk about was that terrible day when Shevraeth brought me to face Galdran before the entire Court. I did not want to know if Nimiar had been there, and had looked at me, and had laughed.

We saw Bran and Shevraeth only at dinner, and that seldom enough, for they were often away. When the weather was particularly bad, they might be gone for several days. On the evenings we were alone, Nee and I would curl up in her room or mine, eating from silver trays and talking.

Branaric and the Marquis managed to be around on most days when the weather permitted gatherings in the old garrison courtyard for swordfighting practice. Even though I was not very good at it, I enjoyed sword work. At least I enjoyed it when not rendered acutely conscious of all my failings, when the bouts were attended by someone tall, strong, naturally gifted with grace, and trained since childhood—such as the Marquis of Shevraeth. So after a couple of particularly bad practices (in which I tried so hard not to get laughed at that I made more mistakes than ever), I stopped going whenever I saw him there.

When Nee and I did join Bran and the Marquis for dinner, for the most part I sat in silence and watched Nee covertly, trying to copy her manners. No one—not even Bran—remarked on it if I sat through an entire meal without speaking.

Thus I was not able to engender any discussions about the Marquise of Merindar, so the letter—and the question of kingship—stayed dormant, except at night in my troubled dreams.

Nee had brought only one seamstress, whom she dispatched with outriders the day after our conversation in the parlor. Armed with one of my drafts on our bankers at Arclor House, this woman was entrusted to hire three more seamstresses and to bring back cloth suitable for gowns and accoutrements.

I don't know what instructions Nimiar gave her seamstress in private. I had expected a modest trunk of nice fabric, enough for a gown or two in the current fashions. What returned, though, just over a week later, was a hired wagon bearing enough stuff to outfit the entire village, plus three determined young journey-seamstresses who came highly recommended and who were ready to make their fortunes.

"Good," Nee said, when we had finished interviewing them. She walked about inspecting the fabulous silks, velvets, linens, and a glorious array of embroidery twists, nodding happily. "Just what I wanted. Melise is a treasure."

"Isn't this too much?" I asked, astounded.

She grinned. "Not when you count up what you'll need to make the right impression. Remember, you are acquiring overnight what ought to have been put together over years. Morning gowns, afternoon gowns, riding tunics and trousers, party dresses, and perhaps one ball gown, though that kind of thing you can order when we get to town, for those take an unconscionable amount of time to make if you don't have a team doing it."

"A team? Doing nothing but sewing? What a horrible life!" I exclaimed.

"Those who choose it would say the same about yours, I think," Nee said with a chuckle. "Meaning your life as a revolutionary. There are many, not just women, though it's mostly females, who like very much to sit in a warm house and sew and gossip all day. In the good houses the sewers have music, or have books read to them, and the products are the better for their minds being engaged in something interesting. This is their art, just as surely as yon scribe regards her map and her fellows regard their books." She pointed toward the library. "And how those at Court view the way they conduct their public lives."

"So much to learn," I said with a groan. "How will I manage?"

She just laughed; and the next day a new arrival brought my most formidable interview yet: with my new maid.

"Her name is Mora," Nee told me, "and she's a connection of my own Ilvet. An aunt, I think. Ilvet promises she is deft and discreet. She was working for one of the northern families—low pay and too much work—but she stayed until her mistress married and adopted into a household even more huskscraping. Mora and the others suddenly found themselves each doing the work of three, while living in chambers that hadn't been altered for four hundred years—right down to the mold on the stones. If you like her, she will then hire your staff, whom you will never really see."

I shook my head. "Strange, to consider having a staff I won't see." But as I went to the interview, my thought was: *You mean, if she likes me.*

Mora was tall and thin, with gray-streaked dark hair. *Her face is more inscrutable even than Shevraeth's,* I thought with dismay. She bowed, then waited, her hands folded, for me to speak.

I took a deep breath. "I gather you're used to sophisticated Court people, and I'd better tell you right out that I'm not

31

sophisticated and haven't been to Court. Well, except once, but that was against my will. It's true that I'm going to Court, but I don't know that I'll stay past the wedding; and then—most likely—it's back here for the rest of my life. I go barefoot all summer, and until now I've never owned more than one hat. And my friends have all been village people."

She said nothing, but there was the faintest crinkling of humor about her eyes.

"On the other hand," I said, "I'm used to cleaning up after myself. I also won't interfere with your hiring whomever you need, and you'll be paid whatever you think fair, at least while we *can* pay. The fortune came to us on someone's whim, so I suppose it could disappear the same way."

Mora bowed. "You honor me," she said, "with your honesty, my lady."

"Does that mean you'll stay?" I asked, after an uncomfortable pause.

She smiled then, just a little. "I believe, my lady," she said, "it is for you to decide if you want me."

I clapped my hands, relieved that this formidable woman had not left in disgust. "Great. Then start today," I said, and grinned. "There's plenty to do if I'm to get properly civilized."

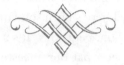

FOUR

MY FIRST GOWN WAS READY SHORTLY THEREAFTER.
It was a dinner gown; I was learning the distinctions between the types of clothing. Morning gowns were the simplest, designed to be practical for working at home. Afternoon gowns were for going visiting, for receiving visitors, and for walking. Dinner gowns were elaborate in the upper half, meant to make one look good while sitting, and narrow in the skirt, so one's skirts wouldn't drape beyond one's cushion. The distinction between party gowns and dinner gowns was blurring, Nee told me, because so frequently now there were dances directly after dinner; quite different again were the ball gowns, which were designed to look good moving. And then there was the formal Court gown, meant for state occasions, and few people had more than one, or possibly two, of these—they were meant to be seen again, and in these, the fashions had changed the least.

"Everyone will retire those they wore for Galdran's affairs, though, either giving them away, or consigning them to attics for their descendants to marvel at, or having them taken apart and remade into new gowns, for the materials are hideously expensive. At the coronation of the new ruler everything will be all new."

"So all these other fashions will change again?" I asked.

"They change all the time." She watched, smiling, as I put on my first dinner gown and started lacing up the front. "Remind me to take you to the Heraldry Archive. There's been someone to draw pictures of what the rulers wear for, oh, centuries. It's astonishing to look through those pictures and see what our ancestors wore. I quite like the silken tunics and loose trousers of four hundred years ago, when we had Theraez of the Desert as our queen. Several generations before that, our climate must have been very warm, for all the hats were sun hats, and short hair was the fashion. No one wore gloves. Quite the opposite of the awful things they wore a hundred years ago—all gaudy, with odd angles, and those huge shoulders on the men, meant to cover up the fact that the king was as vain as he was fat. After him the clothes were more attractive in design, but everything was stiff with jewels and metallic embroidery. It was probably blinding in the sunlight! But that's in living memory, and my grandmother talks of how old all the Court leaders then were, and how very, very formal."

"And now?" I said, taking down my hair and unbraiding it.

"Now we're mostly young, for despite all the talk about Galdran liking young active folk, the truth was, we were there as hostages so our parents would not gainsay him." She smiled. "So though we are young, we prize delicacy of speech, and no one ever gets drunk in public. That kind of behavior, once a luxury, could get one killed under Galdran's rule. So could free speech, which is why fans became so popular. Speaking of fans, now that you know how to open one, and hold it, I'll teach you how to speak with it."

"Speak? With a fan?" I asked.

She grinned. "There are times when words say too much—or too little. For example, watch this." She tapped my wrist lightly with her closed fan. Her wrist was arched, her hand angled downward. "What does that seem to suggest?"

"That I stay where I am," I guessed, mildly intrigued.

She nodded. "But watch this." She tapped my wrist again, still holding the fan closed, but this time her hand was angled differently so that I saw the underside of her wrist.

"It's like a beckon," I said.

"Exactly. The first keeps a suitor at his distance, the second invites him to close the distance, all without speaking a word."

"That's flirting," I said in disgust. "I don't have any need for that. If any Court toady tries that on me, I'll be happy to use my words to send him to the rightabout. That's not why—" *I'm going to Court*, I started to say, but then I closed my mouth.

If she noticed the lapse, she gave no sign. "But it's not just for flirting," she said. "There are so many modes, all of which can change the meaning of one's words. I should add that we often used the fan language to make fun of Galdran or to give ourselves the lie when we had to flatter him. He had a habit—more and more in the last three or four years—of using threats to get flattery. I think he suspected that the end was near."

I whistled. "So the fan language is a kind of flag code? Like the navies use?"

"I guess you could think of it that way," she said. "I liked it because it gave us a bit of freedom, for Galdran never used a fan. Considered it female foolery, even when Savona and the other young men used it right before his face. Stars! Your hair *is* long!" She stood back and admired the waving auburn river of hair that hung just past my knees.

"I promised not to cut it until Mama was avenged, and now I find I can't," I said, and when I saw her odd expression, asked forebodingly, "Don't tell me I'll get laughed at . . . "

"Oh no," she said, brimming with sudden mirth. "It's becoming a fashion, very long hair—coming from the north, of course, where Aranu Crown's declared heir's wife has long silver hair. She's Hrethan, I understand. Not from here, but from their old world. Anyway, everyone is trying to grow theirs; and . . . someone will be jealous."

"Someone?" I repeated, mentally reviewing her descriptions of various Court figures. She did not always name them, I had noticed, particularly when she made her—rare—criticisms. "Is this the same someone you've almost named once before?"

She smiled wryly. "I think I've already said too much. Won't you leave yours down for dinner tonight? It looks quite lovely."

"Not to kneel on at the table," I said, swiftly rebraiding it. "Since there's no one to impress. Now, back to the fans. Let's have some of that code."

"All right," she said. "This mode is called Within the Circle." She twirled her open fan gently in an arc. "It means that the speaker regards the listeners as friends. But if you wave it back— like this—then it alters to the Walled Circle Mode, which indicates trusted friends. It binds the listeners not to speak of what they've heard . . . "

For dinner that night we found Bran and Shevraeth waiting in the parlor next to the dining room. Nee had probably prepared them, I realized. This was new for me, but it was according to the rules of etiquette; and if I looked at it as rehearsal—more of the playacting—I found it easy to walk in beside her, minding my steps so that my skirt flowed gracefully and my floor-length sleeves draped properly without twisting or tripping me up.

Nee walked straight to my brother, who performed a bow, and grinning widely, offered his arm.

This left me with the Marquis, who looked tall and imposing in dark blue embroidered with pale gold, which—I realized as I glanced just once at him—was the exact same shade as his hair. He said nothing, just bowed, but there was mild question in his gray eyes as he held out his arm.

I grimaced, thinking: *You'll have to learn this some time. May's well get it over quickly.* Putting my fingertips so lightly on his sleeve I scarcely felt the fabric, I fell into step beside him as we followed the other two into the dining room. Though this was my home, I didn't plop down cross-legged onto my cushion, but knelt in the approved style.

After I'd fortified myself with a gulp of wine, Bran said, "Life, Mel, you look fine. Getting some more of those duds?"

36

I nodded.

"What have you done with your day?" Nee asked, her fan spread in the attitude I recognized from our fan lesson as Harmonic Discourse.

"We had a bout with the group at the garrison, had a squint at some horses brought from up-mountain. Danric answered mail, and I went over to town with Calder to look at the plans for paving the streets."

This was Tlanth business. I said, "Did you talk to the elders? They want part of their taxes to go to that."

Bran nodded. "It's a fair plan," he said; and I sat back, relieved.

Nee put her chin in her hand. " 'Answered mail,' Vidanric? Is he referring to that formidable bag your equerries brought in this morning?"

"We're finishing the last of the dispersal and reassignment of Galdran's army," Shevraeth said.

"Dispersal?" I repeated, thinking immediately of my plans for evaluating his forming government. Surely it would raise no suspicions to ask about it, since he had introduced the subject. "You've dismantled that gigantic army?"

"A huge standing army with little to do is both—"

" '—a financial burden and a threat,' " I said. "I recognize the quote—and I agree," I added hastily, seeing consternation on Bran's face. "I just...wondered what was happening to them," I finished rather lamely.

To my surprise, Shevraeth said, "I shall be happy to discuss it with you. My decision did not meet with universal approval—there were advocates for extremes at either end—and some of my nearest associates grow tired of the whole affair." Here he saluted Bran with his wineglass, and Bran grinned unrepentantly.

"It's boring," my brother retorted. "And I can't even begin to keep it all in my head. Tlanth's affairs I see as my duty. Dealing with the affairs of the kingdom I regard as a narrow escape."

In disbelief I addressed the Marquis. "Don't you have advisers?"

"Quantities of them," he responded, "most of whom—nearly all, I very much regret to say—are precisely the people one wishes to listen to least: former Galdran toadies who are angling for new privileges, or to keep the ones they have; troublemakers; and then there are mere busybodies. I listen to them all, more to find out the trends of gossip in reaction to what I've done than to seek guidance for future decisions."

"Who are the troublemakers? People who want to rule?"

"Some of them," he agreed. "Among whom are a few with legitimate claims. Then there are those who are backing these claimants, with their own ends in view. Your own names have been put forth."

Bran grinned. "Grumareth kept after me the whole time I was in Athanarel."

"Well, maybe he thinks you'd rule well," I said.

Bran laughed. "He thinks I'd be easy to lead by the nose, yet too stupid to see him doing it."

I looked down at my plate, remembering again the terrible dinner with the Prince of Renselaeus when I had aired my views on how my brother would make a much better king than Shevraeth. Was that argument about to resurface?

But the Marquis said, "Poor Grumareth chose unwisely when he allied with Galdran. His was one of the duchies drained most by the 'volunteer taxes' and the forced levies for the army. I think he dreams of recouping what he lost. His people have to be clamoring for justice."

"He's a foolish man," Nee said, "but his great-niece isn't a fool."

Shevraeth nodded to her. "You're right. And I'm hoping that the duke will remain at Court to busy himself with plots and plans that won't work, so that Lady Elenet can stay in Grumareth and straighten things out."

Nee's eyes were sober as she glanced across the table, but her voice was exactly as pleasant and polite as ever. "So you will not strip the family of lands and title, despite his foolishness in the past?"

"The Duke of Grumareth was always a fool and will always be a fool," Shevraeth said, so lightly it was hard to believe he wasn't joking. His tone altered as he added, "I see no need to ruin the family over his mistakes. There is sufficient intelligence and good-will among them to see that their lands are restored to peace and thereby set on the way to recovering their former prosperity."

Nee smiled. "Trust Elenet for that." That was all she said, but I had a very strong feeling from both their tones of voice that there was an unspoken issue between them. Then I realized that she had been playing with her fan as they talked; I glanced at it, but if she'd used it to make more plain whatever it was that I sensed, it was too late now. She sat back, laying her fan in her lap as she reached for her wine.

"If everyone who compromised with Galdran out of fear, or greed, or even indifference, were to be penalized," Shevraeth went on, "Athanarel would soon be empty and a lot of people sent home with little to do but use their wealth and power toward recovering their lost prestige."

"More war," I said, and thinking again of my secret cause, I ventured a question. "Do you agree with Mistress Ynizang's writings about the troubles overseas and how they could have been avoided?"

Shevraeth nodded, turning to me. "That's an excellent book— one of the first my parents put into my hands when it became apparent I was serious about entering their plans."

"What's this? Who?" Bran asked, looking from one of us to the other.

Shevraeth said, "She is a historian of great repute in the Empress's Court, and I believe what she says about letting social custom and the human habit of inertia bridge an old regime to a new, when there is no active evil remaining."

"Sounds dull as a hibernating snake. Saving your grace." Bran

39

saluted the Marquis with his glass, then said, "Tell my sister about the army."

Shevraeth saluted my brother with his own glass and a slightly mocking smile. "To resume: Dispersal and reassignment. I have relied heavily upon certain officers whom I have come to trust—"

"Which is why you were up here against us last winter, eh?" Bran asked, one brow cocked up. "Scouting out the good ones?"

Old anger stirred deep inside me as I remembered the common talk from a year ago, about Shevraeth's very public wager with the Duke of Savona about how soon he could thoroughly squelch the rustic Tlanths—meaning Branaric and me. Fighting down my emotions, I realized that yet again I had been misled by surface events—and again I had misjudged Shevraeth's true motives.

"Precisely," the Marquis said. "Those who wish to stay are relatively easy; they await reassignment. Those who are unhappy, or incompetent, or for whatever reason are deemed ready for a civilian life are being cut loose with a year's pay. We are encouraging them to get training or to invest in some way so that they have a future, but a good part of that cash will inevitably find its way into the ready hands of pleasure houses. Still, each new civilian leaves with the warning that any bands of ex-soldiers roaming the countryside as brigands are going to find their futures summarily ended."

"So that's where the surplus money went," I said. "What about Galdran's bullies who *loved* their work?"

"The hardest part of our job is to determine who has the necessary qualifications for keeping order, and who merely has a taste for intimidating the populace. Those who fall between the two will be sent for a lengthy stint on border patrol down south, well away from events in the capital."

His readiness to answer my questions caused my mind to glitter with new ideas, like a fountain in the sunlight. I was suddenly eager to try my own theories of government, formed during my half year of reading. I launched a barrage of questions related to the merits of an all volunteer army paid from crown revenues, versus each noble being responsible for a certain number of trained and equipped soldiers should the need arise. To each question Shevraeth readily responded, until we had a conversation—not quite a debate—going about the strengths and weaknesses of each method of keeping the country safe.

Very soon I began to see where my lapses of knowledge were, for he knew the books I quoted from. Further, he knew the sources' strengths and weaknesses, whereas I had taken them as authorities. Still, I was enjoying myself, until I remembered what he'd said about listening to busybodies. Immediately full of self-doubt at the thought, I wondered if I sounded like one of those busybodies. Or worse, had I betrayed my secret quest?

Abruptly I stopped talking and turned my attention to my dinner, which lay cold and untouched on my plate. Stealing a quick glance up, I realized that I'd also kept Shevraeth talking so that his dinner was equally cold. I picked up my fork, fighting against another surge of those old feelings of helpless anger.

Into the sudden silence Branaric laughed, then said, "You've left me behind. What have you been reading, Mel? Life! You should go up to Erev-li-Erval and help take the field against the Djurans. Unless you're planning another revolution here!"

"Were you thinking of taking the field against me?" the Marquis addressed me in his usual drawl.

Aghast, I choked on a bite of food. Then I saw the gleam of humor in his eyes, and realized he'd been joking. "But I'm not," I squawked. "Not at all! I just like, well, reading and thinking about these things."

"And testing *your* knowledge, Danric," Bran added.

"Whether you are testing mine or your own, you really will get your best information firsthand," Shevraeth said to me. "Come to Athanarel. Study the records. Ask questions."

Was he really inviting me straight out to do what I'd resolved so secretly? I had no idea what to make of this. "I promised Nimiar I'd come," I mumbled, and that ended the subject.

Later, Nee sat with me in my room. We were drinking hot chocolate and talking about music, something I usually enjoy. But the dinner conversation was on my mind, and finally I said, "May I ask you a personal question?"

She looked up in query and made the graceful little gesture that I had learned was an invitation.

"Isn't Shevraeth a friend of yours?"

"Yes," she said cautiously.

"Then why the fan, and the careful words when you asked about your friend Elenet?"

Nee set her cup down, her brow slightly furrowed. "We are friends to a degree... Though we all grew up at Court, I was never one of his intimates, nor even one of his flirts. Those all tended to be the leaders of fashion. So I don't really know how close he was to any of them, except perhaps for Savona. It took everyone by surprise to find out that he was so different from the person we'd grown up with." She shrugged. "He was always an object of gossip, but I realized recently that though we heard much about what he did, we never heard what he thought."

"You mean he didn't tell anyone," I said.

"Exactly. Anyway, Elenet *is* an old friend, of both of us, which is complicated by her family's machinations. Her safety is important to me. Yet in referring to it, I don't want to seem one of the busybodies or favor-seekers."

"I don't think you could," I said.

She laughed. "Anyone can do anything, with determination and an inner conviction of being right. Whether they really are right..." She shrugged.

"Well, if he wants to be king, he'll just plain have to get used to questions and toadies and all the rest of it," I said. Remembering the conversation at dinner and wondering if I'd made an idiot of

42

myself, I added crossly, "I don't have any sympathy at all. In fact, I wish he hadn't come up here. If he needed rest from the fatigue of taking over a kingdom, why couldn't he go to that fabulous palace in Renselaeus? Or to Shevraeth, which I'll just bet has an equally fabulous palace?"

Nee sighed. "Is that a rhetorical or a real question?"

"Real. And I don't want to ask Bran because he's so likely to hop out with my question when we're all together and fry me with embarrassment," I finished bitterly.

She gave a sympathetic grin. "Well, I suspect it's to present a united front, politically speaking. You haven't been to Court, so you don't quite comprehend how much you and your brother have become heroes—symbols—to the kingdom. Especially you, which is why there were some murmurs and speculations when you never came to the capital."

I shook my head. "Symbol for failure, maybe. *We* didn't win— Shevraeth did."

She gave me an odd look midway between surprise and curiosity. "But to return to your question, Vidanric's tendency to keep his own counsel ought to be reassuring as far as people hopping out with embarrassing words are concerned. If I were you—and I know it's so much easier to give advice than to follow it—I'd sit down with him, when no one else is at hand, and talk it out."

Just the thought of seeking him out for a private talk made me shudder. "I'd rather walk down the mountain in shoes full of snails."

It was Nee's turn to shudder. "Life! I'd rather do almost anything than *that*—"

A "Ho!" outside the door interrupted her.

Bran carelessly flung the tapestry aside and sauntered in. "There y'are, Nee. Come out on the balcony with me? It's actually nice out, and we've got both moons up." He extended his hand.

Nee looked over at me as she slid her hand into his. "Want to come?"

I looked at those clasped hands, then away. "No, thanks," I said

43

airily. "I think I'll practice my fan, then read myself to sleep. Good night."

They went out, Bran's hand sliding round her waist. The tapestry dropped into place on Nee's soft laugh.

I got up and moved to my window, staring out at the stars.

It seemed an utter mystery to me how Bran and Nimiar enjoyed looking at each other. Touching each other. Even the practical Oria, I realized—the friend who told me once that things were more interesting than people—had freely admitted to liking flirting.

How does that happen? I shook my head, thinking that it would never happen to me. Did I want it to?

Suddenly I was restless and the castle was too confining.

Within the space of a few breaths I had gotten rid of my civilized clothing and soft shoes and had pulled my worn, patched tunic, trousers, and tough old mocs from the trunk in the corner.

I slipped out of my room and down the stair without anyone seeing me, and before the moons had traveled the space of a hand across the sky, I was riding along the silver-lit trails with the wind in my hair and the distant harps of the Hill Folk singing forlornly on the mountaintops.

FIVE

THE BUDS WERE JUST STARTING TO SHOW GREEN ON the trees when Bran said suddenly at dinner one day, "We ought to start to Remalna-city, Mel. Danric has work to do, and Nee hasn't seen her people for all these weeks. And as for me—" He winced. "I'm glad when we have a clear enough day where the construction can go on, but life! The noise and mess make me feel like a cat in a dog kennel."

"Set the date," I said, which I think surprised them all.

But I had already realized that there was little to keep me in Tlanth. Our county was on its way to recovery. By this time the next year we would even have paved roads between the villages and down to the lowlands—everywhere but beyond that invisible line that everyone in Tlanth knew was the border of the Hill Folk's territory.

Nee and Bran began talking about what delights awaited us in the capital. My last order of books had come in three weeks before, and I hadn't ordered more, for Nee and Bran both assured me that the library at Athanarel was fabulous—fantastic—*full*. To all their other words I smiled and nodded, inwardly thinking about the Marquise of Merindar's letter and my own reason for going to Court.

Shevraeth didn't say anything, or if he did, I didn't hear it, for I avoided him whenever possible.

The day before our departure was mild and clear with only an occasional white cloud drifting softly overhead. Bran swooped down on us just after breakfast and carried Nee off for a day alone.

So during the afternoon I retreated to the library and curled up in the window seat with a book on my lap.

But for once the beautifully drawn words refused to make sense, and I gazed instead out the window at the rose garden, which would be blooming well after I was gone. "My last afternoon of peace," I muttered with my forehead against the glass, then I snorted. It sounded fine and poetic—but I knew that as long as I thought that way, the peace had already ended.

And what was I afraid of?

I now knew enough of the rules of etiquette to get by, and I was now the proud possessor of what I once would have thought the wardrobe of a queen. And I wouldn't be alone, for my brother and my sister-to-be would accompany me.

As for the Marquise of Merindar's letter, perhaps its arrival and Shevraeth's on the very same day were coincidences after all. No one had said anything to me about it. And if I were reasonably careful at Court, I could satisfy my quest. . . .

Except, what then?

I was still brooding over this question when I heard a polite tap outside the tapestry, and a moment later, there was the equally quiet impact of a boot heel on the new tile floor, then another.

A weird feeling prickled down my spine, and I twisted around to face the Marquis of Shevraeth, who stood just inside the room. He raised his hands and said, "I am unarmed."

I realized I was glaring. "I hate people creeping up behind me," I muttered.

He glanced at the twenty paces or so of floor between us, then

46

up at the shelves, the map, the new books. Was he comparing this library with the famed Athanarel one—or the equally (no doubt!) impressive one at his home in Renselaeus? I folded my arms and waited for either satire or condescension.

When he spoke, the subject took me by surprise. "You said once that your father burned the Astiar library. Did you ever find out why?"

"It was the night we found out that my mother had been killed," I said reluctantly. The old grief oppressed me, and I fought to keep my thoughts clear. "By the order of Galdran Merindar."

"Do you know why he ordered her murder?" he asked over his shoulder, as he went on perusing the books.

I shook my head. "No. There's no way to find out that I can think of. Even if we discovered those who carried out the deed, they might not know the real reasons." I added sourly, "Well do I remember how Galdran issued lies to cover his misdeeds: Last year, when he commenced the attack against us, he dared to say that it was *we* who were breaking the Covenant!" I couldn't help adding somewhat accusingly, "Did you believe that? Not later, but when the war first started."

"No." I couldn't see his face. Only his back, and the long pale hair, and his lightly clasped hands were in view as he surveyed my shelves.

This was the first time the two of us had conversed alone, for I had been careful to avoid such meetings during his visit. Not wanting to prolong it, I still felt compelled to amplify.

I said, "My mother was the last of the royal Calahanras family. Galdran must have thought her a threat, even though she retired from Court life when she adopted into the Astiar family."

Shevraeth was walking along the shelves now, his hands still behind his back. "Yet Galdran had taken no action against your mother previously."

"No. But she'd never left Tlanth before, not since her marriage. She was on her way to Remalna-city. We only know that it was his own household guards, disguised as brigands, that did the job, because they didn't quite kill the stablegirl who was riding on the luggage coach and she recognized the horses as Merindar horses." I tightened my grip on my elbows. "You don't believe it?"

Again he glanced back at me. "Do you know your mother's errand in the capital?" His voice was calm, quiet, always with that faint drawl as if he chose his words with care.

Suddenly my voice sounded too loud, and much too combative, to my ears. Of course that made my face go crimson with heat. "Visiting."

This effectively ended the subject, and I waited for him to leave.

He turned around then, studying me reflectively. The length of the room still lay between us. "I had hoped," he said, "that you would honor me with a few moments' further discourse."

"About what?" I demanded.

"I came here at your brother's invitation." He spoke in a conversational tone, as though I'd been pleasant and encouraging. "My reasons for accepting were partly because I wanted an interlude of relative tranquillity, and partly for diplomatic reasons."

"Yes, Nimiar told me about your wanting to present a solid front with the infamous Astiars. I understand, and I said I'd go along."

"Please permit me to express my profound gratitude." He bowed gracefully.

I eyed him askance, looking for any hint of mockery. All I sensed was humor as he added, "I feel obliged to point out that... an obvious constraint... every time we are in one another's company will not go unnoticed."

"I promise you I've no intention of trying again for a crown."

"Thank you. What concerns me are the individuals who seem to wish to taste the ambrosia of power—"

"—without the bitter herb of responsibility. I read that one, too," I said, grinning despite myself.

He smiled faintly in response, and said, "These individuals might seek you out—"

My humor vanished. I realized then that he knew about the letter. He *had* to. Coincidence his arrival might be, but this conversation on our last day in Tlanth was not. It could only mean that he'd had someone up in our mountains spying on me, for how else could he know?

My temper flared brightly, like a summer fire. "So you think I'm stupid enough to lend myself to the schemes of troublemakers just for the sake of making trouble, is that what you think?" I demanded.

"I don't believe you'd swallow their blandishments, but you'll still be approached if you seem even passively my enemy. There are those who will exert themselves to inspire you to a more active role."

I struggled to get control of my emotions. "I know," I said stiffly. "I don't want to be involved in any more wars. All I want is the good of Remalna. Bran and I promised Papa when he died." *Even if my brother has forgotten*, I almost added, but I knew it wasn't true. In Bran's view, he had kept his promise. Galdran was gone, and Tlanth was enjoying peace and prosperity. Bran had never pretended he wanted to get involved in the affairs of kings beyond that.

As if his thoughts had paralleled mine, Shevraeth said, "And do you agree that your brother—estimable as he is—would not have made a successful replacement for Galdran Merindar?"

The parallel was unsettling. I said with less concealed hostility, "What's your point?"

"No . . . point," he said, his tone making the word curiously ambiguous. "Only a question."

He paused, and I realized he was waiting for my answer to his.

"Yes," I said. "Bran would make a terrible king. So what's your next question?"

"Can you tell me," he said slowly, "why you seem still to harbor your original resentment against me?"

Several images—spies, lying courtiers—flowed into my mind, to be instantly dismissed. I had no proof of any of it. So I looked

49

out the window as I struggled for an answer. After the silence grew protracted, I glanced back to see if he was still there. He hadn't moved. His attitude was not impatient, and his gaze was on my hands, which were tightly laced in my lap. His expression was again reflective.

"I don't know," I said finally. "I don't know."

There was a pause, then he said, "I appreciate your honesty." He gave me a polite bow, a brief smile, and left.

That night I retreated for the last time to the mountain peaks behind the castle and roamed along moonlit paths in the cool end-of-winter air. In the distance I heard the harpwinds, but this time I saw no one. The harps thrummed their weird threnodies, and from peak to peak reed pipes sounded, clear as winged creatures riding on the air, until the night was filled with the songs of approaching spring, and life, and freedom.

The music quieted my restlessness and buoyed me up with joy. I climbed the white stone peak at Elios and looked down at the castle, silhouetted silvery against the darker peaks in the distance. The air was clear, and I could see on the highest tower a tiny human figure, hatless, his long dark cloak belling and waving, and star-touched pale hair tangling in the wind.

In silence I watched the still figure as music filled the valley between us and drifted into eternity on the night air.

The big moon was high overhead when, one by one, the pipes played a last melody, and at last the music stopped, leaving only the sound of the wind in the trees.

It was time to return, for we would depart early in order to get off the mountain before nightfall. When at last I reached the courtyard and looked up at the tower, no one was there.

"Here's a hamper of good things," Julen said the next day, handing a covered basket into the coach where Nee and I were just settling.

Everyone in the village had turned out to see us off. We made a brave-looking cavalcade, with the baggage coaches and the outriders in their livery, and Branaric and the Marquis on the backs of fresh, mettlesome mounts, who danced and sidled and tossed their heads, their new-shod hooves striking sparks from the stones of the courtyard.

"Thank you," I said, pulling on my new-made traveling gloves. "Be well! 'Ria, keep us posted on Tlanth's business."

"I'll write often," Oria promised, bowed to Nee, and backed away.

"Let's go, then," Bran called, raising his hand. He flashed a grin at us then dropped his hand, and his impatient horse dashed forward.

Our carriage rolled more slowly through the gates; workers paused in their renovations and waved their caps at us. The trees closed in overhead, and we were on the road. I looked back until I had lost sight of the castle, then straightened round, to find Nee watching me, her face wistful within the flattering curve of her carriage hat.

"Regrets about leaving your home?" she asked.

"No," I said—making my first Court white lie.

Her relief was unmistakable as she sat back against the satin pillows, and I was glad I'd lied. "I hope we make it to Carad-on-Whitewater by nightfall," she said. "I really think you'll like the inn there."

"Why?" I asked.

She smiled. "You'll see."

I made a face. "You can't tell me? I think I've already had a lifetime's worth of surprises."

She laughed. "Dancing."

I rubbed my hands together. "Great. Strangers to practice on."

Still smiling, she shook her head. "I confess I find your attitude difficult to comprehend. When I learned, it was a relief to practice with my cousins before I tried dancing with people I didn't know."

"Not me," I said. "Like I told you, if I have to tread on

someone's toes, better some poor fellow I'll never see again—and who'll never see me—than someone who'll be afraid whenever he sees me coming. And as for practicing with Bran . . ."

She tried unsuccessfully to smother a laugh. "Well, he was just as outspoken about his own mistakes when he was learning," she said. "Frequently had a roomful of people in stitches. Not so bad a thing, in those early days," she added reflectively.

I shook my head. "I find it impossible to believe that anyone could regret Galdran's defeat. Besides his family." And, seeing a perfect opportunity to introduce the subject of the Marquise of Merindar, I said, "Even then, didn't they all hate one another?"

"They are . . . a complicated family," she said with care. "But of course they must regret the loss of the perquisites from being related to royalty. All that is gone now. They have only the family holdings."

"And we have his private fortune," I said, wondering if this related to the letter in some way.

She glanced out the window, then said, "Do not feel you have to speak of it, but it distressed me to realize that it is I who has been talking the most over the last days. Now I would very much like to listen."

"To what?" I asked in surprise. "I told you my history, and I don't *know* anything else."

"You know what the Hill Folk are like," she said with undisguised awe.

I laughed. "Nobody really knows what they're like. Except themselves," I said. "But it's true I've seen them. We all have, we who live high enough in the mountains. We do as children, anyway. I still do because I like to go up to them. Most of the others have lost interest."

"What are they like?"

I closed my eyes, drawing forth the green-lit images. "Unlike us," I said slowly. "Hard to describe. Human in shape, of course, but taller, and though they don't move at all like us, I think them very graceful. They can also be very *still*. You could walk right by them and not notice their presence, unless they move."

"Strange," she said. "I think that would frighten me."

I shook my head. "They don't frighten me—but I think I could see how they might be frightening. I don't know. Anyway, they are all brown and green and they don't really wear clothes, but you wouldn't think them naked any more than a tree is naked. They do have a kind of mossy lace they wear ... and flowers and bud garlands—lots of those—and when they are done, they replant the buds and blossoms, which grow and thrive."

"Are they mortal?"

"Oh, yes, though so long-lived they don't seem it—like trees. But they can be killed. I guess there's some grim stuff in our history, though I haven't found it. One thing, though, that's immediate is their sensitivity to herbs, particularly those brought here from other worlds. Like kinthus."

"Oh yes! I remember Bran talking about kinthus-rooting. The berries surely can't hurt them, can they? I mean, we use them for painkillers!"

"We never use kinthus in the mountains," I said. "Lister-blossom is good enough. As for the Hill Folk, I don't know if the berries hurt them. The danger is if there's a fire."

"I know burned kinthus is supposed to cause a dream state," Nee said.

"Maybe in us. The Hill Folk also drop into sleep, only they don't wake up. Anyway, every generation or so there's a great fire somewhere, and so we make certain there's no kinthus that can burn and carry its smoke up-mountain."

"A fair enough bargain," she said. "Tell me about their faces."

"Their faces are hard to remember," I said, "like the exact pattern of bark on a tree. But their eyes are, well, like looking into the eyes of the animals we live among, the ones who make milk. Have you ever noticed that the eyes of the ones we eat—fowl and fish—don't look at yours; they don't seem to see us? But a milk animal will see you, just as you see it, though you can't meet minds. The Hill Folk's eyes are like that, brown and aware. I cannot tell you what I see there, except if I look one in the face, I always want to have a clean heart."

"Very strange," she said, hugging her elbows close. "Yet I think you are lucky."

"Sometimes," I said, thinking of the night before, after my conversation with Shevraeth, when I'd had an angry heart. I was glad I hadn't seen any Hill Folk face-to-face.

But I didn't tell Nee that.

We conversed a little more, on different matters, then I asked her to practice fan language with me again. We made a game of it, and so the time passed agreeably as we progressed steadily down the mountain, sometimes slowly over icy places or snowdrifts. As we got closer to the lowlands the air turned warmer; spring, still a distant promise in the mountains, seemed imminent. The roads were less icy than muddy, but our progress was just as slow.

We stopped only to change horses. Nee and I didn't even get out of the carriage but ate the food that Julen had packed.

It was quite dark, and a sleety rain was just starting to fall when our cavalcade rolled impressively into the courtyard of the Riverside Inn at Carad-on-Whitewater.

What seemed to be the entire staff of the place turned out, all bowing and scurrying, to make our debarkation as easy as possible. As I watched this—from beneath the rain canopy that two eager young inn-helpers held over our heads—I couldn't help remembering last spring's sojourn at various innyards, as either a prisoner or a fugitive, and it was hard not to laugh at the comparison.

We had a splendid dinner in a private room overlooking the river. From below came the merry sounds of music, about as different from the haunting rhythms of the Hill Folk's music as can be, yet I loved it too.

When we had finished, Nee said, "Come! Let's go dance."

"Not me," Bran said. He lolled back on his cushions and

grabbed for his mulled wine. "In the saddle all day. I'll finish this, then I'm for bed."

"I'll go with you," I said to Nee, rising to my feet.

Nee turned to Shevraeth, who sat with both hands round his goblet. "Lord Vidanric? Will you come with us?"

I looked out the window, determined to say nothing. But I was still angry, convinced as I was that he had been spying on me.

"Keep me company," Bran said. "Don't want to drink by myself."

The Marquis said to Nee, "Another time."

I kept my face turned away to hide the relief I was sure was plain to see, and Nee and I went downstairs to the common room, which smelled of spicy drinks and braised meats and fruit tarts.

In one corner four musicians played, and the center of the room was clear save for a group of dancers, the tables and cushions having been pushed back to make space. Nee and I went to join, for we had come in on a circle dance. These were not the formal Court dances with their intricate steps, where each gesture has to be just so, right down to who asks for a partner and how the response is made. These were what Nee called town dances, which were based on the old country dances—line dances for couples, and circles either for men or for women—that people had stamped and twirled and clapped to for generations.

Never lacking for partners, we danced until we were hot and tired, and then went up to the spacious bedrooms. I left my windows wide open and fell asleep listening to the sound of the river.

"I'll go in the rattler with you," Bran said the next morning, to Nee. Grinning at her, he added, "Probably will rain, and I hate riding horseback in the wet. And we never get enough time together as it is."

I looked out at the heavy clouds and the soft mist, thought of that close coach, and said, "I'll ride, then. I don't mind rain—" I looked up, realized who else was riding, and fought a hot tide of embarrassment. "You can go in the coach in my place," I said to Shevraeth, striving to sound polite.

He gave his head a shake. "Never ride in coaches. If you want to know the truth, they make me sick. How about a wager?"

"A wager?" I repeated.

"Yes," he said, and gave me a slow smile, his eyes bright with challenge. "Who reaches Jeriab's Broken Shield in Lumm first."

"Stake?" I asked cautiously.

He was still smiling, an odd sort of smile, hard to define. "A kiss."

My first reaction was outrage, but then I remembered that I was on my way to Court, and that had to be the kind of thing they did at Court. *And if I win I don't have to collect.* I hesitated only a moment longer, lured by the thought of open sky, and speed, and *winning.*

"Done," I said.

SIX

I WENT STRAIGHT BACK TO MY ROOM, SURPRISING Mora and one of her staff in the act of packing up my trunk. Apologizing, I hastily unlaced the traveling gown and reached for my riding gear.

Mora gave me a slight smile as she curtsied. "That's my job, my lady," she said. "You needn't apologize."

I grinned at her as I pulled on the tunic. "Maybe it's not very courtly, but I feel bad when I make someone do a job twice."

Mora only smiled as she made a sign to the other servant, who reached for the traveling gown and began folding it up. I thrust my feet into my riding boots, smashed my fancy new riding hat onto my head, and dashed out again.

The Marquis was waiting in the courtyard, standing between two fresh mares. I was relieved that he did not have that fleet-footed gray I remembered from the year before. On his offering me my pick, I grabbed the reins of the nearest mount and swung up into the saddle. The animal danced and sidled as I watched Bran and Nimiar come out of the inn hand in hand. They climbed into the coach, solicitously seen to by the innkeeper himself.

The Marquis looked across at me. "Let's go."

And he was off, with me right on his heels.

At first all I was aware of was the cold rain on my chin and the exhilaration of speed. The road was paved, enabling the horses to dash along at the gallop, sending mud and water splashing.

Before long I was soaked to the skin everywhere except my head, which was hot under my riding hat, and when we bolted down the road toward the Akaeriki, I had to laugh aloud at how strange life is! Last year at this very time I was running rain-sodden for my life in the opposite direction, chased by the very same man now racing neck and neck beside me.

The thought caused me to look at him, though there was little to see beyond flying light hair under the broad-brimmed black hat and that long black cloak. He glanced over, saw me laughing, and I looked away again, urging my mount to greater efforts.

At the same pace still, we reached the first staging point. To-gether we clattered into the innyard and swung down from the saddle. At once two plain-dressed young men came out of the inn, bowed, and handed Shevraeth a blackweave bag. It was obvious from their bearing that they were trained warriors, probably from Renselaeus. For a moment the Marquis stood conversing with them, a tall mud-splashed and anonymously dressed figure. Did anyone else know who he was? Or who I was? Or that we'd been enemies last year?

Again laughter welled up inside me. When I saw stablehands bring forth two fresh mounts, I sprang forward, taking the reins of one, and mounted up. Then I waited until Shevraeth turned my way, stuck my tongue out at him, and rode out at the gallop, laugh-ing all the way.

I had the road to myself for quite a while.

Though I'd been to Lumm only that once, I couldn't miss the way, for the road to Lumm ran alongside the river—that much I remembered. Since it was the only road, I did not gallop long but pulled the horse back into a slower gait in order to keep it fresh. If I saw pursuit behind me, then would be the time to race again, to keep my lead.

So I reasoned. The road climbed gradually, until the area looked familiar again. Now I rode along the top of a palisade on the north side of the river; I kept scanning ahead for that rickety sheep bridge.

As I topped the highest point, I turned to look out over the valley, with the river winding lazily through it, and almost missed the fast-moving dot half obscured by the fine, silvery curtain of rain.

I reined in my horse, shaded my eyes, and squinted at the dot, which resolved into a horseback rider racking cross-country at incredible speed. Of course it could be anyone, but...

Turning my eyes back to the road, I saw Lumm in the distance, with a couple of loops of river between me and it.

Hesitating only a moment, I plunged down the hillside. The horse stumbled once in the deep mud, sending me flying face first. But I climbed back into the saddle, and we started racing eastward across the fields.

I reached Lumm under a relentless downpour. My horse splashed slowly up the main street until I saw swinging in the wind a sign with a cracked shield. The wood was ancient, and I couldn't make out the device as my tired horse walked under it. I wondered who Jeriab was, then forgot him when a stablehand ran out to take my horse's bridle.

"Are you Countess of Tlanth?" she asked as I dismounted.

I nodded, and she bustled over to a friend, handed off the horse, then beckoned me inside. "I'm to show you to the south parlor, my lady."

Muddy to the eyebrows, I squelched after her up a broad stair into a warm, good-smelling hallway. Genial noise smote me from all directions, and people came and went. But my guide threaded her way through, then indicated a stairway with a fine mosaic rail, and pointed. "Top, right, all across the back is where your party will be," she said. "Parlor's through the double door." She curtsied and disappeared into the crowd.

I trod up the stairs, making wet footprints on the patterned carpet at each step. The landing opened onto a spacious hallway.

I turned to the double doors, which were of foreign plainwood, and paused to admire the carving round the latch, and the painted pattern of leaves and blossoms worked into it. Then I opened one, and there in the middle of a lovely parlor was Shevraeth. He knelt at a writing table with his back to a fire, his pen scratching rapidly across a paper.

He glanced up inquiringly. His hair seemed damp, but it wasn't muddy, and his clothing looked miraculously dry.

I gritted my teeth, crossed my arms, and advanced on him, my cold-numbed lips poonched out below what I knew was a ferocious glare.

Obviously on the verge of laughter, he raised his quill to stop me. "As the winner," he murmured, "I choose the time and place."

"You cheated," I said, glad enough to have the embarrassment postponed.

"If you had waited, I would have shown you that shortcut," he retorted humorously.

"It was a trick," I snarled. "And as for your wager, I might as well get it over now."

He sat back, eyeing me. "Wet as you are—and you have to be cold—it'd feel like kissing a fish. We will address this another time. Sit down and have some cider. It's hot, just brought in. May I request your opinion of that?" He picked up a folded paper and tossed it in my direction. He added, with a faint smile, "Next time you'll have to remember to bring extra gear."

"How come you're not all soggy?" I asked as I set aside my sodden hat and waterlogged riding gloves.

He indicated the black cloak, which was slung over a candle sconce on the wall, and the hat and gloves resting on a side table. "Water-resistant spells. Expensive, but eminently worthwhile."

"That's what we need in Remalna," I said, kneeling on the cushions opposite him and pouring out spicy-smelling cider into a porcelain cup painted with that same leaf-and-blossom theme. "A wizard."

Shevraeth laid his pen down. "I don't know," he said. "A magician is not like a tree that bears fruit for all who want it and demands nothing in return. A wizard is human and will have his or her own goals."

"And a way of getting them that we couldn't very well stand against," I said. "All right. No wizard. But I shall get me one of those cloaks." I drank some of the cider, which was delicious, and while its warmth worked its way down my innards, I turned to the letter he'd handed me.

The exquisite handwriting was immediately familiar—a letter from the Marquise of Merindar. Under my sodden clothing my heart thumped in alarm. Addressed to their Highnesses the Prince and Princess of Renselaeus, the letter went on at length, thanking them for their generous hospitality during her period of grief, and then, in the most polite language, stating that its writer must reluctantly return to her home and family, and take up the threads of her life once again. And it was signed, in a very elaborate script, Arthal Merindar.

I looked up, to find Shevraeth's gaze on me. "What do you think?"

"What am I supposed to think?" I asked slowly, wondering if his question was some kind of a trap. "The Marquise is going back to Merindar, and blather blather blather about her nice year at Athanarel."

"Wants to go back," he said, still mildly. "Do you see a message there?"

"It's not addressed to me," I muttered, hunching up in defense.

"Ostensibly it's addressed to my parents," he said. "Look closely."

I bent over the letter again. At first my conflicting emotions made the letters swim before my eyes, but I forced myself to look

61

again—and to remember my own letter, now hidden in one of my trunks. Then I made a discovery.

"The signature is different from the rest of the writing, which means she must have used a scribe—" I thought rapidly. "Ah. She *didn't* write this herself. Is that a kind of oblique insult?"

"Well, one may assume she intended this to be read by other eyes."

Like my letter, I realized. Which meant . . .

"And since the signature is so different, she wanted it obvious. Yes, I see that," I said, my words slow, my mind winging from thought to thought. Did this mean that Shevraeth *hadn't* spied on me after all—that the Marquise had sent that letter knowing he'd find out?

My gaze was still on the fine scribal hand, but my thoughts ranged back through winter. Of course Bran would have told all his Court friends that he was going home at last, and probably with whom.

I gulped in a deep breath and once again tried to concentrate. "But unless there's a kind of threat in that last bit about taking up the threads of her life, I don't see any real problem here."

He picked up the quill again and ran the feathered part through his fingers. "One of the reasons my parents are both in Remalna-city is to establish someone of superior rank there until the question of rulership is settled."

"You think Arthal Merindar wants to be queen, then?" I asked, and again thought of my letter and why she might have written it.

Unbidden, Shevraeth's words from the day before our departure sounded in my head: ". . . but you'll still be approached if you seem even passively my enemy." Cold shock made me shiver inside when I realized that the Marquise of Merindar might have attributed my refusal to come to Court to unspoken problems between Shevraeth and myself—which would mean her letter was meant either to capitalize on my purported enmity or to make him distrust me.

So did he?

"What is she like?" I asked.

"Like her brother, except much better controlled. She's the only one of the family who is still a danger, but she very definitely is a danger."

"She might be saying the same of you," I said, resolutely trying to be fair. As before, I had no proof, and last year I had gotten myself into trouble for making quick judgments based merely on emotions, not facts. "Not that I think all that much of the Merindars I've met so far, but they do have a claim on the throne. And their marquisate, like Renselaeus, takes its name from the family even if it isn't nearly as old."

It was impossible to read his expression. "You think, then, that I ought to cede to her the crown?"

"Will she be a good ruler?" I countered, and suddenly the shock was gone. My old feelings crowded back into my head and heart. "*I* don't know. Why are you asking me? Why does my answer make any difference at all, unless showing me this letter and asking me these questions is your own way of making a threat?" I got up and paced the length of the room, fighting the urge to grab something and smash it.

"No," he said, dropping his gaze to the papers on the desk. "I merely thought you'd find it interesting." He leaned forward, dipped the point of his pen into the ink, and went on writing.

The argument, so suddenly sprung up, was over. As I stood there watching that pen move steadily across the paper, I felt all the pent-up anger drain out of me as suddenly as it had come, leaving me feeling tired, and cold, and very, very confused.

Shevraeth and I did not speak again; he kept working through his mail, and I, still tired and cold, curled up on a cushion and slipped into uncomfortable sleep.

Waking to the sound of Bran's cheery voice and a bustle and

rustling of people, I got up, feeling horribly stiff. Though I'd tried to stay with exercise through sword practice, I hadn't ridden that hard all winter, and every muscle protested. It did my spirits no good at all to see Shevraeth moving about with perfect ease. Resolving that I'd stay in the coach the rest of the way, crowded or not, I greeted Bran and Nee, and was soon reunited with dry clothing.

The four of us ate dinner together, and Shevraeth was exactly as polite as always, making no reference to our earlier conversation. This unnerved me, and I began to look forward to our arrival at Athanarel, when he would surely disappear into Court life and we'd seldom see one another.

As for the wager, I decided to forget about what had obviously been some kind of aristocratic joke.

SEVEN

So once again on an early spring day, I was en-sconced in a coach rolling down the middle of the Street of the Sun. Again people lined the street, but this time they waved and cheered. And as before, outriders joined us, but this time they wore our colors as well as the Renselaeuses'.

This had all been arranged beforehand, I found out through Nimiar. People expected power to be expressed through visible symbols, such as columns of armed outriders, and fancy carriages drawn by three matched pairs of fast horses, and so forth. Apparently Shevraeth loathed traveling about with such huge entourages—at least as much as Galdran used to love traveling with them—so he arranged for the trappings to be assumed at the last moment.

All this she told me as we rattled along the last distance through Remalna-city toward the golden-roofed palace called Athanarel.

When we reached the great gates, there were people hanging off them. I turned to look, and a small girl yelled, "Astiar!" as she flung a posy of crimson rosebuds and golden daisies through the open window of our carriage.

"They didn't shout last time," I said, burying my face in the posy. "Just stared."

"Last time?" Nee asked.

"When I had the supreme felicity of being introduced to Galdran by the esteemed Marquis," I said, striving for a light tone. "You don't remember?"

"Oh. I remember." Nimiar frowned, looking outside. "Though I was not there. I did not have duty that day. For which I was grateful."

"Duty?"

She gave me a pained smile. "Standing all afternoon in full Court dress was a pleasure for very few. It was a duty, and one strictly observed not out of loyalty or love but out of fear, for most of us."

"You were hostage to your families," I said.

"Essentially," she said, still looking out the window. Her profile was troubled.

"The Renselaeuses are keeping the Marquise of Merindar as a hostage, aren't they?"

Nee looked a little perplexed. "I'm certain she sees it in that light," she said quietly, and then she indicated the cheering people outside the coach. "You spoke of two kinds of crowds, the happy ones such as these, and the silent ones that you saw last year. Yet there is a third kind of crowd, the angry ones that are ready to fall on persons they hate and rend them if only someone brave enough—or foolhardy enough—steps forward to lead. I suspect that the Marquise of Merindar was kept here in part for her own protection from just that kind of crowd."

"Would she make a good queen?"

Nee bit her lip. "I don't know," she said. "I don't trust my ability to assess anyone that way. But I can tell you this: There were times she frightened me more than Galdran did, for his cruelties came out of rage, but hers came out of cold deliberation."

"Cold deliberation," I repeated, thinking of the letter—and of the way Shevraeth had let me know he knew about it. "So far, she and Shevraeth seem two buds on the same branch."

Nee said nothing. The atmosphere had changed, but before I could figure out how, and what it meant, we rolled to a stop before a fine marble terrace.

The carriage doors opened, and I looked out at servants in those fabulous liveries—still the crowned sun of Remalna, but now the green was deeper, and the brown had lightened back to gold.

I disembarked, gazing around. The terrace was part of a building, but in the other directions all I saw was greenery. "We're in a forest, or a garden. Where are the other buildings?"

She smiled again. "You can't see them from here. It's an artful design. Though the Family houses and the lesser guesthouses don't have quite this much privacy."

I looked up at the palace. Its walls were a warm peachy gold stone, with fine carving along the roof and beside each of its ranks of windows. Adjacent, glimpsed through budding trees, was another wing.

"That is the Royal Residence Wing." She pointed. "We're in the primary Guest Wing. On the other side of us, also adjacent, is the State Wing."

I whistled. "Do we have to eat in some vast cavern of a chamber with a lot of ambassadors and the like?"

"There are several dining rooms of varying size and formality, but I've been told we won't be using any of them except occasionally."

We were treading up the broad, shallow steps toward another pair of carved double doors. Someone opened them, and we passed through into a spacious entryway with a fabulous mosiac on the floor: a night sky with all the planets and stars, but with the sun at the center. Light shafted down from stained-glass windows above, overlaying the mosaic with glowing color. It was odd but interesting, and the golds and blues were beautiful.

Downstairs were the more public rooms; we were taken up a flight of beautifully tiled stairs to a long hall of suites. The servants had come up by some more direct way, for they were there before us, busily making the beautifully appointed rooms into a semblance of home.

I glanced around the rooms allotted to me. There was a little parlor, a bedroom, and a dressing room with a narrow, tiled stairway that led to the baths, below the first level. A cunningly hidden, even more narrow stairway led up to where the servants were housed. All three windows overlooked a stream-fed pool surrounded by trees. The rooms were done in soft greens; the tables were antique wood of a beautiful golden shade, the cushions and curtains and hangings all pale blue satin stitched with tiny green ivy and white blossoms.

I wandered through to Nee's suite, which was next to mine. Her rooms were done in quiet shades of rose, and they overlooked a flower garden.

She had been talking to her maids; when she was done and they had withdrawn, she sighed and sat down in a chair.

"What now?" I said.

She opened her hands. "What indeed? Protocol provides no answers. Instead it becomes a ticklish question itself, because there is no sovereign. Under Galdran, the days were strictly divided: Gold, we spent with family; green, we spent at Court; blue was for social affairs—but he even made clear who was to give them, and who was to go."

"Aren't the Prince and Princess setting some kind of schedule?"

"Apparently State work gets done mostly during gold, and twice a week or so they hold court for petitioners at the customary green-time, and all who wish to attend can. But it's not required. The rest of us...do what we will." She lifted her hands. "I expect we'll receive an invitation for dinner from their Highnesses, at second-blue, which will serve as an informal welcome."

I took a deep breath. "All right. Until then we're free? Let's walk around," I said. "I'm not tired or hungry, but I still feel stiff from—from sitting inside that coach for so long." I did not want to refer to my ride or the postponed wager.

If she noticed my hesitation and quick recovery, she gave no sign. She glanced out at the fair sky and nodded. "A good idea."

So we changed into afternoon dresses and walking hats and gloves, and went out. I told Mora that I'd like to have tea when we returned, thinking about how strange it was to be sending orders to a kitchen I'd probably never see. Before this past winter, the kitchen at home in Tlanth had been the center of my life.

Now I was buffered by Mora, and she by runners whose sole purpose seemed to be to wait about, in little anterooms at either end of the wing, to answer the summonses of our own personal servants, to fetch and carry. As Nee and I walked down the broad terrace steps onto a brick path, I reflected that anyone who really wanted to know what was going on at the palace would do better to question the runners than the aristocrats. Except, would they talk to me?

The day was fine, the cool air pleasant with scents of new blooms growing in the extensive gardens. We saw other people walking about, mostly in twos and threes. It was a great chance to practice my etiquette: nods for those unknown, and varying depths of curtsys for those Nee knew—the depth decided by rank and by the degree of acquaintance. Clues to status were in the way she spoke, and the order in which she presented me to people, or them to me if my rank was the higher. It was interesting to see people behave exactly the way she had told me they would—though I realized that, as yet, I couldn't read the tricks of gesture or smile, or the minute adjustments of posture that were additional messages.

For now, everyone seemed pleasant, and I even detected frank curiosity in the smiling faces, which braced me up: It seemed that they were not all accomplished dissemblers.

This was a good discovery to make just before the last encounter.

We strolled over a little footbridge that spanned a stream, then followed the path around a moonflower bed into a clearing beside a tree-sheltered pool.

The tableau we came upon was like a very fine picture. A beautiful lady sat on a bench, her blue skirts artfully spread at her feet, and ribbons and gems in her curling black hair. Watched by three young lords, she was feeding bits of something to the fish in the shallow pool. I gained only hazy impressions of two of the men— one red-haired, one fair—because my eyes were drawn immediately to the tallest, a man of powerful build, long waving dark hair, and a rakish smile. Dressed in deep blue with crimson and gold embroidery, he leaned negligently against the bench. The lady looked up at him with a toss of her head and smiled.

I heard a slight intake of breath from Nee, but when I looked over at her, I saw only the polite smile of her Court mask.

At first the people did not see us—or didn't notice us, I think would be a better way of saying it. For the lady had glanced up and then away, just as she dipped her hand into the beribboned little basket on her lap and, with a quick twist of her wrist, flung a piece of bread out over the light-dappled water of the pool. With a musical *plash*, a golden fish leaped into the air and snapped at the bread, diving neatly back into the water.

"Two to me," the lady cried with a gentle laugh, raising her eyes to the tall man, who smiled down at her, one hand gesturing palm up.

We were close enough now that I could see the lady's eyes, which were the same pure blue of her gown. Just then the tall man glanced over at us, and he straightened up, his dark eyes enigmatic, though he still smiled. He did not turn away, but waited for us to approach.

The lady looked up again, and I think I saw a faint impatience narrow those beautiful eyes; but then she gave us a breathtaking smile as she rose to her feet and laid aside her basket.

"Nimiar? Welcome back, dear cousin," she said in a melodious voice.

"We are returned indeed, Tamara," Nee said. "Your grace, may I present to you Lady Meliara Astiar?" And to me, "The Duke of Savona."

70

The dark eyes were direct, and interested, and very much amused. The famous Duke responded to my curtsy with an elaborate bow, then he took my hand and kissed it. I scarcely heard the names of the other people; I was too busy trying not to stare at Savona or blush at his lingering kiss.

"My dear Countess," Lady Tamara exclaimed. "Why were we not told we would have the felicity of meeting you?"

I didn't know how to answer that, so I just shook my head.

"Though, in truth, perhaps it is better this way," Lady Tamara went on. "I should have been afraid to meet so formidable a personage. You must realize we have been hearing a great deal about your valiant efforts against our former king."

"Well," I said, "if the stories were complimentary, they weren't true."

The fellows laughed. Lady Tamara's smile did not change at all. "Surely you are overly modest, dear Countess."

Savona propped an elegantly booted foot on an edge of the bench and leaned an arm across his knee as he smiled at me. "What is your version of the story, Lady Meliara?"

Instinct made me wary; there were undercurrents here that needed thinking out. "If I start on that we'll be here all night, and I don't want to miss my dinner," I said, striving for a light tone. Again the lords all laughed.

Nee slid her hand in my arm. "Shall we continue on to find your brother?" she addressed me. "He is probably looking for us."

"Let's," I said.

They bowed, Lady Tamara the deepest of all, and she said, "I trust you'll tell us all about it someday, dear Countess."

We bowed and started to move on. One fellow, a young red-haired lord, seemed inclined to follow; but Lady Tamara placed her fingertips on his arm and said, "Now, do not desert me, Geral! Not until I have a chance to win back my losses..."

Nee and I walked on in silence for a time, then she said in a guarded voice, "What think you of my cousin?"

"So that is the famous Lady Tamara Chamadis! Well, she really

71

is as pretty as I'd heard," I said. "But . . . I don't know. Somehow she embodies everything I'd thought a courtier would be."

"Fair enough." Nee nodded. "Then I guess it's safe for me to say—at risk of appearing a detestable gossip—watch out."

I touched the top of my hand where I could still feel the Duke of Savona's kiss. "All right. But I don't understand why."

"She is ambitious," Nee said slowly. "Even when we were young she never had the time for any of lower status. I believe that if Galdran Merindar had shown any interest in sharing his power, she would have married him."

"She wants to rule the kingdom?" I asked, glancing behind us. The secluded little pool was bounded by trees and hidden from view.

"She wants to reign over Court," Nee stated. "Her interest in the multitudes of ordinary citizens extends only to the image of them bowing down to her."

I whistled. "That's a pretty comprehensive judgment."

"Perhaps I have spoken ill," she said contritely. "You must understand that I don't like my cousin, having endured indifference or snubs since we were small, an heir's condescension for a third child of a secondary branch of the family who would never inherit or amount to much."

"She seemed friendly enough just now."

"The first time she ever addressed me as cousin in public," Nee said. "My status appears to have changed since I went away to Tlanth, affianced to a count, with the possible new king riding escort." Her voice took on an acidic sort of humor.

"And what about the Duke of Savona?" I asked, his image vivid in my mind's eye.

"In what sense?" She paused, turning to study my face. "He is another whose state of mind is impossible to guess."

I was still trying to disentangle all my observations from that brief meeting. "Is he, well, *twoing* with Lady Tamara?"

She smiled at the term. "They both are experts at dalliance,

72

but until last year I had thought they had more interest in each other than in anyone else," she said carefully. "Though even that is difficult to say for certain. Interest and ambition sometimes overlap and sometimes not."

As we wound our way along the path back toward Athanarel in the deepening gloom, I saw warm golden light inside the palace windows. With a glorious flicker, glowglobes appeared along the pathway, suspended in the air like great rainbow-sheened bubbles, their light soft and benevolent.

"I'm not certain what you mean by that last bit," I said at last. "As for the first, you said 'until last year.' Does that mean that Lady Tamara has someone else in view?"

"But of course," Nee said blandly. "The Marquis of Shevraeth."

I laughed all the way up the steps into the Residence.

EIGHT

"I THINK YOU SHOULD WEAR YOUR HAIR DOWN," Nee said, looking me over.

"For a dinner? I might kneel on it," I protested.

She smiled. "We'll dine empire style, for Prince Alaerec will be there."

I remembered from my visit to the Renselaeus palace that Shevraeth's father had been wounded in the Pirate Wars many years before. He could walk, but only with difficulty; and he sat in chairs.

"So wear your hair bound with these." She picked up an enameled box and opened it. There lay several snowstone hair ties, with thin silken ribbons hanging down. The ribbons were all white or silver.

I looked at my reflection. My gown was so dark a violet it was almost black, and had tiny faceted snowstones embroidered in lily patterns across the front. Nothing would ever make me look tall or voluptuous—even after a year of excellent food, I was exactly as small and scrawny as ever—but the gown flattered what little figure I had, so I didn't look ten years old. "All right." I simpered at my reflection. "Think I'll start a new fashion?"

"I know you will." She laughed. "I want to watch it happen."

"They might not like me," I said, sitting down on a hassock while Mora's gentle fingers stroked and fingered my hair.

"Mmmm." Nee watched with the air of an artist looking at a painting. "Do not give that a thought. You're *interesting*—something new. I think..." She paused, gestured, and Mora adjusted the thin snowstone band higher on my brow, making it drape at a graceful angle toward the back of my head.

"Think what?" I played nervously with the new fan hanging at my waist.

"What's that?" Nee looked up, her eyes inscrutable for a moment, then she smiled reassuringly. "I think it will be fine."

And it started fine.

Branaric joined us out in the hallway, and the three of us crossed into the State Wing, to an exquisitely decorated parlor where the Prince and Princess of Renselaeus sat in great carved bluewood chairs on either side of a splendid fire. Instead of the customary tiled tiers round the perimeter of the room, the floor had been leveled to the walls, where there were more of the chairs. Several guests sat in these, and I mentally reviewed the etiquette for chairs: knees and feet together, hands in lap.

The Prince wore black and white. The Princess, who was no bigger than I, was a vision in silver and pale blue with quantities of white lace. She had green eyes and silver-streaked brown hair, and an airy manner. Seated at the Princess's right hand was a large, elaborately dressed woman with gray-streaked red hair. Her eyes, so like Galdran's they prompted in me a prickle of alarm, were bland in expression as they met my gaze briefly, then looked away. The Marquise of Merindar? My heart thumped.

"Ah, my dear," Princess Elestra said to me in her fluting voice—that very same voice I remembered so well from my escape from Athanarel the year before. "How delighted we are to have you join us here. Delighted! I understand there will be a ball in your honor tomorrow, hosted by my nephew Russav." She nodded toward the other side of the room, where the newly arrived Duke of Savona stood in the center of a small group. "He seldom bestirs himself this way, so you must take it as a compliment to you!"

"Thank you," I murmured, my heart now drumming.

I was glad to move aside and let Branaric take my place. I didn't hear what he said, but he made them both laugh; then he too moved aside, and the Prince and Princess presented us to the red-haired woman, who was indeed the Marquise of Merindar. She nodded politely but did not speak, nor did she betray the slightest sign of interest in us.

We were then introduced to the ambassadors from Denlieff, Hundruith, and Charas al Kherval. This last one, of course, drew my interest, though I did my best to observe her covertly. A tall woman of middle age, her manner was polite, gracious, and utterly opaque.

"Family party, you say?" Branaric's voice caught at my attention. He rubbed his hands. "Well, you're related one way or another to half the Court, Danric, so if we've enough people to hand, how about some music?"

"If you like," said Shevraeth. He'd appeared quietly, without causing any stir. "It can be arranged." The Marquis was dressed in sober colors, his hair braided and gemmed for a formal occasion; though as tall as the flamboyantly dressed Duke of Savona, he was slender next to his cousin.

He remained very much in the background, talking quietly with this or that person. The focus of the reception was on the Prince and Princess, and on Bran and me, and, in a strange way, on the ambassador from Charas al Kherval. I sensed that something important was going on below the surface of the polite chitchat, but I couldn't discern what—and then suddenly it was time to go in to dinner.

With a graceful bow, the Prince held out his arm to me, moving with slow deliberation. If it hurt him to walk, he showed no sign, and his back was straight and his manner attentive. The Princess went in with Branaric, Shevraeth with the Marquise, Savona with the Empress's ambassador, and Nimiar with the southern ambassador. The others trailed in order of rank.

I managed all right with the chairs and the high table. After we were served, I stole a few glances at Shevraeth and the Marquise of Merindar. They conversed in what appeared to be amity. It was equally true of all the others. Perfectly controlled, from their fingertips to their serene brows, none of them betrayed any emotion but polite attentiveness. Only my brother stood out, his face changing as he talked, his laugh real when he dropped his fork, his shrug careless. It seemed to me that the others found him a relief, for the smiles he caused were quicker, the glances brighter—not that *he* noticed.

Conversation during the meal was light and flowed along like water, sometimes punctuated by the quick, graceful butterfly movements of fans. Music, a comical play recently offered by a famous group of players, future entertainments, the difficulties of the winter—all were passed under review. I sat mute, sipping at the exquisite bluewine, which savored of sunshine and fresh nuts, and listening attentively to the melodic voices.

When the meal was over, the Princess invited everyone to yet another room, promising music after hot chocolate.

Dazzled by the glint of jewels and the gleam of silk in the firelight, I moved slowly until I found myself face-to-face with Princess Elestra.

"Has my son shown you the library yet, my child?" she asked, her gently waving fan flicking up for just a moment at the angle of Confidential Invitation.

"No," I said, instantly ill at ease. "Ah—we just arrived today, you see, and there hasn't been time to see much of anything."

"Come. We will slip out a moment. No one will notice." With a smile, she indicated the corner where Savona was telling some story, illustrating a sword trick with a fireplace poker amid laughter and applause. My brother was laughing loudest of all.

With the smoothest gesture, nod, and bow, she threaded through the crowd. Then we were suddenly in a quiet hall, its richness gleaming in the light of a double row of glowglobes placed in fabulously carved sconces.

"I am told that you like to read," the Princess said as we turned into an even more formal hall. Liveried servants stood at either side of the entry, and when they saw my companion, they bowed, ready for orders. With a little wave, she indicated the tall double doors between two spectacular tapestries dark with age. The servants sprang to open these doors.

As we passed inside, I glanced back at the nearest footman and caught a glimpse of curiosity before his face smoothed into imperviousness.

"A problem, dear child?"

I turned and saw awareness in the Princess's eyes.

So I said carefully, "I don't want to sound critical, Your Highness, but I was thinking how horrible it must be to stand about all day just waiting to open a door, even one as pretty as those."

"But they don't," she responded with a soft laugh. "They trade places regularly. Some stand out there, some are hidden from view waiting for summonses. It is very good training in patience and discretion, for they all want to advance into something better."

She touched a glowglobe, and one by one, in rapid succession, an array of globes flickered, lighting a long room lined with packed bookshelves.

"The books are all arranged by year," she said, nodding at the nearest shelves. "These on this wall concern Remalna. All those there are from other parts of the world. Some real treasures are numbered among that collection. And under the windows are plays and songs."

"Plays, Your Highness?" I repeated in surprise. "Do people write plays down? How can they, when the players change the play each time they do it?"

She nodded, moving along the shelves as though looking for something in particular. "In our part of the world, this is so, and it is common to some of the rest of the world as well. But there are places where plays are written first—usually based on true historical occurrence—and performed as written. It is an old art. At the Empress's Court there is a current fashion for plays written at least four hundred years ago, with all their quaint language and custom and costume."

I thought this over and realized once again how much in the world I was ignorant of. "I thought plays were about dream people, that the events had never happened—that the purpose of plays is to make people laugh."

"There's a fine scholar in the south who has traveled about the world studying plays, and he maintains that, whether or not they are based on real experiences, they are the harbingers of social change," Princess Elestra replied. "Ah! Here we are."

She pulled down a book, its cover fine red silk, with the title in gilt: *The Queen from the Desert.*

"I know that book!" I said.

"It is very popular," she responded, then pulled down four books from nearby, each a different size and thickness. To my surprise, each had the same title. "We were speaking of plays, the implication being that history is static. But even it can change. Look."

I glanced through the histories, all of which were written in a scribe's exquisite hand. Two of them were purported to be taken from the queen's own private record, but a quick perusal of the first few lines showed a vast difference between them. Two of the books were written by Court-appointed historians—the heralds—like the one I'd read. One of them seemed familiar. The other had a lot fewer words and more decoration in the margins. When I flipped through it, I noticed there were conversations I didn't remember seeing in the one I had read.

"So some of these are lies?" I looked up, confused.

"A few are distorted deliberately, but one has to realize that aside from those, which our best booksellers weed out, there is truth and truth," the Princess said. "What one person sees is not always what another sees. To go back to our histories of the desert queen, we can find a fifth one, written a century later, wherein her story is scarcely recognizable—but that one was written as a lampoon of another queen."

"So . . . the scribes will change things?" I said.

She nodded. "Sometimes."

"Why?"

She closed the books and returned them to the shelves. "Occasionally for political reasons, other times because the scribes think they have a special insight on the truth. Or they think the subject was dull, so they enliven his or her words. Court historians are sometimes good, and sometimes foolish . . . and sometimes ambitious. The later histories are often the most trustworthy. Though they are not immediate, the writers can refer to memoirs of two or three contemporaries and compare versions."

"Going back to the memoirs, Your Highness, how does one know one is getting the words of the person whose name is in front?"

She pulled down three more books and flipped to the backs, each showing a seal and names and dates. Below these was written: *Fellowship of the Tower*.

"What is this, Your Highness, a sigil for a guild?"

"It is more than a guild. Men and women who join give up all affiliation with their own land. There are five or six establishments throughout the world. Members of the fellowship are not just scribes, but are sworn to stay with the written truth. If you find a copy of Queen Theraez's memoirs with the Fellowship of the Tower's sigil in back, you can trust that every word—every cross out—scrupulously reproduces the papers kept in the Heraldry Archive, written in the queen's own hand. Their purpose is to spread knowledge, not to comment or to alter or improve."

She closed the books and replaced them, then turned to face me. "This library was a haven for many of us during the late king's reign. He liked appearing suddenly hither and yon, but he never did come in here." She gave me a faint smile. "Are you chilled, my dear? Shall we rejoin the others? You can warm up again by dancing."

"Thank you for showing me the library, Your Highness," I said.

"I hope you will find time for exploring in here during your stay at Athanarel," she replied, leading the way to the doors.

She was kind and unthreatening; and because we were alone, I took a chance. "Did you know I was using your carriage to escape that night?" I blurted. My words sounded sudden, and awkward, and my face burned.

She sighed, looking down at her hand on the door's latch, but she did not open the door. "It was an ill-managed thing, not a memory one wishes to return to. Those were dangerous days, and we had to act quickly." Then she opened the door, and there were the footmen, and when she spoke again, it was about the new musicians that were to play.

We'd reached the reception room before I realized that her answer had admitted to a conspiracy without implicating anyone but herself—and that it had also been a kind of apology. But it was equally clear that she didn't want to return to the subject, and I remembered what Nee had told me during our first real conversation: *They don't talk of the war at all.*

Why? I thought, as we joined the rest of the company. The Renselaeuses won; surely such talk could no longer harm them. And it was impossible to believe that they wanted to protect those who had lost . . . those such as myself.

I shook my head as I made my way to Bran and Nee. *Impossible.*

The reception room was larger now. Folding doors had been thrown back, opening two rooms into one. The second room had the customary tiers along its perimeter, with gorgeously embroidered cushions and low tables for those who did not want to dance. Above, in a cozy gallery, musicians played horns and drums and strings, and in the center of the room, toes pointed and arched wrists held high, eight couples moved through the complicated steps of the taltanne.

The music was stirring and so well played I had to keep my

feet from tapping. Among the Hill Folk it was also impossible to stay motionless when they played their music, yet it was very different from this. Up on the mountains the music was as wild as wind and weather, as old as the ancient trees; and the dances retold stories even older than the trees. This music was more controlled, with its artfully modulated melodies, themes, and subthemes; controlled too were the careful steps of the dance. Controlled, yet still beautiful. *And dangerous,* I thought, as I watched glances exchanged over shoulders and across the precise geometric figures of the dance.

Then the Duke of Savona appeared before me. He bowed, smiled, and held out his arm—and there was no time for thought.

It was my very first dance in Court, and I would have liked to try it with someone I knew. But at Court one didn't dance with one's brother. With the Hill Folk, dance was a celebration of life, sometimes of death, and of the changing of the seasons. Here dances were a form of courtship—one that was all the more subtle, Nee had said once, because the one you danced with might not be the one you were courting.

Savona did not speak until the very end, and then it was not the usual sort of compliment that Nee had led me to expect. Instead, he clasped my hand in his, leaned close so that I could smell his clean scent, and murmured, "Your favorite color, Meliara. What is it?"

No titles, just that soft, intimate tone. I felt slightly dizzy and almost said *Blue,* but I had just enough presence of mind to stop myself. Blue being the primary Renselaeus color, this might be misleading. "Lavender," I said. My voice sounded to my ears like a bat squeak.

The music ended then, and he bowed over my hand and kissed it. Then he smiled into my eyes. "Will you wear it tomorrow?" he asked.

"Certainly. Your grace," I managed.

"Call me Russav." Another bow, and he turned away.

"Here's Geral Keradec." Bran stepped up, took my arm, and turned me to face a tall red-haired young man. "Wants to dance with you, sister."

Desperately I tried to clear my thoughts and respond correctly. Geral—he also insisted on abandoning titles right away—was funny, shy, and mild voiced. Encouraging him to talk, I discovered that he liked music and poetry, and that he was the heir to an old barony.

And so it went for the remainder of the evening. I was never still, never had time to stop or sit down—or to think. Increasingly I felt as if I had stepped down from a quiet pathway expecting to encounter firm stones, but had instead tumbled into a fast-moving river.

Twice I looked across the room to find Savona standing against the wall, his powerful arms crossed, watching me. When my eyes met his, he grinned. After the second time, I just had to know what the Marquis of Shevraeth made of all this, and I darted a fast glance at him under my partner's velvet-sleeved arm as we twirled.

Shevraeth was in the dance at the other end of the room, conversing quietly with his partner. He seemed completely oblivious to everyone else.

And the Marquise of Merindar was not there at all.

NINE

"Savona didn't dance with anyone else," Nee said.

We were curled up in my sitting room. Outside the window, the garden was a silhouette in the faint blue light of dawn.

"We only danced that once. But then he asked me that question about my favorite color," I said. "Ought I to wear it tonight?"

She pursed her lips. "I'll wager my best necklace all the decorations in that ballroom tonight will be lavender, even if he has to empty the entire city today to find them. Did he say anything else?"

"He asked me to call him Russav."

Her eyes widened. "I don't think *anyone* calls him that—except for Vidanric, and sometimes Tamara. I think I told you that he inherited when his parents died under mysterious circumstances, when he was very small. We all grew up calling him Savona."

"Well, I can't think of him as anything but Savona." Again that sense of rushing down a rock-strewn river engulfed me. "What does it all mean?"

"It means you are going to be very, very popular," Nee predicted.

"Is that it?" I said, frowning.

"You mean, what does it signify in personal terms?" she asked, her brows rising. "That question, my dear, you are the one to answer, not I."

"But I can't answer it," I wailed. "I feel like I'm in a whirlwind, and the wrong move will dash me on the rocks."

"You'll learn how to maneuver as you steer your own course," she said. "Everyone began with no experience."

I shook my head. "I think that Savona was born with experience."

She set her cup down. "He was always popular with the wilder children, the ones who liked dares and risks. He and Vidanric both. Only, Vidanric was so small and lightboned he had to work hard at it, while everything came easy to Savona, who was always bigger and faster and more coordinated than anyone else. I think it was the same when they discovered flirting—" She hesitated, then shrugged and closed her lips.

And since the subject had come to include Shevraeth, I didn't want to pursue it. Ever since our conversation on our arrival at Athanarel, Nee had stopped talking about him. I told myself I didn't want to hear any more anyway.

Now she drifted toward the door, her dressing gown trailing behind her. "We'd better get to sleep. We have a very long evening before us."

I nodded, wishing her a good rest. As I crawled into bed, I felt a happy sense of anticipation. Not just because I had a wonderful ball to look forward to—my very first. More important to me was that the day after that was my Name Day and the anniversary of the beginning of the long, terrible time I spent as a prisoner and a fugitive.

My Flower Day had also been last year, but because of the war there had been no music, no dancing, no celebration.

I remembered Bran's words just before I made the fateful spy trip, "Next year I promise you'll have a Name Day celebration to be remembered forever—and it'll be in the capital."

"With us as winners, right?" I'd said. Well, here we were in the capital after all, though we hadn't won the crown. I didn't want a party—not at Court, attended by strangers—but I looked forward to celebrating with Bran.

I didn't have a lavender ball gown, so Mora and her handmaids changed the ribbons on my white-and-silver one. I felt splendid when I looked at myself in the mirror as Mora brushed out my hair and arranged it to fall just right against the back of the silver gown.

Last was the headdress, which Mora's deft fingers pinned securely into place. It was mainly white roses with long white ribbons and one lavender one tied in a bow. I had another new fan, which hung from my waist on a braided silken cord of white.

My spirits were high as I joined Nee and Bran. But instead of walking down the stairs to go into the ballroom with the rest of the guests, Nee and Bran led the way across the hall, to the gallery that overlooked the ballroom, and stopped at the landing at the top of the grand stairway.

And there we found Shevraeth waiting for us, looking formidable and remote in his usual dark colors. Remembering with dismaying intensity that the last time we had talked with one another I had managed—again—to instigate a quarrel, I felt embarrassment chase away my anticipation.

Shevraeth greeted us in his customary calm manner. When he turned at last to Bran, I muttered out of the side of my mouth to Nee, "You mean we have to go down these stairs—with him—and everyone looking at us?"

"We're the guests of honor," she whispered back, obviously trying not to laugh. She looked fabulous in her dark brown velvet gown, embroidered all over with tiny gold leaves dotted with little rubies. "We're supposed to be looked at! We'll open the ball. You remember? I know I told you."

Bran flicked my shoulder. "Brace up, Mel. You'll like it. I promise."

My attempt at a bland face obviously wasn't convincing. I studied the toes of my dancing slippers, wishing with all my strength that I was back in Tlanth, riding the mountain trails with no humans in sight.

"Savona's waiting," Nee whispered to me.

Some invisible servant must have given a signal, for the music started: an entire orchestra filling the vaulted room with the strains of an ancient promenade. Had I been downstairs among the glittering throng, I would have loved it, but I now had Shevraeth standing right beside me, holding out his arm. I just *knew* I would manage to do something embarrassing.

I took a deep breath, straightened my shoulders, and tried my best to smooth my face into a polite smile as I put my hand on his sleeve.

Just before we started down, he murmured, "Think of this as a battle."

"A battle?" I repeated, so surprised I actually looked up at his face. He didn't look angry, or disgusted, or sarcastic. But there was suppressed laughter in the way his gray eyes were narrowed.

He replied so softly I could just barely hear it. "You've a sword in your hand, and vast numbers of ravening minions of some dreaded evil sorcerer await below. The moment you step among them, you'll leap into battle, mowing them down in droves..."

The absolute unlikelihood of it made me grin, on the verge of laughter. And I realized that while he'd spoken we had come safely down the stairs and were halfway along the huge room to the Duke of Savona, who waited alone. On either side people bowed and curtsied, as graceful as flowers in the wind.

I'd almost made it, and my smile was real—until I lost the image and remembered where I was, and who I was with, and I muttered defensively, "I don't really like battles, you know."

"Of course I know," he returned, still in that soft voice. "But you're used to them." And then we were before Savona, who was resplendent in black and crimson and gold; and as the Duke bowed, fanfare after fanfare washed over me like waves of brilliant light.

Because Shevraeth was also a guest of honor, and had the highest rank, it was his choice for the first dance, and he held out his hand to me. Savona went to Nee, and Bran went to Nee's cousin Tamara.

We danced. I moved through the complicated steps with sureness, my whole body in harmony with the singing strings, my eyes dazzled by the swirl of color all around me. Above our dancing figures, and around us, flowers and ribbons and hangings of every shade of violet and lavender made the room seem almost impossibly elegant.

When the dance ended, Shevraeth bowed and handed me to Savona, and once again I danced, relieved that I had somehow managed to get through the first one without any awkwardness at all. *It's the music*, I thought happily as I spun and stepped; *music is truly like magic.*

At the end of that dance I was surrounded by potential partners, and so it went for the rest of the night. I scarcely remembered any of the introductions, but it didn't seem to matter. A succession of smiling, handsome partners and a continual flow of compliments formed a background to the music, which filled me with the light air that makes clouds and rendered it impossible not to dance.

It wasn't until the night was nearly over that I discovered I was thirsty. It was my first quiet moment. Standing near one of the potted shrubs that isolated the food and drink, I sipped at the punch and started picking out individual voices from the chatter around me, and individual dancers from the mass.

I overheard a conversation from the other side of the shrub. "...see Tamara? That's the third time she's gotten him."

Curious, I looked at the dancers and easily found Lady Tamara—dancing with Shevraeth. They made a very handsome couple, her pale blue gown and dark hair, his colors the opposite. Her eyes gleamed through her famous lashes as she smiled up into his face; she then spoke, though the words were inaudible. He, of course, was exactly as unreadable as always.

"Tsk tsk." A new voice joined in, drawling with sardonic amusement, "I suppose it's inevitable. She's always gotten what she's wanted; and beware whoever gets in her way."

"Everything?" the first voice said with a tinkly sort of laugh. "Compassing marriage to either of the cousins?"

"Come now, she's dropped the lesser prospect. Why settle for a duke when there's a king in reach?"

"Perhaps she's been dropped" was the answer. "Or else the glare while Savona danced with the little Tlanth countess was a sham to provide entertainment for our speculation."

Laughing, the speakers moved away. I stood where I was, watching Lady Tamara happily whirling about the room in Shevraeth's grasp, and I realized that he hadn't been near me since the beginning of the evening. Uncomfortable emotions began eroding my enjoyment. I tried to banish them, and also what I'd heard. *It's nothing to do with me*, I told myself firmly, hoping there wasn't some like conversation taking place elsewhere in the room—only with me as its subject. *I didn't do anything wrong.*

Still, it was hard during the remaining dances to recapture the earlier joy, and at the end I was glad to follow Bran and Nee back upstairs to our rooms, Nee yawning all the way. My feet were tired, but I buoyed myself with the reminder that my Name Day came with dawn. *What has Branaric planned?*

He gave me no hints as he bade me a good night outside my rooms.

The windows were bright with sunlight when I woke, and though I could have slept longer, the prospect of my Name Day got me up and dressed.

My first thought was to go to Nee's rooms. She would be a part of anything Bran planned.

I bustled down the hall. As I stretched out my hand to knock outside her tapestry, I heard Bran's genial voice booming from inside: "Enstaeus and Trishe went to kidnap him. We're to meet them at the stable."

And Nee said, "Then we'd better go before Meliara wakens. It'll be easier than trying to explain that she wouldn't enjoy this ride—"

My hand froze. Shock, dismay, and question all kept me from moving, even though I knew I ought to retreat—fast—to my room. Even in the rudest house among the most ignorant people, children grow up knowing that tapestry manners require you to make a noise as soon as you reach someone's room. You don't stand and listen.

Holding my hands straight at my sides so my skirts wouldn't rustle, I backed up one step, two—then Nee's tapestry lifted, and there were the three of us, face-to-face.

Bran snorted a laugh—of course. "Life, sister, you gave me a start!"

Nee's entire face went crimson, though the fault was mine for being there without warning. "Good morning," she said, looking unhappy.

I did my best to assume a sublimely indifferent Court mask. "I just stopped to tell you I was going to the library." And I walked away quickly.

Not enjoy a ride? I thought, and then I remembered that this was Court, and people didn't always say what they thought. Apparently even Nee. *They want to spend some time alone, of course,* I realized, and guilt overwhelmed me. I had monopolized Nee ever since the night in our palace when she offered to show me Court ways.

Well, I was at Court now, and I had made it through a grand ball without causing any disasters or making a complete fool of myself. *So now it is only fair to leave her some time alone with my brother,* I told myself firmly. After all, wasn't that a part of courtship, wanting to be alone with your intended, however much you liked the rest of his family?

90

I hurried down the silent halls toward the library as if I could outrun my emotions, forming a resolve to start making my own way, leaving Nee to get on with her life.

As I neared the State Wing, my heart thumped, and despite the Princess's kind invitation, I hoped I wouldn't encounter any of the Renselaeuses. But no one was about except silent footmen and occasional equerries passing to and fro. When I reached the library, the waiting footmen opened the doors for me, and I passed into the huge room and found myself alone.

I strolled slowly along the shelves, looking at titles without really comprehending them, wondering where I ought to begin. Remembering my conversation with Princess Elestra, I realized what I *really* wanted to see were the originals, the papers written by kings and queens in their own hands. Were they all in the Heraldry Archives, or were some of them here?

My gaze fell on a plain door-tapestry at the other end of the room. *A service access?* I turned and saw a narrow, discreet outline of a door tucked in the corner between two bookshelves; that was the service door, then. Might I find some kind of archive beyond that tapestry?

I crossed the room, heard no noise beyond, so I lifted the tapestry.

The room was small, filled with light. It was a corner room, with two entrances, floor-to-ceiling windows in two walls, and bookshelves everywhere else. In the slanting rays of the morning sun I saw a writing table angled between the windows—and kneeling at the table, dressed in riding clothes, was the Marquis of Shevraeth.

He put down his pen and looked up inquiringly.

Feeling that to run back out would be cowardly, I said, "Your mother invited me to use the library. I thought this might be an archive."

"It is," he said. "Memoirs from kings and queens addressed specifically to heirs. Most are about laws. A few are diaries of Court life. Look around." He picked up the pen again and waved it toward

91

the shelves. "Over there you'll find the book of laws by Turic the Third, he of the twelve thousand proclamations. Next to it is his daughter's, rescinding most of them." He pushed a pile of papers in my direction. "Or if you'd like to peruse something more recent, here are Galdran's expenditure lists and so forth. They give a fairly comprehensive overview of his policies."

I stepped into the room and bent down to lift up two or three of the papers. Some were proposals for increases in taxes for certain nobles; the fourth was a list of people "to be watched."

I looked at him in surprise. "You found these just lying around?"

"Yes," he said, sitting back on his cushion. The morning light highlighted the smudges of tiredness under his eyes. "He did not expect to be defeated. Your brother and I rode back here in haste, as soon as we could, in order to prevent looting; but such was Galdran's hold on the place that, even though the news had preceded us by two days, I found his rooms completely undisturbed. I don't think anyone believed he was really dead—they expected one of his ugly little ploys to catch out 'traitors.' "

I whistled, turning over another paper. "Wish I could have been there," I said.

"You could have been."

This brought me back to reality with a jolt. Of course I could have been there—but I had left without warning, without saying good-bye even to my own brother, in my haste to retreat to home and sanity. And memory.

I glanced at him just in time to see him wince slightly and shake his head. Was that regret? For his words—or for my actions that day?

"What you said last night," I demanded, "about battles and me being used to them. What did you mean by that?"

"It was merely an attempt to make you laugh."

"I did laugh," I admitted, then frowned. "But did you *really* intend some kind of courtly double meaning? Hinting that I'm used to battles in the sense that I lost every one I was in? Or merely that I get into quarrels?"

"Neither." His tone was flat. "Forgive my maladroitness."

"Well, I *don't* get into quarrels," I said, suddenly desperate to explain, to accuse. "Except with—"

There came a tap outside the opposite doorway then.

I shut my mouth; and for a moment, there we were, in silence, me wishing I could run but feeling I ought not to. There was—something—I had to do, or say, though I had no idea what.

So I watched him rise, move the few steps to the other tapestry, and lift it. I did not see whoever was outside—I realized he was shielding me from sight. I could not hear the voice beyond, but I heard his: "Please inform Lady Trishe I will be along shortly. Thank you." He dropped the tapestry back into place and stood with his back to it, looking at me across the width of the room. "It seems," he said, "that seeking your opinion will not cease to embroil us in argument, whatever the cause. I apologize. I also realize trying to convince you of my good intentions is a fruitless effort, but my own conscience demanded that I make the attempt."

I couldn't think of any reply to make to that, so I whirled around and retreated into the library, my insides boiling with a nasty mixture of embarrassment and anger. Why did I always have to bring up that war—and pick a fight? What kind of answer was I looking for?

All I do is repeat the humiliations of last year. As if I haven't had enough of those, I thought grimly. And the worst thing was, I wouldn't dare to go near that room again, despite his offer at the beginning of the encounter—an encounter which was thoroughly my own fault.

Well, I'd have to console myself with the big room. Stopping along the row of biographies, I selected the histories of three well-hated tyrants, figuring they'd be good company for me, and I retreated to my rooms.

It was a while before my mind was quiet enough for reading. The conversation with Shevraeth I was determined not to think about. What was the use? It was over, and it was clear it wasn't going to be repeated.

Recalling the name he'd mentioned, Lady Trishe—one of the names Bran had spoken earlier that morning—I realized it was Shevraeth they were planning to go riding with. *She wouldn't enjoy this ride* was what Nee had said, meaning that I wouldn't enjoy it because Shevraeth would be along. What it probably also meant, I realized glumly, was that *they* wouldn't enjoy having *me* along if I glared at Shevraeth and started squabbling.

I grabbed up a book and flung myself down on my nest of pillows. At frequent intervals I set the book aside and listened, expecting to hear the noise of their return. But the sun marched across the sky without their reappearance, and just after sunset Nee knocked to ask if I was ready to go to a concert officially scheduled for the ambassadors.

I changed hastily, expecting my brother to appear. But what happened was that we went to the concert. Bran—indifferent to music—had gone off elsewhere with other friends. The choir was wonderful, and the songs from over the sea were beautiful, though I heard them through a damp veil of self-pity.

I finally had to admit to myself that my brother had forgotten all about my Name Day, and Nee had no idea. Before the revolt, my brother and I had been close. Obviously, more had changed since Galdran's defeat than I'd realized.

The main person in his life now is Nee—as it should be, I told myself as she and I walked across the flagged courtyard to the Residence Wing. But my mood stayed sober as I contemplated how life would change when we all returned to Tlanth. *I'm not oath-sworn as a countess, not until we gather before the new monarch when he or she is crowned; and Bran is the legal heir. And a county can't have two countesses . . .*

94

When we reached our hall, Nee offered to share hot chocolate with me. Shaking my head, I pleaded tiredness—true enough—and retreated to my rooms.

And discovered something lying on the little table in the parlor where letters and invitations were supposed to be put.

Moving slowly across the room, I looked down at an exquisite porcelain sphere. It was dark blue, with silver stars all over it, and so cunningly painted that when I looked closer it gave the illusion of depth—as if I stared deeply into the sky.

Lifting it with reverent care, I opened it and saw, sitting on a white silk nest, a lovely sapphire ring. Trying it on my fingers, I found to my delight it fit my longest one.

Why couldn't Bran give me this in person? There were times when I found my brother incomprehensible, but I knew he thought the same of me.

Puzzled, but content, I fell asleep with my ringed hand cradled against my cheek.

TEN

WHEN I HEARD BRANARIC CALL A MORNING GREET-
ing outside Nee's parlor, I rushed out and batted aside her tapestry.
They both looked at me in surprise as I hugged Bran. "Thank you.
It's really lovely!"

"Huh?" Bran looked half pleased, but half confused. Nee
looked completely confused.

"The gift egg! This ring!" I stuck out my hand. "The finest
Name Day gift I ever had!" I laughed.

Bran blinked, then grimaced. "Burn me, Mel—I forgot. I mean,
it ain't from me, the date went right out of my head. Life! I talked
to Nee about planning a boat party—didn't I?" He turned suddenly
to Nee, who looked stricken. He sighed. "But I guess I think we're
still back three or four months." He held out his arms and hugged
me. "I'm sorry."

I said with an unsteady laugh, "Well, I'll admit to being disappointed yesterday, until I found this—but if you didn't put it in
my room, who did?"

Nee also gave me a hug. I sensed how bad she felt. "We'll make
up for it," she whispered, and then, louder, "Was there a letter
with it?"

"No. But who else would know?"

"It might not be a Name Day gift at all, though it's awfully expensive for an admirer to start with," Nee said slowly.

"Savona, you think?" I felt my cheeks go red.

"Could be, except my understanding is, he usually writes love letters to go with gifts."

"Love letters," I said, grimacing. "I don't want those."

Nee and Branaric both grinned.

"Well, I don't," I protested. "Anyway, what ought I to do?"

Nee's maid brought coffee, which filled the room with its aromatic promise. When the woman was gone, Nee said, "You can put it away, which of course will end the question. Or you can wear it in public, to signify your approval, and see if anyone claims it, or even looks conscious."

Which is what I did. A sudden spring shower prevented our going out immediately, but late in the afternoon the sky cleared and the air was balmy enough for one to carry one's walking gloves instead of wear them. I chose a dark gown to show off the ring, had my hair brushed out, and walked out with Nee, Branaric having disappeared earlier.

There were even more blooms in the garden than on my previous walk, scarcely two days before. Everyone seemed to be out and about—talking, laughing, watching the fish and ducks and swans. It was while we were walking along the big pool, admiring the swans and their hatchlings, that we found ourselves annexed by two energetic ladies, Lady Trishe and Lady Renna. The latter was tall, thin, and mild in manner, though Nee had told me she was a formidable rider—not surprisingly, as she was heir to the Khialem family, who were known for horse breeding. She had recently married, and her husband, second son to a baron whose family's lands bordered hers, was another horse-mad type.

Lady Trishe was the one who caught the eye. Also tall, with bright golden hair now worn in loose curls around her shoulders, she looked like the personification of spring in her light green gown. Nee had said she was a popular hostess.

They greeted us with expressions of delight, and Trishe said, "Have they finished their ride, then?"

Nee stiffened ever so slightly beside me. "That I do not know. Branaric went on ahead. It was too wet for my taste."

"You also did not want to go with them, Lady Meliara?" Trishe turned to me. "There has been much said in praise of your riding."

"About your everything," a new voice spoke with cool amusement from behind, and we turned to see Lady Tamara leading a small party of ladies and gentlemen. Tamara also wore her hair down, a cascade of glossy curls to her waist, with tiny gems braided into it. "Good day, Countess," she said, waving her fan slowly. I'd noticed that she always carried a fan, even at informal gatherings when the others didn't. "Is there any end to your accomplishments, then? Yesterday the air rang with acclaim for your grace on the ballroom floor. Shall you lead the way on horseback as well?" And she curtsied, a formal reverence, coming up with her fan spread half before her face in the mode denoting Modesty Deferring to Brilliance.

I was being mocked. Nothing in her manner gave it away, yet I knew that that particular fan gesture was not for social occasions but reserved for literary or artistic exchanges.

I bowed back, exactly the same bow, and because they all seemed to expect me to speak, I said, "I haven't had a chance to go riding as yet."

"I am surprised," Tamara exclaimed, her smile gentle but her hands making artful swirls with the fan. "But, I confess, not as surprised as I was that you did not join us at Petitioners' Court today."

Nee said quickly, "Court is not obligatory. You know that, Cousin."

"Obligatory, no indeed. Cousin." Now Tamara's fan gestured gracefully in query mode, but at a plangent angle. I couldn't get the meaning of it, and the other ladies were silent. "Surely the forming government would benefit from her advice?"

Was she referring to my having led a revolt, however unsuccessful, or was she digging at me for having lost a crown? I suspected the latter, not from any sign she gave but from the others' reactions, and I stood in silence, trying to find something to say that wouldn't start trouble. It was a relief when the sounds of laughter and voices heralded new arrivals.

We all turned, and my brother appeared with four other gentlemen. Branaric called jovially, "Found you, Mel, Nee." And he bowed to the other ladies, who in turn greeted the arrivals: Geral, Savona, Lord Deric of Orbanith, and Shevraeth.

"What's toward?" the Duke asked.

Tamara's gaze was still on me. I saw her open her mouth, and before she could say anything that might sting me with embarrassment, I stuck out my hand and said, "Look at my ring!"

Surprise, and a few titters of laughter, met my sudden and uncourtier-like gesture.

Trishe took my hand, turned it over so the ring caught the light. She made admiring noises, then looked up and said, "Where? Who?"

"Yesterday." I sneaked a look at Savona. He was grinning.

"Which finger?" Tamara asked, glancing down.

"The one it fits best," I said quickly, which raised a laugh. I cast a desperate look at Nee, who was biting her lip. I hadn't even thought to ask about meaning in ring fingers, though I ought to have, I realized belatedly. Rings would be a symbol just like flowers and fan language.

"I've seen it before," Trishe said, frowning in perplexity. "I know I have. It's very old, and they don't cut stones like this anymore."

"Who is it from?" Savona asked.

I looked up at him, trying to divine whether secret knowledge lay behind his expression of interest.

"Of course she cannot tell," Tamara said, her tone mock chiding—a masterpiece of innuendo, I realized. "But... perhaps a hint, Countess?"

"I can't, because it's a secret to me, too." I looked around.

Nothing but interest in all the faces, from Savona's friendly skepticism to Shevraeth's polite indifference. Shevraeth looked more tired than ever. "The best kind, because I get the ring and don't have to do anything about it!"

Everyone laughed.

"Now that," Savona said, taking my arm, "is a direct challenge, is it not? Geral? Danric? I take you to witness." We started strolling along the pathway. "But first, to rid myself of this mysterious rival. Have you kissed anyone since yesterday? Winked? Sent a posy-of-promise?" He went on with so many ridiculous questions I couldn't stop laughing.

The others had fallen in behind. Conversations crossed the group, preventing it from breaking into smaller groups. Before too long Tamara brought us all together again. She was now the center of attention as she summoned Savona to her side to admire a new bracelet.

This was fine with me. I did not like being the center, and I felt jangled and uneasy. Had I betrayed myself in any important way? Had I been properly polite to Shevraeth? The few times he spoke I was careful to listen and to smile just like the others.

When I found myself on the edge of the group, I slipped away and hastened back to the Residence. In my room, I found Mora sewing. She looked at me in surprise, and hastily got to her feet to curtsy.

"Never mind that," I said. "Tell me, who brings letters and things?"

"The runners, my lady," she said.

"Can you find out who sent a runner?" When she hesitated, I said, "Look, I just want to find out who gave me these gifts. I know under the old king, people could be bribed. Is that true now? Please, speak plain. I won't tell anyone what you tell me, and I won't make trouble."

Mora pursed her lips. "There are times when the runners can be bribed, my lady," she said carefully. "But not all of them. Were it to get out, they could lose their position."

"So everyone belowstairs doesn't know everything?"

"No, my lady. Many people use personal runners to deliver things to the palace runners; and the loyal ones don't talk."

"Ah hah!" I exclaimed. "Then, tell me this: Can something be returned along the same route, even though I don't know to whom it's going?"

She thought a bit, then nodded. "I think that can be arranged."

"Good. Then let me pen a message, and please see that it gets sent right away." I dived down onto the cushions beside the desk, rummaged about, and came up with pen and writing paper. On the paper I wrote: *The gifts are beautiful, and I thank you, but what do they mean?*

I signed my name, sealed the letter, and handed it to Mora.

She left at once, and I was severely tempted to try to follow her, except I'd promised not to make trouble. And if I were caught at it, I suspected that the servants involved might get into trouble. I decided to look at this whole matter as a kind of challenge. I'd find some clever way of solving the mystery without involving anyone innocent.

So I pulled on a cloak and went out to take another walk. The sky was already clouding up again, and a strong, chilly wind kicked up my skirts. The weather reminded me of home, and I found it bracing. I set out in a new direction, away from the aristo gardens and the outlying great houses.

The buildings were still in the same style, but plainer. Presently I found myself midway between the royal stables and the military compound. My steps slowed. I remembered that the prison building was not very far from the stables, and I had no desire to see it again.

I turned around—and nearly bumped into a small group of soldiers in Renselaeus colors. They all stopped, bowed silently, and would have stepped out of my way, but I recognized one of them from my ride to Renselaeus just before the end of the war, and I cried, "Captain Nessaren!"

"My lady." Nessaren smiled, her flat cheeks tinged slightly with color.

"Is your riding assigned here now?"

"As you see, my lady."

The others bowed and withdrew silently, leaving us alone.

"Are you not supposed to talk to the civs?" Raindrops stung my face.

Her eyes crinkled. "They usually don't talk to us."

"Is this a good duty, or is it boring now that nothing is going on?"

Her eyes flickered to my face then down to the ground, and her lips just parted. After a moment she said, "We're well enough, my lady."

Which wasn't quite what I had asked. Resolving to think that over later, I said, "You know what I miss? The practice sessions we had when we were riding cross-country last year. I did some practice at home . . . but there doesn't seem to be opportunity anymore."

"We have open practice each day at dawn, in the garrison court when the weather's fine, the gym when it isn't. You're welcome to join us. There's no hierarchy, except that of expertise, by order of the Marquis himself."

"The Marquis?" I repeated faintly, realizing how close I'd come to making an even worse fool of myself than my spectacular attempts so far.

"There every day," she said. "Others as well—Lady Renna. Duke of Savona there most days, same as Baron Khialem. You wouldn't be alone."

I won't be there at all. But out loud I just thanked her.

She bowed. Her companions were still waiting at a discreet distance, despite the spatter of rain, so I said, "I won't keep you any longer."

As she rejoined her group, I started back toward the Residence. The wind had turned chill, and the rain started falling faster, but I scarcely noticed. *Was* there still some kind of danger? Instinct attributed Nessaren's deliberate vagueness to a military reason.

If the threat was from the borders, it seemed unlikely that

I'd find Renselaeus warriors roaming around the royal palace Athanarel. So, was there a threat at home?

Like a rival for the kingship? My thoughts went immediately to the Marquise of Merindar—and to the conservation with Shevraeth at the inn. The Marquise had made no attempt to communicate with me, and I had not even seen her subsequent to that dinner the night of my arrival. In the days since, I'd managed to lose sight of my purpose in coming.

When I'd surprised Shevraeth in the archive, it had seemed he was actually willing to discuss royal business—at least that portion that pertained to cleaning up after Galdran—for why else would he offer me a look at the old king's papers? But I'd managed to turn the discussion into a quarrel, and so lost the chance.

I groaned aloud. What was *wrong* with me? As I hurried up the steps to our wing, I promised myself that next time Shevraeth tried to talk to me, I'd listen, and even if he insulted me, my family, and my land, I'd keep my tongue between my teeth.

"My own conscience demands that I make the attempt." Would there even be another try?

I sighed as I opened my door, then Nessaren and Shevraeth and the rain went out of my mind when I saw that my letter table was not empty.

Two items awaited me. The first was a letter—and when I saw the device on the heavy seal, my heart sped: the Marquise of Merindar.

I ripped it open, to find only an invitation to a gathering three weeks hence. No hint of any personal message.

Laying it aside, I turned my gaze to the other object.

Sitting in the middle of the table was a fine little vase cut from luminous starstone, and in it, bordered by the most delicate ferns, was a single rose, just barely blooming.

One white rose. I knew what that meant, thanks to Nee: *Purity of Intent.*

ELEVEN

MY GLIMPSES OF SHEVRAETH WERE RARE OVER THE
next three weeks, and all of those were either at State events or else
at big parties held by mutual Court friends. I did not see the
Marquise of Merindar or her two children at all—Nee said they
rarely attended Court functions and entertained only in their family's house on the outskirts of Athanarel's garden, though the State
rooms in the Residence could be hired by anyone. The Marquise's
invitation sat on my table, looking rather like a royal summons.

Very different were the invitations that I received from the
Court young people, for as Nee had predicted, I *had* become popular. At least on the surface, everyone was friendly, even Lady
Tamara Chamadis, though her tone, and her fan, hinted that she
didn't find me amusing because she thought I was a wit.

Others were more forthright in offering their friendship. Not
just the ladies, either. To my vast surprise, I seemed to have col-
lected several flirts. The Duke of Savona sought me out at every
event we both attended, insisting on the first dance at balls—and
lots more through the evening. He was an excellent dancer, and I
thoroughly enjoyed him as a partner. His outrageous compliments
just made me laugh.

My second most devoted admirer was Lord Deric Toarvendar,

Count of Orbanith. He was not content to meet me at balls but showered invitations on me—to picnics, riding parties, and other events that had to do with sport.

Among intimates, I'd discovered, young courtiers didn't write invitations, they spoke them, usually at the end of some other affair. Some people were overt—which meant they wanted others to overhear and thus to know they'd been excluded—but most were more subtle about it.

Not that Deric was particularly subtle. He made it obvious that he thought I was fun and funny, as good a loser as I was a winner. In the weeks after I received that rose, we had competed at all kinds of courtly games, from cards to horse racing. He was entertaining, and—unlike Certain Others—easy to understand, and also easy to resist when his flirting, wine- and moonlight-inspired, intensified to wandering hands and lips.

The night before the Merindar party, I had made myself easy to understand by planting a hand right in the middle of his chest and pushing him away. "No," I said.

He found that funny, too, and promptly offered to drive me to the Merindar party himself.

I accepted. By then I'd pretty much decided that he was the one who had sent me the ring and the rose, for despite his enthusiastic dedication to sport and his one energetic attempt at stealing a kiss, he was surprisingly shy about discussing anything as intimate as feelings.

This was fine with me. I felt no desire to tax him about it; if I did and it proved I was right, it might change a relationship I liked just where it was.

The night of the Merindar party, the weather was cold and rainy, so Deric drove his handsome pony-trap to the Residence to pick me up. It was not that long a distance to the Merindar house.

The Family houses were built around the perimeter of the

palace at Athanarel's extensive gardens, a tiny city within the city of Remalna. None of these were castles, and thus could never have been defended. They were palaces, designed for pleasure and entertaining—and for secret egress.

The finest two were at opposite ends, the one belonging to the Merindar family, and the other to the Chamadis family.

The Merindar palace most nearly resembled a fortress, for all its pleasing design; there were few windows on the ground level, and those on the upper levels seemed curiously blind. And all around the house stood guards, ostensibly to protect the Merindar family from grudge-holding citizens. I had discovered that this was in fact not new; Galdran Merindar had kept guards stationed around the house during his reign. As king, he had not had to give a reason.

"The food will be excellent, the music even better, but watch out for the Flower and the Thorn," Deric said to me at the end of the journey, just before we disembarked from the pony-trap. "Of the two, the Flower is the more dangerous," he added.

"Flower—is that the Marquise's son or daughter?"

"Lord Flauvic," Deric said with a twist to his lips and an ironic gleam in his black eyes. "You'll understand the moment you get a squint at him and hear his pretty voice. It was your brother gave him the nickname last year, after Flauvic returned from his sojourn at Aranu Crown's Court in Erev-li-Erval. He spent almost ten years there as a page."

"A page," I repeated, impressed.

"Ten successful years," he added.

I considered this, making a mental note to stay away from Lord Flauvic—who had also been recently named his mother's heir, bypassing his older sister, Lady Fialma, the one called the Thorn. I'd learned about pages in my reading, for they had not been in use in Remalna for at least a century, and a good thing, too. Unlike runners, who were from obscure birth and kept—as servants—outside the main rooms until summoned, pages were from good homes and waited on their superiors within the State rooms. Which meant they were privy to everything that went on—a very, very dangerous privilege. According to my reading, pages who made political mistakes were seldom executed. Instead they were sent home before their term of indenture was over, which was a public disgrace and, as such, a lifelong exile from the provinces of power. Those who finished their time successfully tended to return home well trained and formidably adept at political maneuvering. A page trained at the Empress's Court would be formidable indeed.

The only other thing I had known about Flauvic was that the Marquise had sent him out of the kingdom when he was small in order to keep him alive, the year after his father and two of his uncles had met mysterious deaths. I hadn't met him yet—apparently he never attended any State events or social events outside of his own home, preferring to remain there deep in his studies. An aristocratic scholar.

Studying what? I wondered, as we were bowed inside the house by blank-faced Merindar servants.

The grandeur around us was a silent testimony to wealth and power. The air was scented with a complex mixture of exotic flowers and the faintest trace of tanglewood incense, denoting peace and kindred spirits.

"Easy over the fence," Deric said softly beside me.

We were already at the parlor. I suppressed a grin at the riding term, then stepped forward to curtsy to the Marquise.

"My dear Countess," Lady Arthal said, smiling as she pressed my hand. "Welcome. Permit me to introduce my children, Fialma and Flauvic. The rest of the company you know."

Lady Fialma was tall, brown-haired, with cold eyes and the elevated chin of one who considers herself to be far above whomever she happens to be looking at—or down on. She was magnificently gowned, with so many glittering jewels it almost hurt the eyes to look at her. She would have been handsome but for a very long nose—which was the more obvious because of that imperious tilt to her head—and thinly compressed lips.

"Welcome," she said, in so faint and listless a voice that it was almost hard to hear her. "Delighted to . . ." She shrugged slightly, and her languidly waving fan fluttered with a dismissive extra flick.

Lord Flauvic, on the other side of their mother, was startlingly beautiful. His coloring was fair, his long waving hair golden with ruddy highlights. His eyes were so light a brown as to seem gold, a match for his hair. ". . . meet you, Countess," he said, finishing his sister's sentence. Politeness? Humor? Insult? Impossible to guess. His voice was the pure tenor of a trained singer, his gaze as blank as glass as he took my hand and bowed over it. Of medium height and very slender, he was dressed in deep blue, almost black, with a rare scattering of diamonds in his hair, in one ear, and on his clothing.

I realized I was staring and looked away quickly, following Deric into the next room. He fell into conversation with Branaric, Shevraeth, and Lady Renna Khialem, the subject (of course) horses. Deric's manner reminded me of someone relieved to find allies. Next to Bran sat Nee, completely silent, her hands folded in her lap.

Under cover of the chatter about horse racing, I looked around, feeling a little like a commander assessing a potential battlefield. Our hosts, despite their gracious outward manner, had made no effort to bind the guests into a circle. Instead, people were clumped in little groups, either around the magnificent buffet, or around the fireplace. As I scanned them, I realized who was there—and who was not there.

Present: counts, countesses, a duke, a duchess, heirs to these titles, and the only two people in the marquisate: Shevraeth and our hostess.

Absent: anyone with the title of baron or lower, except those —like Nee—who had higher connections.

Absent also were the Prince and Princess of Renselaeus.

"My dear Countess," a fluting voice said at my right ear, and Lady Tamara's soft hand slid along my arm, guiding me toward the lowest tier near the fireplace. Several people moved away, and we sank down onto the cushions there. Tamara gestured to one of the hovering foot-servants, and two glasses of wine were instantly brought. "Did I not predict that you would show us the way at the races as well?"

"I won only once," I said, fighting against embarrassment.

Deric was grinning. "Beat me," he said. "Nearly beat Renna."

"I had the best horse," I countered.

For a moment the conversation turned from me to the races the week before. It had been a sudden thing, arranged on the first really nice day we'd had, and though the course was purported to be rough, I had found it much easier than riding mountain trails.

As Deric described the last obstacles of the race in which I had beaten him, I saw the shy red-haired Lord Geral listening with a kind of ardent expression in his eyes. He was another who often sought me out for dances but rarely spoke otherwise. Might my rose and ring have come from him?

Tamara's voice recalled my attention ". . . the way with swords as well, dear Countess?"

I glanced at her, sipping at my wine as I mentally reached for the subject.

"It transpires," Tamara said with a glinting smile, "that our sharpest wits are also experts at the duel. Almost am I willing to rise at dawn, just to observe you at the cut and the thrust."

I opened my mouth to disclaim any great prowess with the sword, then realized that I'd walk right into her little verbal trap if I did so. Now, maybe I'm not any kind of a sharp wit, but I wasn't going to hand myself over for trimming so easily. So I just smiled and sipped at my wine.

Fialma's faint, die-away voice was just audible on Tamara's other side. "Tamara, my love, that is not dueling, but mere sword-play."

Tamara's blue eyes rounded with perplexity. "True, true, I had forgotten." She smiled suddenly, her fan waving slowly in query mode. "An academic question: Is it a real duel when one is favored by the opponent?"

Fialma said, "Is it a real contest, say, in a race when the better

109

rider does not ride?" She turned her thin smile to Shevraeth. "Your grace?"

The Marquis bowed slightly, his hands at an oblique angle. "If a stake is won," he said, "it is a race. If the point draws blood, it is a duel."

A murmur of appreciative laughter met this, and Fialma sighed ever so slightly. "You honor us," she murmured, sweeping her fan gracefully in the half circle of Intimate Confidence, "with your liberality...." She seated herself at the other side of the fireplace and began a low-voiced conversation with Lady Dara, the heir to a northern duchy.

Just beyond Fialma's waving fan, Lord Flauvic's metal-gold eyes lifted from my face to Shevraeth's to Tamara's, then back to me.

What had I missed? Nee's cheeks were glowing, but that could have been her proximity to the fire.

Branaric spoke then, saluting Shevraeth with his wineglass. "Duel or dabble, I'd hie me to those practices, except I just can't stomach rough work at dawn. Now, make them at noon, and I'm your man!"

More laughter greeted this, and Bran turned to Flauvic. "How about you? Join me in agitating for a decent time?"

Lord Flauvic also had a fan, but he had not opened it. Holding it horizontally between his fingers in the mode of the neutral observer, he said, "Not at any time, Tlanth. You will forgive me if I am forced to admit that I am much too lazy?"

Again laughter, but more subdued. Heads turned. As the smiling Marquise approached, she said, "You are all lazy, children." She gestured at the artfully arranged plates of food. "Come! Do you wish to insult my tastes?"

Several people converged on the table, where waiting servants piled indicated dainties on little plates. The Marquise moved smoothly through the milling guests, smiling and bestowing soft words here and there. To my surprise, she made her way to me, held out her hand, and said, "Come, my dear. Let's see what we can find to appeal to you."

I rose, trying to hide my astonishment. Deric's face was blank, and Bran looked puzzled. Behind him, Shevraeth watched, his expression impossible to interpret. As I followed the Marquise, I glanced at her son, and was further surprised to see his gaze on me. His fingers manipulated his fan; for just an instant he held it in the duelist's "guard" position, then his wrist bent as he spread the fan open with languid deliberation.

A warning? *Of course it is—but why?*

With a regal gesture the Marquise indicated a door—a handsome carved one—and a lackey sprang to open it. A moment later we passed inside a lamp-lit conservatory and were closed off in the sudden, slightly unsettling silence vouchsafed by well-fitted wooden doors. "I find young Deric of Orbanith a refreshing boy," she said. "He's been my daughter's friend through their mutual interest in horses since they were both quite small."

I cudgeled my mind for something diplomatic to say and came up with, "I hope Lady Fialma will join us for the next race, your grace."

"Perhaps, perhaps." The Marquise stretched out a hand to nip away a dead leaf from one of her plants. She seemed completely absorbed in her task; I wondered how to delicately turn the discussion to the purpose of her letter when she said, "A little over a year ago there appeared at Court a remarkable document signed by you and your esteemed brother."

Surprised, I recalled our open letter to Galdran outlining how his bad ruling was destroying the kingdom. The letter, meant to gain us allies in the Court, had been the last project we had worked on with our father. "We didn't think anyone actually saw it," I said, unnerved by the abrupt change of subject. "We did send copies, but I thought they had been suppressed."

One of her brows lifted. "No one but the king saw it—officially. However, it enjoyed a brief but intense covert popularity, I do assure you."

"But there was no response," I said.

"As there was no protection offered potential fellow rebels,"

111

she retorted, still in that mild voice, "you ought not be surprised. Your sojourn here was brief. Perhaps you were never really aware of the difficulties facing those who disagreed with my late brother."

"Well, I remember what he was going to do to *me*," I said.

"And do you remember what happened instead?"

I turned to stare at her. "I thought—"

"Thought what, child? Speak freely. There is no one to over-hear you."

Except, of course, the Marquise. But was she really a danger? The Renselaeuses now gripped the hilt-end of the sword of power, or she would have been home long since.

"The Princess Elestra hinted that they helped me escape," I said.

"Hinted," she repeated. "And thus permitted you to convince yourself?"

"You mean they didn't?"

She lifted one shoulder slightly. "Contradiction of the con-queror, whose memory is usually adaptable, is pointless, unless..." She paused, once more absorbed in clearing yellowed leaves from a delicate plant.

"Unless what, your grace?" Belatedly I remembered the nice-ties.

She did not seem to notice. "Unless one intends to honor one's own vows," she murmured. "I have not seen you or your respected brother at Court. Have you set aside those fine ideals as expressed in your letter?"

"We haven't, your grace," I said cautiously.

"Yet I have not seen you at Petitioners' Court. That is, I need hardly point out, where the real ruling takes place."

But Shevraeth is there. Remembering the promise I had made that last day at Tlanth, I was reluctant to mention my problems with him. I said with care, "I haven't been asked to attend—and I do not see how my presence or absence would make much dif-ference."

112

"You would learn," she murmured, "how our kingdom is being governed. And then you would be able to form an idea as to whether or not your vows are in fact being kept."

She was *right*. This was my purpose in coming.

Ought I to tell her? Instinct pulled me both ways, but memory of the mistakes I had made in acting on hasty judgment kept me silent.

She bent and plucked a newly bloomed starliss, tucked it into my hair, then stepped back to admire the effect. "There are many among us who would be glad enough to see you and your brother honor those vows," she said, and took my arm, and led me back to the reception room.

At once I was surrounded by Nee and Deric and Renna—my own particular friends—as if they had formed a plan to protect me. Against what? Nothing happened after that, except that we ate and drank and listened to a quartet of singers from the north performing ballads whose words we could not understand, but whose melancholy melodies seemed to shiver in the air.

The Marquise of Merindar did not speak to me again until it was time to leave, and she was gracious as she begged me to come visit her whenever I had the inclination. There was no reference to our conversation in the conservatory.

When at last Deric and I settled into his carriage, he dropped back with a sigh of relief. "Well, that's over. Good food and good company, but none of it worth sitting mum while Fialma glared daggers at me."

Remembering the Marquise's opening statement, I realized suddenly what I'd missed before—some of what I'd missed, anyway—and tried unsuccessfully to smother a laugh. It seemed that Deric was deemed an appropriate match for the daughter of a Merindar.

Deric grinned at me, the light from glowglobes flickering in his black eyes. "Cowardice, I know. But burn it, that female scares me."

I remembered the gossip about Lady Fialma and her recent return from Erev-li-Erval, where she was supposed to have contracted an appropriately brilliant marriage alliance but had failed. Which was why the Marquise had passed her over for the heirship of Merindar.

But that wasn't all; as Deric drove away and I mounted the steps of the Residence, I realized that he could, in fact, be subtle when he wanted. And that there were consequences to bluntness that one could not always predict. He had asked me to accompany him as a hint to the Merindars that he was courting me, and therefore wouldn't court Fialma.

Interesting, though, that he asked to take me to that party right *after* I had rejected his attempts to kiss me.

I'll never understand flirting, I thought, fighting the impulse to laugh. *Never.*

In my rooms, I sat at the window, looking out at the soft rain and thinking about that conversation with the Marquise. Was she, or was she not, inviting me to join her in opposing Shevraeth's rule?

Ought I to attend Petitioners' Court, then, and begin evaluating the Renselaeus policies? Where was the real truth between the two families?

I remembered the hint that the Marquise had dropped. According to her, Princess Elestra had not, in fact, had anything to do with my escape. If she hadn't, who, then? The Marquise? Except why didn't I find out before? Who could I ask?

Deric? No. He showed no interest whatever in Crown affairs. He lived for sport. Renna as well. Trishe and the others?

I bit my lip, wondering if my opening such a discussion would be a betrayal of the promise to Shevraeth. I didn't know any of these people well enough to enjoin them to secrecy, and the thought of Shevraeth finding out about my purpose in coming made me shudder inside.

Of the escape, at least, I could find out some of the truth. I'd write to Azmus, our trusted spy during the war, who had helped me that night. Now he was happily retired to a nice village in Tlanth. I moved to my writing table, plumped down onto the pillows without heeding my expensive gown, and reached for a pen. The letter was soon written and set aside for dispatch home.

Then I sat back on the pillows. As I thought about the larger question, a new idea occurred to me: Why not ask the Secret Admirer who'd sent the ring and the rose?

He certainly knew how to keep a secret. If he was only playing a game, surely a serious question would show him up. I'd phrase it carefully. . . .

I remembered the starliss in my hair and pulled it out to look down into the silver-touched white crown-shaped petals. I thought about its symbolism. In Kharas it was known as Queensblossom; that I'd learned from my mother long ago. Nowadays it symbolized ambition.

My scalp prickled with a danger sense. Once again I dipped my quill. I wrote:

Dear Unknown,
    You probably won't want to answer a letter, but I need some advice on Court etiquette, without my asking being noised around, and who could be more closemouthed than you? Let's say I was at a party, and a high-ranking lady approached me . . .

TWELVE

As soon as I finished the letter I asked Mora to have it sent, just so I wouldn't stay awake changing my mind back and forth during the night.

When I woke the next morning, that letter was the first thing on my mind. Had I made a mistake in writing it? I'd been careful to make it seem like a mental exercise, a hypothetical question of etiquette, describing the conversation in general terms and the speakers only as a high-ranking lady and a young lady new to Court. Unless the unknown admirer had been at the party, there would be no way to connect me to the Marquise. And if he had been at the party—as Deric, Savona, and Geral, all of whom flirted with me most, had been—wouldn't his not having given away his identity make him obliged to keep my letter secret as well?

So I reasoned. When Mora came in with my hot chocolate, she also brought me a gift: a book. I took it eagerly.

The book was a memoir from almost three hundred years before, written by the Duchess Nirth Masharlias, who married the heir to a principality. Though she never ruled, three of her children married into royalty. I had known of her, but not much beyond that.

There was no letter, but slipped in the pages was a single petal of starliss. The text it marked was written in old-fashioned language, but even so, I liked the voice of the writer at once:

. . . and though the Count spoke strictly in Accordance with Etiquette, his words were an Affront, for he knew my thoughts on Courtship of Married Persons . . .

I skipped down a ways, then started to laugh when I read:

. . . and mock-solemn, matching his Manner to the most precise Degree, I challenged him to a Duel. He was forced to go along with the Jest, lest the Court laugh at him instead of with him, but he liked it Not . . .

. . . and at the first bells of Gold we were there on the Green, and lo, the Entire Court was out with us to see the Duel. Instead of Horses, I had brought big, shaggy Dogs from the southern Islands, playful and clumsy under their Gilt Saddles, and for Lances, we had great paper Devices which were already Limp and Dripping from the Rain. . . .

Twice he tried to speak Privily to me, but knowing he would apologize and thus end the Ridiculous Spectacle, I heeded him Not, and so we progressed through the Duel, attended with all proper Appurtenances, from Seconds to Trumpeteers, with the Court laughing themselves Hoarse and No One minding the increasing Downpour. In making us both Ridiculous I believe I put paid to all such Advances in future . . .

The next page went on about other matters. I laid the book down, staring at the starliss as I thought this over. The incident on this page was a response—the flower made that clear enough—but what did it mean?

And why the mystery? Since my correspondent had taken the trouble to answer, why not write a plain letter?

Again I took up my pen, and I wrote carefully:

Dear Mysterious Benefactor:

I read the pages you marked, and though I was greatly diverted, the connection between this story and my own dilemma leaves me more confused than before. Would you advise my young lady to act the fool to the high-ranking lady—or are you hinting that the young one already has? Or is it merely a suggestion that she follow the duchess's example and ward off the high-ranking lady's hints with a joke duel?

If you've figured out that this is a real situation and not a mere mental exercise, then you should also know that I promised someone important that I would not let myself get involved in political brangles; and I wish most straightly to keep this promise. Truth to tell, if you have insights that I have not—and it's obvious that you do—in this dilemma I'd rather have plain discourse than gifts.

The last line I lingered over the longest. I almost crossed it out, but instead folded the letter, sealed it, and when Mora came in, I gave it to her to deliver right away. Then I dressed and went out to walk.

In the past, when something bothered me, I'd retreat up into the mountains to think it through. Now I strolled through Athanarel's beautiful garden, determined to review the entire sequence of events as clearly as memory permitted.

During the course of this I remembered one vital hint, which I then wondered how I could be so stupid as to forget: Lord Flauvic's little gesture with the fan. *On guard.*

That, I decided, I could pursue.

Running and walking, I cut through the gardens. The air was cold and brisk, washed clean from rain. The sky was an intense, smiling blue.

Growing up in the mountains as I had, I'd discovered that maintaining a true sense of direction was instinctive. As I homed in on Merindar House, taking the straightest way rather than the ordered paths, I found ancient bearded trees and tangled grottos. Just before I reached the house, I had to clamber over a mossy wall that had begun to crumble over the centuries.

Pausing to run my fingers over its small, weather-worn stones, I wondered if the wall had been set during the time my mother's family had ruled. Had one of my ancestors looked on then, and what had been her hopes and fears? What kind of life had she seen at Athanarel?

Vaulting over into the tall grass on the other side, I turned my attention to the problem at hand. For there was a problem, I realized as I emerged from the protective shelter of silvery-leaved argan trees and looked across the carefully planted gardens at the house. Its blind windows and slowly strolling guards served as a reminder of the hidden eyes that would observe my walking up and demanding to talk to the heir.

I stepped back beyond the curtain of breeze-stirred leaves and made my way over a log that crossed a little stream, then crossed the rough ground on a circuit round the house as I considered the matter.

I had no conscious plan in mind, but it turned out I did not need one; when I reached the other side of the house, I glimpsed through a wall of vines a splendid terrace, and seated at a table on it was Lord Flauvic. Exquisitely dressed in pale shades of peach and gray, he was all alone, absorbed in reading and writing.

I stooped, picked up some small gravel, and tossed it in his direction.

He went very still. Just for a moment. Then his head turned deliberately. When he saw me he smiled slightly. Moving with swift grace, he swung to his feet and crossed the terrace. "Serenades," he said, "are customarily performed under moonslight, or have fashions here changed?"

"I don't know," I said. "No one's serenaded me, and as for my serenading anyone else, even if I wanted to, which I don't, my singing voice sounds like a sick crow."

"Then to what do I owe the honor of this delightful—but admittedly unorthodox—visit?"

"That." I demonstrated his gesture with my hands. "You did that when your mother took me away last night. I want to know what you meant by it."

His fine brows lifted just slightly, and with leisurely grace he stepped over the low terrace wall and joined me among the ferns. "You do favor the blunt, don't you?"

It was phrased as a question, but his lack of surprise hinted fairly broadly that he'd heard gossip to this effect. My chin came up; I said, "I favor truth over style."

He retorted in the mildest voice, "Having endured the blunt style favored by my late Uncle Galdran, which had little to do with truth as anyone else saw it, I beg you to forgive me when I admit that I am more dismayed than impressed."

"All right," I said. "So there can be truth with style, as well as the opposite. It's just that I haven't been raised to think that I'd find much truth in Court, though there's plenty of style to spare there."

"Will I seem unnecessarily contentious if I admit that my own life experience has engendered in me a preference for style, which at least has the virtue of being diverting?" It seemed impossible that Flauvic was exactly my age. "Not so diverting is the regrettable conviction that truth doesn't exist." His golden eyes were wide and curiously blank.

"Doesn't exist? Of course it does," I exclaimed.

"Is your truth the same as mine? I wonder." He was smiling just slightly, and his gaze was still as limpid as the stream rilling at our feet, but I sensed a challenge.

I said gloomily, "All right, then, you've neatly sidestepped my question—if you even intended to answer it."

He laughed, so softly I just barely heard it, and bowed, his hands moving in a quick airy gesture. I gasped when I saw the bouquet of flowers in his hands. As I reached, they poofed into

120

glowing cinders of every color, which then swirled around and re-formed into butterflies. Then he clapped his hands, and they vanished.

"Magic!" I exclaimed. "You know magic?"

"This is merely illusion," he said. "It's a kind of fad in Erevli-Erval. Or was. No one is permitted to study true magic unless invited by the Council of Mages, which is overseen by the Empress."

"I'd love to learn it," I exclaimed. "Real magic or not."

We were walking, randomly I thought; in the distance I heard the sweet chiming bells announcing second-gold.

Flauvic shrugged slightly. "I could show you a few tricks, but I've forgotten most of them. You'd have to ask a play magician to show you—that's how we learned."

"Play magician?" I repeated.

"Ah," he said. "Plays here in Remalna are still performed on a bare stage, without illusion to dress it."

"Well, some players now have painted screens and costumes, as in two plays here during recent days. I take it you haven't seen them?"

"I rarely leave the house," he said apologetically.

We reached a path just as the beat of horse hooves sounded from not far ahead. I stepped back; Flauvic looked up as two riders trotted into view.

My first reaction was blank dismay when I saw Savona and Shevraeth riding side by side. The three lords greeted one another with practiced politeness; and when the newcomers turned to me, I curtsied silently.

By the time I had realized that the very fineness of their manners was a kind of message, somehow it was agreed—amid a barrage of mutual compliments—that Flauvic's escort could be dispensed with and the two would accompany me back to the Residence. Savona swung down from his mount and took the reins in hand, falling in step on my left side. Shevraeth, too, joined me on foot, at my right. They were both informally dressed—just returning from the swordfighting practice, I realized. Meanwhile Flauvic had disappeared, as if he'd dissolved into the ground.

All my impressions and speculations resolved into one question: Why did they think I had to be accompanied? "Please don't think you have to change your direction for my sake," I said. "I'm just out wandering about, and my steps took me past Merindar House."

"And lose an opportunity to engage in converse without your usual crowd of swains?" Savona said, bowing.

"Crowd? Swains?" I repeated, then laughed. "Has the rain affected your vision? Or am I the blind one? I don't see any swains. Luckily."

A choke of laughter on my right made me realize—belatedly—that my comment could be taken as an insult. "I don't mean you two!" I added hastily and glanced up at Savona (I couldn't bring myself to look at Shevraeth). His dark eyes narrowed in mirth.

"About your lack of swains," Savona murmured. "Deric would be desolated to hear your heartless glee."

I grinned. "I suspect he'd be desolated if I thought him half serious."

"Implying," Savona said with mendacious shock, "that I am not serious? My dear Meliara! I assure you I fell in love with you last year—the very moment I heard that you had pinched a chicken pie right from under Nenthar Debegri's twitchy nose, then rode off on his favorite mount, getting clean away from three ridings of his handpicked warriors."

Taken by surprise, I laughed out loud.

Savona gave me a look of mock consternation. "Now don't— please don't—destroy my faith in heroism by telling me it's not true."

"Oh, it's true enough, but heroic?" I scoffed. "What's so heroic about that? I was hungry! Only got one bite of the pie," I added with real regret. I was surprised again when both lords started laughing.

"And then you compounded your attractions by keeping my

122

lazy cousin on the hop for days." He indicated Shevraeth with an airy wave of the hand.

Those memories effectively banished my mirth. For it wasn't just Galdran's bullying cousin Baron Debegri who had chased me halfway across the kingdom after my escape from Athanarel. Shevraeth had been there as well. I felt my shoulders tighten against the old embarrassment, but I tried not to show it, responding as lightly as I could. "On the contrary, it was he who kept me on the hop for days. Very long days," I said. And because the subject had been broached and I was already embarrassed, I risked a quick look at the Marquis and asked, "When you said to search the houses. In the lake town. Did you know I was inside one?"

He hesitated, looking across at Savona, who merely grinned at us both. Then Shevraeth said somewhat drily, "I...had a sense of it."

"And outside Thoresk. When you and Debegri rode by. You looked right at me. Did you know that was me?"

"Will it make you very angry if I admit that I did? But the timing seemed inopportune for us to, ah, reacquaint ourselves." All this was said with his customary drawl. But I had a feeling he was bracing for attack.

I sighed. "I'm not angry. I know now that you weren't trying to get me killed, but to keep me from getting killed by Debegri and Galdran's people. Except—well, never mind. The whole thing is stupid."

"Come then," Savona said immediately. "Forgive me for straying into memories you'd rather leave behind, and let us instead discuss tonight's prospective delights."

He continued with a stream of small talk about the latest entertainments—all easy, unexceptionable conversation. Slowly I relaxed, though I never dared look at Shevraeth again.

So it was another unpleasant surprise when I glanced down an adjoining pathway to find the tight-lipped face of Lady Tamara framed in a truly spectacular walking hat.

Tight-lipped for the barest moment. In the space of a blink she was smiling prettily, greeting me with lavish compliments as she fell in step on my right. Shevraeth moved to the outside of the path to make room, his gray still following obediently behind.

The conversation went on, but this time it was Tamara who was the focus. When we reached the bridge just before the rose garden where several paths intersected, she turned suddenly to me. "You did promise me, my dear Countess, a little of your time. I think I will hold you to that promise, perhaps tomorrow evening?"

"I—well—" Answers and images cartwheeled wildly through my mind. "I think—that is, if I haven't forgotten—"

She spoke across me to Savona. "You'll have the evening free?"

He bowed; though I hadn't heard or seen anything untoward in that brief exchange, I saw her eyes narrow just the slightest degree. Then she looked up over her shoulder at Shevraeth. "And you, Vidanric?"

"Regrettably, my mother has a previous claim on me," he said.

Tamara flicked a curtsy, then turned back to me. "I'll invite a few more of your many friends. Do not distress me with a refusal."

There was no polite way to get around that, or if there was, it was beyond my skills. "Of course," I said. "Be delighted."

She curtsied gravely, then began talking with enviable ease about the latest play.

Silent, I walked along until we came to an intersection. Then I whirled to face them all. "I fear I have to leave you all now. Good day!" I swept a general curtsy then fled.

When I returned from that night's dinner party at Nee's family's house, I found two letters on my table. One was immediately recognizable as Oria's weekly report on Tlanth's affairs, which I left for later; Tlanth had been flourishing peacefully. All my problems were here.

The second letter was sealed plainly, with no crest. I flung myself onto my pillows, broke the seal impatiently, and read:

My Dear Countess:

You say you would prefer discourse to gifts. I am yours to command. I will confess my hesitancy was due largely to my own confusion. It seems, from my vantage anyway, that you are surrounded by people in whom you could confide and from whom you could obtain excellent advice. Your turning to a faceless stranger for both could be ascribed to a taste for the idiosyncratic if not to mere caprice.

I winced and dropped the paper to the table. "Well, I asked for the truth," I muttered, and picked it up again.

But I am willing to serve as foil, if foil you require. Judging from what you reported of your conversation with your lady of high rank, the insights you requested are these: First, with regard to her hint that someone else in power lied about rendering assistance at a crucial moment the year previous, you will not see either contender for power with any clarity until you ascertain which of them is telling the truth.

Second, she wishes to attach you to her cause. From my limited understanding of said lady, I suspect she would not so bestir herself unless she believed you to be in, at least potentially, a position of influence.

There was no signature, no closing.

I read it through three times, then folded it carefully and fitted it inside one of my books.

Pulling a fresh sheet of paper before me, I wrote:

Dear Unknown:

The only foil—actually, fool—here is me, which isn't any pleasure to write. But I don't want to talk about my past mistakes, I just want to learn to avoid making the same or like ones in future. Your advice about the event of last year (an escape) I thought of already and have begun my investigation. As for this putative position of power, it's just that. I expect you're being confused by my proximity to power—my brother being friend to the possible king and my living here in the Residence. But believe me, no one could possibly be more ignorant or less influential than I.

With a sense of relief I folded that letter up, sealed it, and gave it to Mora to send along the usual route. Then I went gratefully to sleep.

I dressed carefully for Tamara's party, choosing a gown that became me well—the effect of knowing one looks one's best is enormously bracing—but which was subdued enough that even the most critical observer could not fault me for attempting to draw the eye from my beautiful hostess.

Neither Bran nor Nee was invited, which dismayed me. I remembered Tamara having promised to invite my friends, and I knew I would have refused had I known Bran and Nee would be overlooked. But Nee insisted it would be a terrible slight not to go, so alone I went.

And nothing could have been more gracious than my welcome. With her own hands Tamara pressed a glacé of iced punch on me. The liquid was astringent with citrus and blended fruit flavors. "Do you like it, Countess?" she said, her brows raised in an anxious line. "It is a special order. I tried so hard to find something new to please you."

"It's wonderful," I said, swallowing a second sip. My throat burned a little, but another sip of the cool drink soothed that. "Lovely!"

"Please drink up—I'll get you another," she said, smiling as she led me to the honored place by the fire.

And she waited on me herself, never permitting me to rise. I sat there and sipped at my punch cup, which never seemed to be empty, and tried to follow the swift give and take of the conversational circle. The talk reminded me of a spring river, moving rapidly with great splashes of wit over quite a range of territory. Like a river, it wound and doubled back and split and re-formed; as the evening progressed I had more and more difficulty navigating in it. I was increasingly distracted by the glowing candles, and by the brilliance with which the colorful fabrics and jewels and embroidery reflected back the golden light. Faces, too, caught my eye, though at times I couldn't follow what the speakers said. With a kind of fixed attention I watched the swift ebb and flow of emotion in eyes, and cheeks, and around mouths, and in the gesturing of hands with or without fans.

Then suddenly Tamara was before me. "But we have strayed far enough from our purpose. Come, friends. I bid you to be silent. The Countess did promise to entertain us by describing her adventures in the late war."

I did? I thought, trying to recall what she'd said—and what I'd promised. My thoughts were tangled, mixing present with memory, and finally I shook my head and looked around. Every face was turned expectantly toward me.

My vision seemed to be swimming gently. "Uh," I said.

"Mouth dry?" Tamara's voice was right behind me. "Something to wet it." She pressed a chilled goblet into my hands.

I raised it and saw Savona directly across from me, a slight frown between his brows. He glanced from me to Tamara, then I blocked him from my view as I took a deep sip of iced—bristic.

A cold burn numbed my mouth and throat, and my hand started to drop. Fingers nipped the goblet from mine before I could spill it. I realized I had been about to spill it and looked aside, wondering how I'd gotten so clumsy. My hand seemed a long way from my body.

Even farther away was Tamara's voice. "Did you really fight a duel to the death with our late king?"

"It was more of a duel to the—" I felt the room lurch as I stood up.

That was a mistake.

"A duel," I repeated slowly, "to—" I wetted my lips again. "To—burn it! I actually had a witty saying. Fer onsh...once. What's wrong with my mouth? A duel to the dust!" I giggled inanely, then noticed that no one else was laughing. I blinked, trying to see, to explain. "He knocked me outa the saddle...y'see...an' I fell in the—in the—"

Words were no longer possible, but I hardly noticed. The room had begun to revolve with gathering speed. I lost my footing and started to pitch forward, but before I could land on my face, strong hands caught my shoulders and righted me.

I blinked up into a pair of very dark eyes. "You're not well," said Savona. "I will escort you back to the Residence."

I hiccuped, then made a profound discovery. "I'm drunk," I said and, as if to prove it, was sick all over Lady Tamara's exquisite carpet.

THIRTEEN

I WOKE UP FEELING TERRIBLE, IN BODY AND IN SPIRIT.
I recalled Nee's exhortations about drinking, and control, and
how it was a sure way to social ruin. Our grandparents had apparently considered it fashionable to drink until one was insensate, but
during Galdran's threat, that had changed. Was I socially finished?

A light scent like fresh-cut summer grass reached me; I turned
my head, wincing against the pounding inside my skull, and saw a
teacup sitting on a plate beside my bed. Steam curled up from it.
For a time I watched the steam with a strange, detached sort of
pleasure. My eyes seemed to ache a little less; the scent made me
feel incrementally better.

"Can you drink this, my lady?" a soft voice murmured.

I turned my head. "Mora," I croaked. "I think I got drunk."

"Yes, my lady."

I sighed, closing my eyes.

"Please, my lady. Do drink my elixir. It's a special one."

Groaning and wincing, I sat up, took the cup, and sipped the
liquid in it. The taste was bitter and made me shiver, but within
the space of two breaths I felt a wondrous coolness spread all
through me. When I gulped down the rest, the coolness banished
most of the headache.

I looked up at Mora gratefully. She gave me a short nod of satisfaction, then said, "I have laid out your dressing gown." And noiselessly she left.

So I was alone with my regret. I sighed, and for a long, pleasant moment envisioned myself sneaking out in my nightdress, grabbing a horse from the stables, and riding hard straight for home. Tlanth was safe. Tlanth was friendly and honest and respectful. *Mother was right*, I thought aggrievedly. Court was nothing but betrayal in fine clothing.

I certainly hadn't meant to get drunk. And Tamara had certainly made it easy for me, keeping my cup filled; but of course she hadn't forced me to drink it. *Whether she meant it to happen or not, there is little purpose in blaming her*, I thought morosely. That was the coward's way out.

And so was sneaking back to Tlanth, leaving Nee and Bran to face the inevitable gossip.

No, I'd have to brave it out; and if people really did snub me, well, a snub wasn't permanent like a sword through one's innards. I'd live. I'd just spend my time in the library until the wedding, and *then* ride home.

This plan seemed eminently reasonable, but it left me feeling profoundly depressed. I rose at last, reaching for my dressing gown so I could go downstairs to the bath. My spirits were so glum I almost overlooked the two letters waiting on my writing table.

When I did see them, my heart gave one of those painful thumps, and I wondered if these were letters of rejection. The top one had my name written out in a bold, slanting hand, with flourishing letter-ends and underlining. I pulled it open.

My Dear Meliara:

You cannot deny me the pleasure of your company on a picnic this afternoon. I will arrange everything. All you need to do is appear and grace the day with your beautiful smile. To meet you will be some of our mutual friends . . .

Named were several people, all of whom I knew, and it ended with a promise of undying admiration. It was signed *Russav*.

Could it be an elaborate joke, with me as the butt, as a kind of revenge for my social lapse? I reread the note several times, dismissing automatically the caressing tone—I knew it for more of his flirtatious style. Finally I realized that I did not see Tamara's name among the guests, though just about all of the others had been at the party the night before.

A cold sensation washed through me. I had the feeling that if anyone was being made a butt, it was not Meliara Astiar, social lapse notwithstanding.

I turned to the next letter and was glad to see the plain script of my Unknown:

Meliara—

In keeping faith with your stated desire to have the truth of my observations, permit me to observe that you have a remarkable ability to win partisans. If you choose to dismiss this gift and believe yourself powerless, then of course you are powerless; but the potential is still there—you are merely pushing it away with both hands.

Ignorance, if you will honor me with permission to take issue with your words, is a matter of definition—or possibly of degree. To be aware of one's lack of knowledge is to be merely untutored, a state that you seem to be aggressively attempting to change. A true ignorant is unaware of this lack.

To bring our discourse from the general to the specific, I offer my congratulation to you on your triumph in the Affair Tamara. She intended to do you ill. You apparently didn't see it, or appeared not to see it. It was the most effective—perhaps the only effective—means of scouting her plans for your undoing. Now her reputation is in your hands.

This is not evidence of lack of influence.

And it ended there.

Two utterly unexpected communications. The only facts that seemed certain were that the Unknown had been at that party and like Savona (maybe it was he?) had sat up very late penning this letter. Or both letters.

I needed very much to think these things out.

Nee tapped outside my door and asked if I'd like to go down to the baths with her.

"How do you feel?" she asked, looking concerned, as we walked down the stairs.

I felt my face burn. "I suppose it's all over Remalna by now."

She gave me a wry smile. "I think I received six notes this morning, most of which, I hasten to add, affirm their partisanship for you."

Partisan. The term used by the Unknown.

"For me?" I said. "But I got drunk. Worse, I got sick all over Tamara's carpet. Not exactly courtly finesse." I ducked my head under the warm water.

When I came up, Nee said, "But she was the one who served an especially potent punch, one they all knew you probably hadn't tasted before, as it's a Court delicacy . . ." She hesitated, and I hazarded a guess at what she was leaving out.

"You mean, people might want to see Tamara in trouble?"
She nodded soberly.

"And apparently I can do something about that?"

"All you have to do is give her the cut," Nee said quietly. "When you appear in public, you don't notice her, and she'll very shortly come down with a mysterious ailment that requires her to withdraw to the family estate until the next scandal supplants this one."

"Why would she do it?" I asked. "I am very sure I never did anything to earn her enmity."

Nee shrugged. "I can't say I understand her, cousins though we be. She's always been secretive and ambitious, and I expect she sees you as competition. After all, you appeared suddenly, and it seems effortless how you have managed to attract the attention of the most eligible of the men—"

I snorted. "Even I know that a fad can end as suddenly as it began. Savona could get bored with me tomorrow, and all the rest would follow him to the next fad, just as if they had ribbons tied round their necks and somebody yanked."

Nee smiled as she wrung out her hair. "Well, it's true, but I think you underestimate the value of Savona's friendship."

"But it isn't a friendship," I retorted without thinking—and I realized I was right. "It's just a flirtation. We've never talked about anything that really matters to either of us. I don't know him any better now than I did the first day we met." As I said the words I felt an unsettling sensation inside, as if I were on the verge of an important insight. Pausing, I waited; but further thoughts did not come.

Nee obviously thought that sufficed. "If more people recognized the difference between friendship and mere attraction, and how love must partake of both to prosper, I expect there'd be more happy people."

"And a lot fewer poems and plays," I said, laughing as I splashed about in the scented water.

Nee laughed as well.

We talked more about what had happened, and Nee maintained that Savona's picking me up and walking out was the signal that had finished Tamara.

This made me wonder, as I dressed alone in my room, if there had been an unspoken struggle going on all along between the two of them. If so, he'd won. If she'd been the more influential person, his walking out with me would not have mattered; her followers would have stayed and dissected my manners, morals, and background with delicacy and finesse and oh-so-sad waves of their fans.

And another thing Nee maintained was that it was my forthright admission that I was drunk that had captivated Savona. Such honesty was considered risky, if not outright madness. This inspired some furious thinking while I dressed, which produced two resolutions.

Before I could lose my courage, I stopped while my hair was half done, and dashed off a note to my Unknown:

I'll tell you what conclusion I've reached after a morning's thought, and it's this: that people are not diamonds and ought not to be imitating them.

I've been working hard at assuming Court polish, but the more I learn about what really goes on behind the pretty voices and waving fans and graceful bows, the more I comprehend that what is really said matters little, so long as the manner in which it is said pleases. I understand it, but I don't like it. Were I truly influential, then I would halt this foolishness that decrees that in Court one cannot be sick; that to admit you are sick is really to admit to political or social or romantic defeat; that to admit to any emotions usually means one really feels the opposite. It is a terrible kind of falsehood that people can only claim feelings as a kind of social weapon.

Apparently some people thought it took amazing courage to admit that I was drunk, when it was mere unthinking truth. This is sad. But I'm not about to pride myself on telling the truth. Reacting without thinking—even if I spoke what I thought was true—has gotten me into some nasty situations during the recent year. This requires more thought. In the meantime, what think you?

I signed it and got it sent before I could change my mind, then hastily finished dressing. *At least,* I thought as I slipped out the door, *I won't have to see his face when he reads it, if he thinks it excessively foolish.*

Wrapping my cloak closely about me, I ran down the Residence steps, immediately left the flagged pathway, and faded into the garden.

One thing I still remembered from my war days was how to move in shrubbery. With my skirts bunched in either hand so the hems wouldn't get muddy, I zigzagged across the grounds so that no one would see me. I emerged from behind a scree of ferns and tapped at the door at the wing of the Chamadis House where I knew that Tamara had her rooms.

The door was opened by a maid whose eyes widened slightly, but her voice was blank as she said, "Your ladyship?" She held the door close, as if to guard against my entry; I expect she would have denied me had not Tamara herself appeared in the background.

"Who is it, Kerael?" The drawl was completely gone, and her voice was sharp with repressed emotion—I almost didn't recognize it.

In silence the maid opened the door wider, and Tamara saw me. Her blue eyes were cold and angry, but her countenance betrayed the marks of exhaustion and strain. She curtsied, a gesture replete with the bitterest irony; it was the bow to a sovereign.

I felt my neck burn. "Please. Just a bit of your time."

She gestured obliquely, and the maid stepped aside; I walked in. A moment or two later we stood facing one another alone in a lovely anteroom in shades of celestial blue and gold.

She took up a stance directly behind a chair, her back straight, her hands laid atop the chair back, one over the other, the image of perfect control. She was even beautifully gowned, which made me wonder if she had been expecting someone else to call.

She stared at me coldly, her eyes unblinking; and as the silence grew protracted, I realized she would not speak first.

"Why did you get me drunk?" I asked. "I'm no rival of yours."

She made a quick, sharp gesture of negation. A diamond on her finger sparkled like spilled tears, and I realized her fingers were trembling.

"It's true," I said, watching her bury her hands in the folds of her skirts. "What little you know of me ought to make one thing plain: I don't lie. That is, I don't do it very well. I don't fault you for ambition. That would be mighty two-faced when my brother and I plotted half our lives to take the crown from Galdran. Our reasons might be different, but who's to fault that? Not me. I gave that over last year. As for Savona—"

"Don't," she said.

"Why?" I demanded. "Can't you see he's just flirting with me? I don't know much of romance—well, nothing, if you only count experience—but I have noticed certain things, and one is that in a *real* courtship, the two people endeavor to get to know one another." Again I had that sensation of something important hovering just out of my awareness, but when I paused, frowning—trying to perceive it—my thoughts just scattered.

"I think," she said, "you are being a trifle too disingenuous."

I sighed. "Humor me by pretending I am sincere. You know Savona. Can't you see him making me popular just to . . . well, prove a point?" I faltered at the words *pay you back for going after Shevraeth and a crown?*

Not that the meaning escaped her, for I saw its impact in the sudden color ridging her lovely cheeks. Her lips were pressed in a thin line. "I could . . . almost . . . believe you had I not had your name dinned in my ear through a succession of seasons. Your gallantry in facing Galdran before the Court. The Astiar bravery in taking on Galdran's army with nothing but a rabble of half-trained villagers on behalf of the rest of the kingdom. Your running almost the length of the kingdom with a broken foot and successfully evading Debegri's and Vidanric's warriors. The duel-to-the-death with Galdran."

I had to laugh, which I saw at once was a mistake. But I couldn't stop, not until I saw the common omission in all of this: my disastrous encounters with Shevraeth. Had he spoken about my defeats, surely this angry young lady would have nosed it all out— and it was apparent she'd have no compunction about flinging it in my teeth.

No. For some incomprehensible reason, he hadn't talked about any of it.

This realization sobered me, and I gulped in a deep, shaky breath.

Tamara's grimness had given way to an odd expression, part anger, part puzzlement. "You will tell me that your heroism is all lies?" she asked.

"No," I said. "But it's—well, different. Look, if you really want to hear my story, we can sit down and I'll tell you everything, from how I ran about barefoot and illiterate in the mountains joyfully planning our easy takeover, right down to how Galdran knocked me clean out of my saddle after I warded a single blow and nearly lost my arm in doing it. I think he attacked me because I was the weakest—it's the only reason that makes sense to me. As for the rest—" I shrugged. "Some of it was wrong decisions made for the right reasons, and a little of it was right decisions made for the wrong reasons; but most of what I did was wrong decisions for the wrong reasons. That's the plain truth."

She was still for a long, nasty space, and then some of the rigidity went out of her frame. "And so you are here to, what, grant mercy?"

I closed my eyes and groaned. "Tamara. *No one* knows I'm here, and if you don't like my idea, then no one *will* know I was here unless *you* blab. I won't. I just wondered, if I invite you to come with me to Savona's picnic this afternoon, think you things might just go back to how they were?"

She flushed right up to her hairline, a rose-red blush that made her suddenly look like a young girl. "As his supplicant? I bow to your expertise in wielding the hiltless knife." And she swept a jerky curtsy, her hands shaking.

"Life! I didn't mean that," I said hastily. "Yes, I think I can see it's a bad idea. All right, how's this: You and I go out for a walk. Right now. You don't even have to talk to me. But wouldn't that shut up all the gossipmongers—leastwise pull the teeth of their gossip—if we seem to be on terms of amity, as if last night was just a very good joke?"

Again her posture eased, from anger to wariness. "And in return?"

"Nothing. I don't need anything! Or what I need no one can give me, which is wisdom." I thought of my mistakes and winced. Then said, "Just let things go back to the way they were, except you don't have to think of me as an enemy. I'm not in love with Savona any more than he is with me, and I don't see myself changing my mind. If I did, I don't believe he'd like it," I added, considering the elusive Duke. "No, I don't think I could fall in love with him, handsome though he is, because I don't accept any of that huff he gives me about my great beauty and all that. I'd have to trust a man's words before I could love him. I think."

She took a deep, slightly shaky breath. "Very well."

And so we went.

It wasn't a very comfortable walk. She hardly exchanged five words with me; and every single person who saw us stared then hastily recovered behind the remorselessly polite mask of the true courtier. It would have been funny if I had been an observer and not a participant, an idea that gave me a disconcerting insight into gossip. As I walked beside the silent Tamara, I realized that despite how entertaining certain stories were, at the bottom of every item of gossip there was someone getting hurt.

When we were done with a complete circuit of the gardens and had reached her house again, I said, "Well, that's that. See you at the ball tonight, right?"

She half put out a hand, then said, "Your brother's wedding is nearing."

"Yes?"

"Did you know it is customary for the nearest relation to give a party for the family that is adopting into yours?"

I whistled. "No, I didn't. And I could see how Nee would feel strange telling me. Well, I'm very grateful to you."

She curtsied. Again it was the deep one, petitioner to sovereign, but this time it was low and protracted and wordlessly sincere.

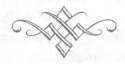

FOURTEEN

ON THE SURFACE, SAVONA'S PICNIC WAS A DELIGHT.
All his particular friends—except Shevraeth—were there, and not
one of them so much as mentioned Tamara. Neither did I.

When a lowering line of clouds on the horizon caused us to
pack up our things and begin the return journey, I wondered how
many notes would be dispatched before the morrow.

Savona escorted me back to the Residence. For most of our
journey the talk was in our usual pattern—he made outrageous
compliments, which I turned into jokes. Once he said, "May I count
on you to grace the Khazhred ball tomorrow?"

"If the sight of me in my silver gown, dancing as often as I can,
is your definition of grace, well, nothing easier," I replied, wondering what he would do if I suddenly flirted back in earnest.

He smiled, kissed my hand, and left. As I trod up the steps
alone, I realized that he had never really *talked* with me about any
serious subject, in spite of his obvious admiration.

I thought back over the picnic. No serious subject had been
discussed there, either, but I remembered some of the light, quick
flirtatious comments he exchanged with some of the other ladies,
and how much he appeared to appreciate their flirting right back.
Would he appreciate it if I did? *Except I can't*, I thought, walking

down the hall to my room. Clever comments with double meanings; a fan pressed against someone's wrist in different ways to hint at different things; all these things I'd observed and understood the meanings of, but I couldn't see myself actually performing them even if I could think of them quickly enough.

What troubled me most was trying to figure out Savona's real intent. He certainly wasn't courting me, I realized as I pushed aside my tapestry. What other purpose would there be in such a long, one-sided flirtation?

My heart gave a bound of anticipation when I saw a letter waiting and I recognized the style of the Unknown.

You ask what I think, and I will tell you that I admire without reservation your ability to solve your problems in a manner unforeseen by any, including those who would consider themselves far more clever than you.

That was all.

I read it through several times, trying to divine whether it was a compliment or something else entirely. *He's waiting to see what I do about Tamara*, I thought at last.

"And in return?" That was what Tamara had said.

This is the essence of politics, I realized. One creates an interest, or, better, an obligation, that causes others to act according to one's wishes. I grabbed up a paper, dipped my pen, and wrote swiftly:

Today I have come to two realizations. Now, I well realize that every courtier in Athanarel probably saw all this by their tenth year. Nonetheless, I think I finally see the home-thrust of politics. Everyone who has an interest in such things seems to be waiting for me to make some sort of capital with respect to the situation with Tamara, and won't they be surprised when I do nothing at all!

Truth to say, I hold no grudge against Tamara. I'd have to be a mighty hypocrite to fault her for wishing to become a queen, when

I tried to do the same a year back—though I really think her heart lies elsewhere—and if I am right, I got in her way yet again.

Which brings me to my second insight: that Savona's flirtation with me is just that, and not a courtship. The way I define courtship is that one befriends the other, tries to become a companion and not just a lover. I can't see why he so exerted himself to seek me out, but I can't complain, for I am morally certain that his interest is a good part of what has made me popular. (Though all this could end to-morrow.)

"Meliara?" Nee's voice came through my tapestry. "The concert begins at the next time change."

I signed the letter hastily, sealed it, and left it lying there as I hurried to change my gown. *No need to summon Mora,* I thought; she was used to this particular exchange by now.

Not many were at that night's concert, and none of Court's leading lights. By accident I overheard someone talking and discovered that most of them had been invited to Merindar House to see some players from Erev-li-Erval.

When I heard this, I felt strange. So, I hadn't been invited. I suspected that this was a message from the Marquise, to whom I had given no answer. Either that or she had simply decided I was not worth her attention after all.

Well, what *had* I done to investigate the rival rulers and how they might rule? Shevraeth's policies I might learn something of if I could nerve myself to attend Petitioners' Court sessions. But how to investigate the Marquise of Merindar as a potential ruler?

Before my eyes rose an image of the beautiful and utterly unreadable Flauvic. I felt an intense urge to find him, ask him, even though I had learned firsthand that he was very capable of turning off with oblique replies whatever he did not wish to answer directly.

The problem was, he never left Merindar House, and I had no

excuse to visit there that wouldn't cause all kinds of speculation.

As the singers spun away the evening with lovely melodies, my mind kept returning to the problem, until at last I got what seemed to me to be an unexceptionable idea.

When I returned from the concert I wrote, in my very best hand, a letter to Flauvic requesting the favor of his advice on a matter of fashion. I sent it that night, and to my surprise, an answer awaited me when I woke in the morning. In fact, two answers awaited: one, the plain paper I had grown used to seeing from my Unknown, and the second, a beautifully folded and sealed sheet of imported linen paper.

This second one I opened first, to find only a line, but Flauvic's handwriting was exquisite: He was entirely at my disposal, and I was welcome to consult him at any time.

The prospect was daunting and fascinating at the same time. Resolving to get that done directly after breakfast, I turned eagerly to the letter from the Unknown:

I can agree with your assessment of the ideal courtship, but I believe you err when you assume that everyone at Court has known the difference from age ten—or indeed, any age. There are those who will never perceive the difference, and then there are some who are aware to some degree of the difference but choose not to heed it. I need hardly add that the motivation here is usually lust for money or power, more than for the individual's personal charms.

But I digress. To return to your subject, do you truly believe, then, that those who court must find themselves of one mind in all things? Must they study deeply and approve each other's views on important subjects before they can risk contemplating marriage?

Well, I had to sit down and answer that.

I scrawled out two pages of thoughts, each following rapidly on the heels of its predecessor, until I discovered that the morning was already advancing. I hurried through a bath, put on a nice gown, and grabbed up a piece of fruit to eat on the way to Merindar House.

Again I made certain that no one knew where I was going. When I emerged from the narrow pathway I'd chosen, just in view of the house, the wind had kicked up and rare, cold drops of rain dashed against my face, promising a downpour very soon.

The servant who tended the door welcomed me by name, his face utterly devoid of expression, offered to take my hat and gloves, which I refused, then requested that I follow him.

This time I visited a different part of the house; the room was all windows on one side, but the air was cool, not cold, with a faint trace of some subtle scent I couldn't quite name. Directly outside the windows was a flowery hillock, down from which poured a small waterfall that splashed into a pool that reached almost to the long row of windows.

Flauvic was standing by the middle window, one slim hand resting on a golden latch. I realized that one window panel was, in fact, a door, and that a person could step through onto the rocks that just bordered the pool. Flauvic was looking down, the silvery light reflecting off rain clouds overhead, and water below throwing glints in his long golden hair.

He had to know I was there.

I said, "You do like being near to water, don't you?"

He looked up quickly. "Forgive me for not coming to the door," he said directly—for him. "I must reluctantly admit that I have been somewhat preoccupied with the necessity of regaining my tranquillity."

I was surprised that he would admit to any such thing. "Not caused by me, I hope?" I walked across the fine tiled floor.

He lifted a hand in a gesture of airy dismissal. "Family argument," he said. Smiling a little, he added, "Forbearance is not, alas, a hallmark of the Merindar habit of mind."

Again I was surprised, for he seemed about as forbearing as anyone I'd ever met—but I was chary of appearing to be a mere flatterer, and so I said only, "I'm sorry for it, then. Ought I to go? If the family's peace has been cut up, I suppose a visitor won't be welcome."

143

Flauvic turned away from the window and crossed the rest of the floor to join me. "If you mean you'd rather not walk into my honored parent's temper—or more to the point, my sister's—fear not. They departed early this morning to our family's estates. I am quite alone here." He smiled slightly. "Would you like to lay aside your hat and gloves?"

"Not necessary," I said, stunned by this unexpected turn of events. Had the Marquise given up her claim to the crown, or was there some other—secret—reason for her sudden withdrawal? If they had argued, I was sure it had not been about missing social events.

I looked up—for he was half a head taller than I—into his gold-colored eyes, and though their expression was merely contemplative, and his manner mild, I felt my neck go hot. Turning away from that direct, steady gaze, I just couldn't find the words to ask him about his mother's political plans. So I said, "I came to ask a favor of you."

"Speak, then," he said, his voice just a shade deeper than usual.

I looked over my shoulder and realized then that he was laughing. Not out loud, but internally. All the signs were there; the shadows at the corners of his mouth, the sudden brightness of his gaze. He was laughing at me—at my reaction.

I sighed. "It concerns the party I must give for my brother's coming marriage," I said shortly, and stole another quick look.

His amusement was gone—superficially, anyway.

"You must forgive my obtuseness," he murmured. "But you could have requested your assistance by letter."

"I did. Oh." I realized what he meant, and then remembered belatedly one of Nee's more delicate hints about pursuit—and pursuers. "*Oh!*" So he *hadn't* guessed why I'd come; he thought I'd come courting. And, well, here we were alone.

My first reaction was alarm. I did find him attractive—I realized it just as I was standing there—but in the way I'd admire a beautifully cut diamond or a sunset above sheer cliffs. Another person, finding herself in my place, could probably embark happily into dalliance and thus speed along her true purpose. But the prospect simply terrified me.

He touched my arm, lightly, just enough to guide us back to his window. "It is not merely the sight of water that I find salubrious," he said. "Its function as a metaphor for study is as . . . as adaptable—"

"You were going to say fluid," I cut in, almost giddy with relief at the deft change of subject.

Once again I saw that brightness in his eyes that indicated internal laughter. "I wasn't," he insisted. "I would never be so maladroit."

Forgive my maladroitness . . . For an instant I was back in that corner room in the State Wing, with Shevraeth standing opposite me.

I dismissed the memory as Flauvic went on, "As adaptable, to resume our discourse, as its inherent properties. The clarity, the swift change and movement, the ability to fill the boundaries it encounters, all these accommodating characteristics blind those who take its utility and artistry for granted and overlook its inexorable power."

As if to underline his words—it really was uncanny—the threatening downpour chose that moment to strike, and for a long moment we stood side by side as rain thundered on the glass, running down in rivulets that blurred the scene beyond.

Then he turned his back to it. "How may I be of service?"

"My brother's party. I want it to be special," I said. "I should have been planning it long before. I just found out that it's a custom, and to cover my ignorance I would like to make it *seem* I've been planning it a long time, so I need some kind of new idea. I want to know what the latest fashion for parties in the Empire's Court is, and I thought the best thing I could do would be to come to you."

"So you do not, in fact, regard me as an arbiter of taste?" He placed a hand over his heart, mock-solemn. "You wound me." His tone said, *You wound me again.*

Once again I blushed, and hated it. "You *know* you're an arbiter of taste, Flauvic," I said with some asperity. "If you think I'm here just to get you to parrot out Erev-li-Erval's latest fad, then you're—well, I know you don't believe it. And I didn't think you fished for compliments."

He laughed out loud, a musical sound that suddenly rendered him very much more like the age we shared. It also made him, just for that moment, devastatingly attractive. I realized that I had to get out of there before I got myself into trouble that it would take a lifetime to get out of.

"There's never any one fad," he said. "Or if there is, it changes from day to day. A current taste is for assuming the mask of the past."

"Such as?" I looked out at the rain streaming down the windowpanes.

"Such as choosing a time from history, say six hundred years ago, and everyone who comes must assume the guise of an ancestor of that time."

"Well, my mother was a Calahanras, but it seems to me—and I know I'm not exactly subtle—that it would not be in the best of taste to assume the guise of royalty for this party."

"But you have your father's family. For example, Family Astiar and Family Chamadis have intermarried, ah, twice that I know of. One of those was a love match, almost three hundred years ago. Your brother and prospective sister would be charming in the guises of Thirav Astiar and Haratha Chamadis. It would also be a compliment to Nimiar, for it was her ancestor Haratha who considerably boosted the family's prestige by her part in the Treaty of the Seven Rivers."

"Oh!" I was delighted. "I knew you'd think of something! But is there a part for me? I have to be prominent, being hostess."

"You don't know your own family's history?" He raised a brow slightly.

"We barbarians are ignorant, yes," I retorted, "mostly because my father burned most of our books after my mother died."

"He did?" Flauvic's blank gaze seemed curiously intent. "Now, why was that—do you know?"

"I don't have any idea. Probably will never find out. Anyway, there was no history of any kind for me to read until I began last year by ordering new books, and very few of those mention the Astiar family."

He bowed, gesturing apology. "Forgive me," he said. "I had not known. As for your part, that's a shade more difficult, for Thirav had no sisters. However, there were two female cousins, either of whom you might assume the guise of. Ardis was the more prominent of the two."

"Ardis. I suppose there are no portraits..."

"...but you could safely order a gown based on court fashions of the time," he finished. "The point here is, if people are to get their costumes ordered in time, you must be speedy with your invitations."

"Costumes are easily ordered," I said, smiling sourly. "What you mean is, to give everyone time to dive into their family histories if they aren't as well read as you are."

"Precisely," he said with a gentle smile. "It is a shame that so few have the time or inclination for scholarship these days. There is much entertainment to be afforded in perusing the mistakes of our forebears."

He said it exactly like he said everything else, but once again that sense of warning trickled through me. "For what purpose?" I asked, daring my real subject. "To advise new rulers?"

"Mere curiosity," he murmured, still smiling. "I never involve myself in political skirmishes."

So that was that.

"Thanks for the advice," I said briskly. "I'd better get to my own studies."

"You do not wish to stay for some refreshment?" he asked.

I shook my head, pointing at the window, which was now clear.

The downpour, as downpours will, had slackened just as suddenly as it had come, and there was a brief glimpse of blue through the tumbling clouds. "I think I'd better go now, before it comes back."

He bowed, silent and gracious, and I was very soon gone.

I decided that that would be my last visit to the heir to the Merindars, at least uninvited and when he was alone. Meanwhile, there was his suggestion for my party to be researched.

What time was it? Just then the bells for first-green pealed. Green—time for Petitioners' Court, Nee had said. Which meant that the Renselaeuses ought to be safely ensconced in the throne room.

Despite the fact that I was somewhat damp from the rain that had begun again in earnest just before I reached the Residence, I sped down the halls to the State Wing, slowing to a sedate walk just before I reached the areas where the door servants would be found.

My heart thumped hard when I reached that last hallway, but the big library was empty. Relieved and grateful, I dashed inside and started scouring the shelves. I knew I would not find anything directly relating to the Astiars—they weren't particularly famous for anything. I'd have to find memoirs or histories that might mention them. The best source for researching the Chamadis family, of course, would be a history of the Battle of the Seven Rivers, or else a history about relations between Remalna and Denlieff. Chamadis lands being on the border, there was sure to be mention of them—and maybe the marriage with the Astiars.

Unfortunately there was only one book that dealt with that battle, and it was written by the ambassador at the time, who featured himself so prominently that the negotiations for the treaty were presented only through a long and self-praising catalog of the entertainments he gave. There was just one brief mention of Lady Harantha.

Remembering what the Princess had told me about histories, I had to grin as I replaced the dusty book for what would probably be another hundred years. So now where?

Of course I knew where.

I turned toward the corner, staring at the tapestries to the little alcove where the memoirs for the heirs were stored. Bunching my skirts in either hand so they wouldn't rustle, I moved stealthily to the tapestry and stood listening. No voices, certainly, and no sounds beyond the drumming of the rain against the near windows.

So I lifted the tapestry—and looked across the room into a pair of familiar gray eyes. Dressed splendidly in black and gold, as if for Court, Shevraeth knelt at the desk, writing.

For the third time that day, my face went hot. Resolutely reminding myself of my promise not to initiate any quarrels, I said, "Harantha Chamadis. Thirav Astiar. The Treaty of Seven Rivers. Is there a record?"

Shevraeth didn't say a word. He lifted his pen, pointed at a particular shelf, then bent his head and went right back to his task.

For a moment I watched his pen traversing swiftly over the paper in close lines. Then my gaze traveled to the smooth yellow hair, neatly tied back, and from there to the lines of his profile. For the very first time I saw him simply as a person and not as an adversary, but I did not give myself the space to gauge my reactions. The curl of danger, of being caught at my observations and once again humiliated, caused me to drag my gaze away, and I trod to the shelf to which I'd been directed.

A few swift glances through the books, and I found the memoirs of the queen of that time. A quick glance through showed the names I wanted repeated on a number of pages. Gripping the book in one hand and brushing back a strand of my wet hair with the other, I said, "Do you need my reason—"

He cut in, lightly enough: "Just put it back when you're done."

He kept his gaze on his writing, and his pen scarcely paused. Scrawl, dip, scrawl, dip.

Two or three more words—then the pen stopped, and he glanced up again. "Was there something else?" he asked. Still polite, but very remote.

I realized I'd been staring for a protracted time, my reactions frozen as if behind a layer of ice. I said in a rush, "The party, for Bran and Nee. Do you—should I send you—"

He smiled just a little. "It would cause a deal of talk if you were to avoid inviting any of my family."

"Oh." I gulped. "Yes. Indeed."

He dipped his pen, bent his head, and went back to his task.

I slipped out the door and fled.

FIFTEEN

FLAUVIC'S REMARK ABOUT SCHOLARSHIP, I DECIDED before the day ended, was a kind of double-edged sword. When I discovered my ancestor Ardis was not so much prominent as notorious, my first reaction was a snort of laughter, followed by interest—and some indignation.

The queen's memoir, which was replete with gossip, detailed Ardis's numerous and colorful dalliances. Her ten-year career of flirtation came to a close not long after she became engaged to a Renselaeus prince. This engagement ended after a duel with the third Merindar son—no one knew the real reasons why—and though both men lived through the duel, neither talked of it afterward. Or to her. She wound up marrying into a minor house in the southwest and passed the rest of her days in obscurity.

She was beautiful, wealthy, and popular, yet it appeared, through the pages of this memoir anyway, that the main business of her life had been to issue forth in the newest and most shocking gown in order to shine down the other women of the Court, and to win away lovers from her rivals. There was no hint that she performed any kind of service whatever.

In short, she was a fool.

This made me drop the book and perform a fast and furious

review of my conversations with Flauvic. Did he think I was a fool? Did he think that I would find Ardis in the records and admire her?

Or was this some kind of oblique challenge? Was he hinting that I ought to do more than my ancestor—such as get involved in a fight for the crown?

The answer seemed pretty obvious. I decided not to communicate with Flauvic about my foolish ancestor. Instead, I'd use his idea but find my *own* time period and historical personages. A much more elegant answer.

This time I planned my foray. When I saw Shevraeth dancing at the Khazhred family ball that night, I excused myself after a short time as quietly as I could, retreated to the Residence, changed out of my gown, lit a candle, and sped through the library to the alcove.

It was empty. I knelt at the desk, which was bare except for pen and ink, and leafed through book after book, names and events filling my mind and overlaying the present until I felt as if I existed in two times at once—as in a dream.

And I realized that if Flauvic had intended some kind of obscure statement through his choice of the time and the ancestors, I could do the same.

For instance, Branaric and I were also descendants of royalty through the Calahanras family. The Calahanras rulers had been some of the best kings and queens this kingdom had ever known; it would be a nice gesture to Flauvic, I thought wryly, if I were to assume the guise of one of my Calahanras ancestors. I could select one who was not famous—thus who wouldn't draw attention to me and away from my brother and his betrothed.

Furthermore, I realized I ought to know something of the ancestors of the other guests, if I could, in case there was some ancient scandal or disgrace that I might accidentally dredge up. So I read until my vision flickered with the candle flames. Before I left, I held my candle up, scanning that barren desk. Why would Shevraeth work there when he had what was rumored to be a fabulous suite of rooms in the Royal Wing—including at least one study?

Because he could be alone, of course.

Except for a certain snotty countess bounding in and starting quarrels.

Sighing to myself, I retreated to my rooms to think out my strategy. I didn't notice the waiting letter until I sank down on my pillows. I grabbed it, saw the familiar handwriting, and tore into the envelope eagerly.

It was a long response to my letter, talking freely about all manner of things. Several times I laughed out loud. Other times I felt the impulse to go hunting books again, for he made easy reference to historical events and people he assumed I was familiar with. It was a relief that, though he knew I was ignorant, he did not think I was stupid. Despite my tiredness, I sat up most of the night happily penning my reply.

And so passed the next several days.

I prowled around the various Court functions to mark where Shevraeth was, and if I spotted him I'd invariably sneak back to the State Wing and slip into the memoirs room to read some more—when I wasn't writing letters.

My response to the Unknown had caused a lengthy answer in kind, and for a time we exchanged letters—sometimes thrice a day. It was such a relief to be able to express myself freely and without cost. He seemed to appreciate my jokes, for his style gradually metamorphosed from the carefully neutral mentor to a very witty kind of dialogue that verged from time to time on the acerbic— just the kind of humor that appealed most to me. We exchanged views about different aspects of history, and I deeply enjoyed his trenchant observations on the follies of our ancestors.

He never pronounced judgment on current events and people, despite some of my hints; and I forbore asking directly, lest I inadvertently say something about someone in his family—or worse, him. For I still had no clue to his identity. Savona continued to flirt with me at every event we met at. Deric claimed my company for every sporting event. And shy Geral always gravitated to my side at balls; when we talked—which was a lot—it was about music. Though others among the lords were friendly and pleasant, these three were the most attentive.

None of them hinted at letters—nor did I. If in person the Unknown couldn't bring himself to talk on the important subjects that increasingly took up time and space in his letters, well, I could sympathize. There was a person—soon to be king—whom I couldn't bring myself to face.

Anyway, the only mention of current events that I made in my letters was about my own experience. Late one night, when I'd drunk a little too much spiced wine, I poured out my pent-up feelings about my ignorant past, and to my intense relief he returned to me neither scorn nor pity. That did not stop me from going around for a day wary of smiles or fans hiding faces, for I'd realized that though the letters could be pleasant and encouraging, I could very well be providing someone with prime material for gossip. Never before had I felt the disadvantage of not knowing who he was, whereas he knew me by name and sight.

But no one treated me any differently than usual; there were no glances of awareness, no bright, superior smiles of those who know a secret. So it appeared he was as benevolent as his letters seemed, yet perfectly content to remain unknown.

And I was content to leave it that way.

At the end of those three days my life changed again when I received a surprise visitor: Azmus, our former spy.

Bran and Nee had already departed for some early morning event. Unspoken between us was the understanding that they would go off to enjoy purely social affairs for Shevraeth's personal friends, and I would stay behind. They didn't mention them ahead of time, they just went.

So I was alone that morning when Mora came in and said, "The vendor you summoned is here to show you some new wares."

"Vendor?" I asked, surprised.

"I think—you wished to see him," Mora said quietly, and so I thanked her, my surprise changing to intense curiosity.

A moment later there was Azmus's round face and snub nose. He was dressed as a goldsmith, and he even carried a bulging satchel.

"Azmus!" I exclaimed in delight. "I didn't think you'd come— I hope you didn't think I'd summoned you." I finished on an apologetic note. "If anyone has earned retirement, it is you."

Azmus grinned. "Neither Khesot nor I like retirement," he said, his voice so quiet it was just above a whisper. "Makes us feel too old. I believe Oria informed you that he's now the head of your border riders—"

"Yes."

"—and as for me, I was glumly sitting at home planning out a garden when your most welcome letter came."

"You can speak to be heard," I said, and grinned. "I think Mora knew who you were—and even if she's listening, I believe she's got our interests to heart. As to why I wrote; oh, Azmus, I truly need help. The Marquise of Merindar wrote me last winter, hinting that I ought to join her, and the one time I spoke with her she twitted me for not keeping the vows of our letter last year. But I do want to keep those vows, and those we made to Papa as well! *Ought* I to help her gain the throne? Would she be better than Shevraeth? Or will he make a good king? I can't find out on my own—either the courtiers don't care, or they take sides, and the one person I could ask..." I thought of my unknown admirer, and sighed. "Well, I can't ask him, either, lest my asking be misconstrued."

He bowed his head slightly, his brows knit. "May I speak freely, my lady?" he said at last.

"Please," I said, and hastened to point to the pillows. "Sit down, Azmus. Speak plainly with me. I desperately need that."

He pursed his lips. "First. Have you gone to Petitioners' Court, or talked to the Renselaeuses? When his grace the Marquis of Shevraeth was up at Tlanth during winter, he rode around the county with Lord Branaric and answered questions very freely, no matter who asked."

"No. I . . . keep running afoul of him."

"Running afoul on political questions?" he asked.

"It never gets that far." I felt my face burn. "Purely personal questions—usually with me misconstruing his motivations. I can't ask him."

Once again he pursed his lips, but this time his countenance seemed more serious. "We can begin with your question to me, then. The Princess of Renselaeus did indeed aid us in our escape that day, though it was indirect aid. I retraced the steps not long after, for my own peace of mind. The Marquise had no involvement whatever with the escape. If she spoke to her brother on your behalf, there's no way of knowing. From what I know of her, I doubt it. But it is entirely possible," he amended scrupulously.

"Ah-hah," I said. "So *she* lied to me. Go on."

"It wasn't a lie so much as indirection," Azmus said. "She did make certain that copies of your letter to Galdran were given into important hands." He grinned. "Her servant was most discreet, yet most insistent that the copies be distributed through the Marquise. I didn't mind, so long as they got read."

"Yet from what you hint about her character, there ought to be a reason beyond altruisim, am I right?"

"You are." He nodded. "More than one person in Court was overheard surmising that it was her way of undermining her brother's position even more thoroughly than he was doing on his own."

"Shev—it's been hinted that she wants the throne."

He nodded again. "Of course I have never overheard her say anything to prove it, nor have I intercepted any correspondence to prove it. But I can well believe it."

"She has recently gone home," I said. "Do you think she gave up?"

He shook his head. "She has never retreated in her life. Every movement was an advance, even when it seemed she retreated. If she went back to her estates, then she has some kind of plan."

I thought furiously. "Her initial request to go home was denied—this was just before we came. Shevraeth showed me her letter. And the other day, I visited Lord Flauvic, and he said that he'd had some kind of argument with his mother and sister, just before they left for Merindar."

Azmus's eyes lowered to his plump hands. "You have established a relationship with Lord Flauvic?"

I grimaced. "Well, let's say I had the opportunity. But I suspect that even if I had continued talking to him, I'd be no more knowledgeable than I am now. He's very good at deflecting questions and giving misleading answers."

Azmus nodded slowly. "We can assume, then, that he wishes this news of the family fight to get about."

"I'm not telling anyone," I said. "Not even about my visit to him."

Azmus's face went bland.

"But you knew," I said, not even making it a question.

"Those who wanted to know, knew," he said.

"So there *is* someone spying on me?" I cried.

"Not on you. On the Merindar House. I arrived two days ago and resumed some of my old contacts and found this out. I also found out that the Merindars have their own spy network, and not just here at Athanarel."

"Spies! Did one intercept my letter to you?" I asked in alarm.

"I did not think a proper answer to your questions ought to be put on paper—though your letter did arrive at my home with its seal intact. I do know how to unseal and seal a letter again, and I know how to tell the difference when it's been done," he assured me. "It appears that the Renselaeus family never did release my name after they identified me, and so most folk believe me to be a retired goldsmith. The letter arrived unmolested."

"Well that's good to know." I sighed in relief. "I hadn't even

157

thought about tampering. Maybe it's best that I stay ignorant and foolish," I added bitterly. "You know how successful Bran and I were with our revolt, and messing with politics is just as likely to leave me mud-covered now."

"If you so choose," Azmus said, "I will return to Tlanth."

"I don't know." I played restlessly with my fan. "I want to do the right thing, yet I can't outthink Flauvic—I proved that recently, over a relatively simple question of social usage—and your re-minder about the letters makes me realize I could stupidly do some-thing disastrous without meaning to."

"If you want information," he said in his low tones, "I am willing to take up my old connections and provide it. You need write to no one or speak to no one. It's common enough for people to summon their own artisans for special projects." He patted his satchel. "You are wealthy enough to enable me to sustain the cover."

"You mean I should order some jewelry made?"

He nodded. "If you please, my lady."

"Of course—that's easy enough. But to backtrack a bit, what you said about spies on both sides worries me. What if the Renselaeuses find out you're here? Will they assume I'm plotting?"

"I have taken great care to avoid their coverts," he said. "The two who met me face-to-face last year are not in Athanarel. And none of the family has actually seen me."

Once again I sighed with relief. Then an even more unwelcome thought occurred. "If my movements are known, then other things have been noticed," I said slowly. "Are there any I ought to know about?"

He gave his nod. "It is known, among those who observe, that you do not attend any private social functions that are also attended by the Marquis of Shevraeth."

So much for my promise, I thought dismally. Yet Shevraeth hadn't said anything. "So . . . this might be why Flauvic granted me that interview?"

"Possibly," he said.

"I take it servants talk."

"Some," he agreed. "Others don't."

"I suppose the Merindar ones don't."

He smiled. "They are very carefully selected and trained, exceedingly well paid—and if they displease, they have a habit of disappearing."

"You mean they're found dead, and no one does anything?"

He shook his head, his mouth now grim. "No. They disappear."

I shuddered.

"So whatever I find out must be by observation and indirection."

"Well, if you can evaluate both sides without endangering yourself," I said, deciding suddenly, "then go ahead. The more I think about it, the less I like being ignorant. If something happens that might require us to act, you can help me choose the correct thing to do and the way to do it."

He bowed. "Nothing would please me more, my lady," he promised.

"Good," I said, rising to fetch my letter from the Marquise. "Here's her letter. Read it—and as far as I care, destroy it." I handed it to him, relieved to have it gone. "So, what's in your bag? I will want something special," I said, and grinned. "For someone special."

SIXTEEN

THE UNKNOWN WAS NOT LIKELY TO WEAR THE JEW-elry I sent. I knew that. Yet it gave me pleasure to plan the design and select just the right gem.

It was a ring I wanted, a fitting return for my own ring, which I wore frequently. Around it Azmus etched laurel leaves in an abstract, pleasing pattern. Leaves, spring, circles—all symbols that complemented the friendship. The gemstone was the best ekirth that Azmus could find, carefully faceted so it glittered like a nightstar, so deep a blue as to seem black, except when the light hit it just so and it would send out brilliant shards of color: gold, blue, crimson, emerald.

Ekirthi traditionally symbolized mystery, but I didn't think an old meaning so bad a thing. I sent it the night following Azmus's second visit. After wasting much paper and time in fruitless endeavor to write a graceful note to accompany it, I decided to simply send it in a tiny cedar box that my mother had apparently brought from Erev-li-Erval and that I'd had all my life.

There was no response the next morning, when I rose early, which disappointed me just a little, but I shrugged off the reaction and dressed swiftly. For I'd found out that Trishe was having a riding party before breakfast, and I intended to encounter it by accident.

Encountering a party by accident is a chancy business. You can't just appear at the party's destination and affect surprise to find everyone gathered there, not unless you want to seriously discommode either the host or yourself. Probably Savona or Tamara—or Flauvic—were expert at managing such a thing gracefully, but I knew I wasn't.

So what I had to do was take a ride on my own, find their path, and see to it that we fell in together. That was the easy part.

The hard part was reacting with delight and no hint of embarrassment when I did find them, for of course most of them exclaimed in various kinds of surprise when they saw me, especially Nee and Bran. A quick glance showed me that Shevraeth was indeed with them, riding next to a young lady I had never seen before.

I reined in my borrowed mount and reached forward to stroke her braided mane, pretending not to notice Nee's confusion. On the periphery of the group I saw the golden-haired hostess, Lady Trishe. She smiled, but her eyes showed worry. I turned to my brother. For once, I hoped, his disastrous habit of loudly saying whatever he thought would be a boon.

"Bran! You're up already. What a surprise to find you out here!" And of course for Bran it was a surprise. His usual habit on days when he had no engagements was to sleep in, or if he did rise betimes, he'd go with some of his cronies to the gymnasium and take up the swords for a bout or two.

Bran looked at me now, saying in his clear voice, "Not as surprising as finding you here, Mel. We take a morning ride once a week, unless it rains. Trishe puts on a breakfast spread in some nice grassy spot—"

And here I was able to cut in and say in an equally jovial and penetrating voice, " 'Tis true I haven't seen much of anyone these mornings, but I've been locked up studying for a special project. But I'm nearly done, and so I find myself free."

Then Trishe had her opportunity to come forward and request that I join them, which I professed myself honored to do, and the awkward moment passed. I urged my mount in on the other side of Trishe's and, in the friendliest voice I could assume, told her how they would all know about my secret project very soon.

I didn't actually look at little red-haired Lady Arasa Elbanek or her skinny, long-nosed brother, but I could sense them both listening avidly. This meant, I thought happily as I dropped back to ride next to Nee, that my confidential conversation with Trishe would be all over Athanarel before the bells for green-change rang.

So I congratulated myself on a fine, subtle social save—until we reached Trishe's picnic site. In the chaos of dismounting and tendering the horses to the waiting servants, I happened to catch Shevraeth's gaze. Those gray eyes, always so accursedly observant, were now narrowed with humor, but his mouth was mock-solemn as he said, "I have the honor to introduce to you Lady Elenet Kheraev of Grumareth."

I curtsied, wondering where I'd heard that name before. Elenet was a tall, slim young lady with a heart-shaped face and wide-set gray-blue eyes. Her hair was fine and somewhat thin, of a tint midway between blond and brown, but it had been dressed by a master hand; and her gown, though of sober hues that suited her subdued coloring, was as finely made as any of Fialma's. She gave me a quiet smile, but there was no time for conversation because Trishe beckoned and everyone had to follow along a narrow path up a short hill, where we found blankets and baskets spread out invitingly on the grass overlooking one of the ponds.

A quick side-glance showed Trishe addressing a hurried question to one of her servants, which was answered with a nod. So they had enough cups and plates—probably carried against breakage. Good. Then I wouldn't have to pretend I'd already eaten.

Next transpired the sort of flutter of well-bred activity attendant upon being seated and served with cups of gently steaming hot chocolate and light, flaky little pan-breads covered with fresh greenhouse berries. During the course of this I got a chance to scan the company and assess positions and attitudes. Not that I could believe everything I saw, I knew. Most of them were probably dissembling as much as I and probably more successfully. But, bent as I was on eradicating negative gossip, I made myself wander from group to group, chocolate cup in hand.

First to my hostess, who sat with Lady Renna, her husband, and some of the other horse-mad people. We talked a little about horses, and the coming races, and who was likely to bet on—or against—whom. Then I passed on to Arasa, sitting with Geral and the Turlee heir. On the outskirts of this conversation hovered Arasa's sour, clapper-tongued brother Lord Olervec, tolerated only because his sister was so popular.

Arasa, whose blue silk gown flattered her attractive, plump figure, seemed perfectly happy to share her two swains with me. She greeted me with a smile and complimented me sunnily on my gown. "Were you hinting about a special party?" she asked, hugging herself. "Oooh, I do hope so!"

"I was," said I, watching Geral and Alcanad Hazhlee watch her. I dropped some hints about costumes and mysteries, and she giggled and shivered. I realized that I was very probably talking to the present-day equivalent of my forebear Ardis. It was hard not to laugh at the idea.

As I bowed to them and moved away, I wondered if she were in fact as empty-headed as she seemed. Everyone liked her, but with the sort of tolerant attitude one expresses when one admits to a taste for spun sugar. Her name was coupled almost constantly with this or that gentleman by those who liked that kind of gossip. Such as, for instance, her brother.

Next was the foursome I had been bracing myself to face all along: Tamara, Savona, the newly met Lady Elenet, and the Marquis of Shevraeth. Very conscious of Olervec's pale eyes following me, I forced myself to greet the Marquis first: "Good morning," I said, as if we'd been talking just the day before. "How much I wish to thank you for putting me in the way of finding the proper books for my project."

Again that laughter was evident in his glance as he sketched a bow. "If you have any further questions," he said, "it would be my pleasure to accommodate you."

"I'd be honored." I curtsied, my hands making the fan gesture of Unalloyed Gratitude. The shadow of humor in the corners of his mouth deepened.

Then I turned to the others. Savona grinned at me, one hand moving slightly in the fencer's salute of a good hit. I fought the urge to blush as Tamara murmured, "You'll be in the race tomorrow?"

"Of course," I said, lifting my hands. "I have to prove whether my wins last time were luck, skill—or the kindness of well-wishers."

Tamara smiled a little. "And once you've proved which it is?"

"Why then I either celebrate, commiserate—or fulminate!"

They all laughed at that, even the quiet Elenet, though her laughter was so soft I scarcely heard it.

I turned to Shevraeth and said, "Will you be there?"

"I hope to be," he said.

"Riding your gray?"

"Is that a challenge?" he replied with a hint of a smile.

I opened my mouth, then a stray memory brought back our private wager before we reached Athanarel and nothing could prevent the heat that burned up my neck into my face; so I quickly bent over, making a business of ordering one of the flounces on my gown. After I had straightened up I'd have an excuse for a red face, or at least enough of one to pass the notice of the three who (presumably) knew nothing of that unpaid wager.

"I think," I said, retying a ribbon and patting it into place, then unbending with what I hoped was an expression of nonchalance, "I'd better find out if my luck is due to skill or kindness before I make any pledges."

"Very well," he said. "A friendly race will suffice."

When the conversation came to a natural close, I retreated to Nee's side and finished the rest of the picnic with her and Bran.

The morning was chill and the sky steadily darkened. Trishe

gave a signal to the servants as soon as the last plate was picked up; it was not a morning to linger.

Scattered drops of rain rustled the leaves overhead as we pulled our gloves on and resettled our hats. Within moments the sweetly chiming harness bells announced that the mounts waited below, and very soon the company was in motion again. I rode back with Nee and Bran, and despite the increasing cold and the strengthening rain I had that inner glow of satisfaction that comes with having attempted the right thing—and actually managing to carry it off.

When we returned to the Residence I decided I had better make the most of my virtuous mood. I sat down at my desk, drew forth the papers I had ordered, which resembled age-yellowed paper from the past, and in my very best writing, began my invitations. I would not insult my brother and Nee by foisting the job off on a scribe.

The historical period I had selected for my party was five hundred years before. The king, young and popular and handsome, had married a lady from the house of Noarth, forebears of the Chamadis family. Those two sterling historical personages would do for Bran and Nee. The king, Jhussav, had had a sister, whose guise I could adopt without causing any kind of political repercussions. She had departed on a world tour not long after she reached my age, and had settled somewhere else. It was a quiet time in our history—no wars or great changes—and there were no exceptionally villainous members of any of the families whose names were prominent now, nor were there any great fools. We could enjoy the masquerade, dress like our ancestors, eat food that was fashionable then, and everyone could find out the idiosyncrasies of their forebears, without embarrassment, and come to the party to do some playacting.

I was thus congratulating myself on having successfully routed Flauvic when a chilling thought made me drop my pen and groan.

Flauvic! What could have possessed me to forget to look up the Merindars? I had checked on everyone else except the forebears of the one who had given me the idea.

No use scolding myself, I thought as I hurried out into the hallway. As I'd done my reading, pausing to run through names of friends, acquaintances, and neutral parties, the Merindars had somehow stood outside of this group. They did not spring naturally to mind, either, when I considered my guest lists. But of course I had to invite Flauvic, and his mother and sister if they returned.

Had I read their names as I did my research? I couldn't remember, which made me fear that something distasteful had been done to them or by them, either of which would be disastrous to call attention to now.

My friendly guise of the morning notwithstanding, I had no wish to blunder into the memoir room if Shevraeth was working there. *This time I will be more stealthy*, I vowed....

The thought vanished when I happened to glance out one of the many arched windows lining the long hallway and saw two figures in one of the private courtyards.

The glass was old and wavery, but something about the tall figure made me stumble to a halt and reach to unlatch the window. As I did, my mind went back to another time when I stood inside a building with distorted glass and stared out at the Marquis of Shevraeth. And somehow he had sensed I was there.

I opened the window just a crack, telling myself that they could see me if they chanced to look up, so it wasn't really spying. He was walking side by side with Lady Elenet, his head bent, his hands clasped behind him. His manner was completely absorbed. I could not hear her voice, but I could see urgency in her long hands as she gestured, and intensity in the angle of her head. Then she glanced up at him and smiled, just briefly, but the expression in her face made me back away without closing the window. I had seen that look before, in the way Nee and Bran smiled at one another, and in the faces of Lady Renna and her new husband. It was love.

Almost overwhelming was the sense that I had breached their privacy, and instinctively I started back to my room until I realized I was in retreat. Why? No one had seen me. And now I knew I would not accidentally encounter Shevraeth in the alcove where he kept the royal memoirs.

Still, it was with shaking hands and pattering heartbeat that I raced back to the archive room and searched through the appropriate years looking for mentions of the Merindars. In one old, crumbling book there was a dull listing of everyone who attended formal Court functions, and the Merindars showed up there. The next book revealed the fact that the most prominent of them five hundred years ago was an elderly man. This was certainly innocuous enough.

I closed the book, carefully replaced it, and left.

The rain had turned the sky to slanting sheets of gray by afternoon, a steady, pelting shower that kept the humans from promenading the paths. Even the spring birds were quiet and invisible.

As Bran had gone off in pursuit of some kind of pleasure, Nee joined me in my room. I'd bade Mora to bring us hot chocolate, which had arrived creamy and perfect as always. Nee poured it out, then settled at my desk to read her letters. For a time I stood at the window, toying with my cup and breathing the gentle, aromatic steam rising up. For some reason the scent of chocolate threw me back to my first taste of it—at the Renselaeus palace. I looked out at the rain and thought about my past.

My thoughts lengthened into reverie, which was broken only by the sound of Nee's voice. "Something amiss?"

I turned my back to the shower-drenched garden. Nee laid down her pen and looked at me from over her cup, held in both hands. Her manner indicated it was not the abstract question of one who would hardly spare the time to listen to the answer. She was in a mood for converse.

So I shrugged, and forced a smile. "Thinking about the rain," I said.

"Rain?" Her brows arched in inquiry.

"Here I stand, regretting our missed opportunity to walk. A year ago I would have happily run up in the hills, whether it rained or not. And I was thinking that I could go out, in spite of the weather, but I wouldn't enjoy it like I used to."

She gestured in amicable agreement. "There's no fault in misliking the feel of a water-soaked gown."

"That's part of it," I said, seizing on the image. "Last year I wore the same clothes year round. My only hat was a castoff that Julen found me somewhere. I loved the feel of rain against my face, and never minded being soaked. I never noticed it! Now I own carriage hats, and walking hats, and riding hats, and ball headdresses—and none of them except the riding hats can get wet, and even those get ruined in a good soak. My old hat never had any shape to begin with, or any color, so it was never ruined." I turned to face the window again. "Sometimes I feel like I didn't lose just my hat, I lost my *self* that horrible night when I walked into Bran's trap."

Nee was silent.

I ran my thumb around the gilt rim of the cup a couple of times, then I made myself face her. "You think I'm being foolish?"

She put her palms together in Peaceful Discourse mode. "Yes I do," she said, but her tone was not unkind. "One doesn't lose a self, like a pair of gloves or a pin. We learn and change, or we harden into stone."

"Maybe I've changed too fast. Or haven't changed enough," I muttered.

"Have you compromised yourself in any important way?" she asked.

I opened my mouth to say *Of course, when we were forced to give up our plans to defeat Galdran,* but I knew it would be an untruth as soon as it left my lips. "I think," I said slowly, "I lost my purpose that day. Life was so easy when all I lived for was the revolt, the accomplishment of which was to bring about all these wondrous miracles. Nothing turned out to be the way we so confidently expected it to. Nothing."

"So . . ." She paused to sip. ". . . if you hadn't walked into that trap, what would be different?"

"Besides the handsomeness of my foot?" I forced a grin as I kicked my slippered toes out from under my hem. No one could see my scarred foot, not with all the layers of fine clothing I now wore, but the scars were there.

She smiled, but waited for me to answer her question.

I said, "I suppose the outcome in the larger sense would have been the same. In the personal sense, though, I suspect I would have been spared a lot of humiliation."

"The humiliation of finding out that your political goals were skewed by misinformation?"

"By ignorance. But that wasn't nearly as humiliating as—" *my encounters with a specific individual.* But I just shook my head, and didn't say it.

"So you blame Vidanric," she said neutrally.

"Yes . . . no . . . I don't know," I said, trying not to sound cross. "I don't." I looked down, saw my hand fidgeting with the curtain and dropped it to my side. "Tell me about Elenet. Why haven't I met her before? Or is she another who abjured Court?"

"On the contrary," Nee said, and she seemed as relieved as I was to have the subject changed. "She grew up with the rest of us. In fact, she was my greatest friend until she went back to Grumareth. As young girls we were both very minor members of our families, largely ignored by the others. She's solitary in habit. Serious. Though her humor comes out in her art."

"Art?"

"Yes. She's very, very gifted at painting. The fan she made for me is so beautiful and so precious I use it maybe once a year. She makes them only when she wishes to. Screens as well. They can change a room."

"I remember you talking about her once."

"She went home two years ago, when she was unexpectedly made the heir to Grumareth." Nee's mouth tightened. "It was another of Galdran's workings, though no one could point to any

169

proof. Until two years ago the Duke of Grumareth had been a very bright man working hard to counter Galdran's worse excesses. Then there was some kind of power struggle and the Duke had one of the accidents that has decimated so many of our families. Galdran got rid of most of the rest of the smart ones in that family, either by accidents or by sending them out of the kingdom. Elenet's mother then moved back to her family in Denlieff, leaving Elenet here. Galdran settled on the present duke, Elenet's great-uncle, to take the title and quiet, obedient Elenet to be heir. The new duke stayed here to pay lip service to Galdran, and Elenet was sent back to run the province."

The memory of my first formal dinner back in Tlanth, when Shevraeth and Nee fenced verbally over the question of reversion of titles, came clear. Nee had defended her friend. "She's done a good job?"

"A superlative job," Nee said fervently. "No one expected it of her, except me. Just because she seldom speaks doesn't mean she doesn't notice, or think. She's saved her people untold grief, deflecting Galdran when she could, and her great-uncle the rest of the time."

"Do you know what brings her here now?"

"I don't," Nee said. "I've scarcely had an opportunity to exchange two words with her. I trust I'll have the chance tonight. I expect, though, that she's here partly because Grumareth has finally gone home ill."

I'd scarcely noticed the absence of the obnoxious duke. Full of patently false flattery and obsequiousness mixed with superciliousness, he was thoroughly repellent—and stupid. Luckily he favored the older generation as gambling cronies, only paying lip service to those young people he thought would somehow advantage him. He'd apparently decided we Astiars were not worth his exalted efforts; though he'd courted my brother all the year before, he'd largely ignored us both since my arrival.

"Ill? But no one admits to being sick—it always means something else."

"Probably gambling debts," Nee said, shrugging. "That's what it usually is, with *him*. Elenet will have informed him they haven't the wherewithal for his latest squanderings, and he'll have gone home to save face until they can raise what's needed."

"You mean they are that close to ruin?"

Nee grinned. "Oh, not as bad as they were, thanks to Elenet. It's just that his foolishness is now the very last priority, over land improvement. It's she who governs the finances, not he. He's so afraid of anyone finding out, he perforce permits it. I shall make certain the two of you have a chance to talk. I think you will really like her."

"Thank you," I said, sweeping a curtsy. "I'm flattered."

SEVENTEEN

THE NEXT DAY'S RACE WAS CANCELED ON ACCOUNT of rain. My invitations had been delivered, however, causing a spate of notes to cross and recross the elegant pathways, borne by patient runners under drooping rain canopies.

Bran and Nee were delighted—and I think Nee was just a little relieved as well. With every appearance of enthusiasm, they both summoned their clothier staffs to start planning their costumes.

I also received a note from Azmus saying that he needed to talk to me, so I asked Mora to help me arrange my schedule for the following day so that I could see him alone when everyone else was to be busy. Mora gave no sign that I knew she knew all my affairs—she just said she'd help, and did.

I also received a note from the Unknown, the first in two days. I pounced on it eagerly, for receiving his letters had come to be the most important part of my day.

Instead of the long letter I had come to anticipate, it was short.

I thank you for the fine ring. It was thoughtfully chosen and I appreciate the generous gesture, for I have to admit I would rather impute generosity than mere caprice behind the giving of a gift that cannot be worn.

Or is this a sign that you wish, after all, to alter the circum-
scriptions governing our correspondence?

I thought—to make myself clear—that you preferred your ad-
mirer to remain secret. I am not convinced you really wish to re-
linquish this game and risk the involvement inherent in a contact
face-to-face.

I dropped the note on my desk, feeling as if I'd reached for a blos-
som and had been stung by an unseen nettle.

My first reaction was to sling back an angry retort that if gifts
were to inspire such an ungallant response, then he could just return
it. Except it was I who had inveighed, and at great length, against
mere gallantry. In a sense he'd done me the honor of telling the
truth—

And it was then that I had the shiversome insight that is probably obvious by now to any of my progeny reading this record: that
our correspondence had metamorphosed into a kind of courtship.

A *courtship.*

As I thought back, I realized that it was our discussion of this
very subject that had changed the tenor of the letters from my
asking advice of an invisible mentor to a kind of long-distance
friendship. The other signs were all there—the gifts, the flowers.
Everything but physical proximity. And it wasn't the unknown gentleman who could not court me in person—it was I who couldn't
be courted in person, and he knew it.

So in the end I sent back only two lines:

You have given me much to think about.
Will you wear the ring, then, if I ask you to?

I received no answer that day, or even that night. And so I sat
through the beautiful concert of blended children's voices and tried
not to stare at Elenet's profile next to the Marquis of Shevraeth,
while feeling a profound sense of unhappiness, which I attributed
to the silence from my Unknown.

The next morning brought no note, but a single white rose.

Despite Nee's good intentions, there was no opportunity for any real converse with Elenet after that concert. Like Nee, Elenet had unexpectedly risen in rank and thus in social worth. If she'd been confined to the wall cushions before, she was in the center of social events now.

But the next morning Nee summoned me early, saying she had arranged a special treat. I dressed quickly and went to her rooms to find Elenet there, kneeling gracefully at the table. "We three shall have breakfast," Nee said triumphantly. "Everyone else can wait."

I sank down at my place, not cross-legged but formal kneeling, just as Elenet did. When the greetings were over, Nee said, "It's good to have you back, Elenet. Will you be able to stay for a while?"

"It's possible." Elenet had a low, soft, mild-toned voice. "I shall know for certain very soon."

Nee glanced at me, and I said hastily, "If you are able to stay, I hope you will honor us with your presence at the masquerade ball I am hosting to celebrate Nee's adoption."

"Thank you." Elenet gave me a lovely smile. "If I am able, I would be honored to attend."

"Then stay for the wedding," Nee said, waving a bit of bread in the air. "It's only scarce days beyond—midsummer eve. In fact, if Vidanric will just make up his mind on a day—and I don't know why he's lagging—you'll have to be here for the coronation, anyway. Easier to stay than to travel back and forth."

Elenet lifted her hands, laughing softly. "Easy, easy, Nee. I have responsibilities at home that constrain me to make no promises. I shall see what I can contrive, though."

"Good." Nee poured out more chocolate for us all. "So, what think you of Court after your two years' hiatus? How do we all look?"

"Older," Elenet answered. "Some—many—have aged for the better. Tastes have changed, for which I am grateful. Galdran never would have invited those singers we had last night, for example."

"Not unless someone convinced him that they were all the rage at the Empress's Court and only provincials would not have them to tour."

"It must be expensive to house so many," Elenet observed.

"Princess Elestra brought them." Nee picked up her fan, snapped it open, and gestured in Acknowledgment of Superior Aesthetics mode, which caused Elenet to smile. "Apparently they have those children up in Renselaeus every year, and I understand one or two of their own youth have been deemed good enough to join the choir and travel the world. It's a long association." She leaned back on her pillows. "It's been like that of late, Elenet. You really must stay and enjoy it while the Princess is still arranging royal entertainments. Remember those long, hideous nights of watching Galdran win at cards?"

"I never watched him," Elenet admitted. "I watched the others, always. It took consummate skill to lose to him."

"I take it people had to lose," I said.

They both looked at me quickly, as if they'd forgotten I was there. *So others can lose themselves in memories of the past,* I thought. And obviously not good memories, either.

"Yes," Nee said. "If you didn't, he got his revenge. Mostly, though, if you wanted to live—if you wanted your family to be safe—then you pretended to be much stupider than he was."

Elenet made a quick gesture of warding. "Banish those old fears. Let us talk of pleasant things. Have you been keeping up with your own music?"

"I blush to say no," Nee admitted, "but a beautiful harp awaits me when we remove to Tlanth, and then I know I will have the time to practice every day. Maybe even make my own songs again."

I looked at her in surprise—I hadn't known that she wrote music.

175

"Your songs are beautiful," Elenet said.

"But sad," Nee said, wrinkling her nose. "I promised myself no more sad songs, and so I stopped. Now I think I can make happy ones. You?" Nee asked.

"Every day," Elenet said. "Acquit me of heroic efforts, though! It has been my solace to sit at my harp each morning, just before first-gold."

"If I painted like you do, I'd have solace enough," Nee said, sighing.

Elenet's smile was slight, and her eyelids lowered as she stared down at her hands. "It seems that my . . . sad songs . . . took a different form."

"No more sad songs for you, either," Nee said, touching her friend's wrist. "You've earned happiness. I command you to have it!"

All three of us laughed, and the remaining conversation was about inconsequentials, such as gowns and materials, and then music again, before Nee realized it was late and we all had things to do. We parted with mutual compliments and expressions of esteem.

Azmus leaned forward and said, "I have only one fact to give you: The Duke of Grumareth met with the Marquise and her daughter on their way to Merindar."

"On their way?" I repeated. "Merindar is north, and Grumareth west."

Azmus's round, pleasant face hardened into a kind of sardonic amusement. "For a half day's journeying, their path could lie together."

"Which could be innocuous," I said. "Anything else?"

"Only that the rain forced them to stop at an inn for a full time-change. Admittedly the rain was heavy that day, but it was also intermittent; yet only after second-green did both parties deem it possible to ride on."

"I take it you got this from inn servants, or Grumareth's?"

"One of the duke's people." Azmus nodded. "They are loyal enough to their land, but some loathe the Merindars with deadly passion."

"Ah-hah!" I exclaimed. "So, what now?"

Azmus's gaze was serious. "It is time for the truth, my lady, if you will honor me with the privilege of speaking frankly."

"Do," I said, hiding the wail of dismay that shivered through my head. Everyone seemed to want to tell me the truth, when I wasn't sure I wanted to hear it. *Except Flauvic, who says there is no truth.*

"I can pursue this," he said, "but it will take a great deal of work, and it will also be costly."

"How so?" I asked uneasily. "Bribery?"

He shook his head. "Not at all. The person who gives information for bribes is usually worthless; someone else could be paying a higher price either for the information you want—or for you to get the wrong information. I told you before that the Merindars' servants are mum. What I must do is reassemble many of my old contacts and gather the information we need by finding patterns. This is exhaustive and complicated if it is to be done well—and without causing comment."

"Patterns?"

He nodded, smiling. "The very first lesson I learned when I first began spying for my lord your father was that information that cannot be gathered on where someone is can usually be inferred by where the individual isn't. This is particularly true for runners." He looked at me expectantly.

I drew a deep breath. "So. What you're saying is that you—and whomever else you need—must visit all the likely inns along likely paths and find out if Merindar runners have been there, and when, and how long?"

"That's close enough," he said. "Bear in mind that the best of them take different routes quite often, but humans are creatures of habit, and they are also creatures of comfort. At some point they will go where they know there are clean beds or a particularly good table set, or where they can do their own listening. And of course, there are their horses."

"But wealthy people like the Merindars and the Renselaeuses have horses stabled all over the kingdom," I protested. "I noticed that last year."

"Yes, but good stablehands know those horses, and thus know when they're taken out, and for how long, and where they went. For one stablehand to talk about the fine roan Windrunner and how he did in the bad weather last week is merely horse talk and seldom raises comment. But Windrunner's movements put together with Jerrec of Ilvan-town's movements make a pattern."

"I see. So you want to know if I'll pay for it?"

He shook his head. "I want to know, my lady, what you will do with the information."

My first thought was that the Marquise would probably make any servant disappear who spoke thus with her. But I had given Azmus the right. He loved a challenge, this I knew, but he also loved the kingdom. When I first took charge of Tlanth's accounting books, I had discovered that Azmus had been paid only sporadically over the years. He had used his ostensible trade as goldsmith in order to pursue his clandestine vocation on our behalf. My father, and then my brother and I, had helped little, beyond sending him back to Remalna-city with a basket of fresh food and one of our good mounts after he'd made one of his reports.

So he was not in any sense a mere lackey to go silently and carry out my whims. He was a co-conspirator, and he wanted to discuss the goal.

So what was my goal?

Images fled through my mind, chased by phantom emotions: my descending on Shevraeth to inform him of whatever it was the Marquise was planning; my sending him an anonymous letter with the same information. Fine, triumphant gestures, but to what end? And why?

I shook my head, as if that would dispel the images. If I was going to dip my hand into public affairs, then I had to dismiss personal considerations.

"To help the new king," I said. "To make certain that no Merindar sits again on that throne, because none of them are worthy."

Azmus smiled, clapped his hands to his knees and bowed with slow deliberation. "I shall communicate with you as soon as I know something, my lady," he said, and slipped out.

EIGHTEEN

THE DAYS IMMEDIATELY FOLLOWING PASSED VERY swiftly.

Now that summer had begun, the spring rains, which had held off for weeks, inundated us steadily. I noticed worried conversations once in a while, among people whose lands lay along the coast, and runners dashed and splashed back and forth to report on crops and roads and floods.

Meanwhile, the peculiar life of Athanarel continued. We did not have a king, yet the government was somehow carried forward, and foreign diplomats attended the constant round of social events, and they all seemed content with things as they were. Not so the more serious of the courtiers, but as yet the questions everyone most wanted to ask—"When will we have a king? Why does he wait?"—were as yet discussed only in quiet corners of informal parties and never by those most closely concerned.

The weather curtailed outside activities. For now the races and picnics were set aside for inside diversions: readings, music, dancing, parties, chocolate, and talk. I think four new dances were introduced during that time, but what I really enjoyed was the resumption of sword work. Parties to pursue the martial arts were organized, and fencing tourneys replaced racing for those who liked competition.

I competed only for fun, and no one bet on me, not even Savona, because, despite my enthusiasm, I wasn't very good. Neither was Bran, though he shared my enthusiasm. The others who favored the blade had been well-trained from childhood, and our lack showed. But this did not stop either of us from trying.

One of the topics of conversation was my party, which was perhaps the more anticipated because people kept inside perforce had more time to spend on their costumes. My own involvement with the preparations had escalated accordingly, about which I'll have something to say anon.

From Flauvic, of course, nothing was seen, nor did he entertain—but after enough days had passed that I had quite given up on him, I received a witty note, gracefully written by his own hand, stating that he would attend my party.

And so, on the surface, all was serene enough. Tamara remained cool but friendly, and Nee told me over chocolate one morning when Elenet was not there that Tamara never mentioned me but in praise.

Trishe held her weekly breakfast parties in her rooms at Khialem House; Derec and Geral continued to flirt with me; Savona continued his extravagant compliments; I was often in company with Shevraeth now, and we both smiled and conversed, but always, it seemed, with other people.

And on most mornings, Elenet joined Nee and me for breakfast. Sometimes Bran was there, and sometimes not. I cannot say that I came to know Elenet any better as the days wore on. She was reserved and never made any reference to anything personal. Still, when she was there, we had some of our best discussions of reading, music—always music—art, and history.

One morning when we three were alone, Nee leaned forward and said, "Elen, you've been closeted with Vidanric a lot, I've noticed. Has he said aught about a coronation? I confess it makes me nervous to have it not decided—as if they are waiting for something terrible to happen."

Elenet's expression did not change, but high on her thin cheeks appeared a faint flush. "I trust we will hear something soon," she murmured. And she turned the conversation to something general.

Were they in love? I knew that she was. Elenet would make a splendid queen, I told myself, and they both certainly deserved happiness. I found myself watching them closely whenever we were all at an event, which occurred more and more often. There were no touches, no special smiles, none of the overt signs that other courting couples gave—but she was often by his side. I'd inevitably turn away, thinking to myself that it was none of my business. It wasn't as if I didn't have admirers, both the social kind and one real one—though I didn't know his name. Still, the subject made me restless, which I attributed to my knowledge of how badly I had behaved to Shevraeth. I knew I owed him an apology, or an explanation, two things I could not bring myself to offer lest—someone—misconstrue my motives. And think me angling for a crown.

So I hugged to myself the knowledge of my Unknown. No matter how my emotions veered during those social occasions, it was comforting to realize that I would return to my room and find a letter from the person whose opinions and thoughts I had come to value most.

I *preferred* courtship by paper, I told myself. No one feels a fool, no one gets hurt. And yet—and yet—though I loved getting those letters, as the days went by I realized I was becoming slightly impatient of certain restraints that I felt were imposed on us.

Like discussing current events and people. I kept running up against this constraint and finding it more irksome as each day passed. We continued to range over historical events, or the current entertainments such as the Ortali ribbon dancers or the piper-poets from faraway Tartee—all subjects that I could have just as well discussed with an erudite lady.

The morning of Nee's question to Elenet about coronations, I found the usual letter waiting when I returned to my room. I decided to change everything. Having scanned somewhat impatiently down the well-written comparison of two books about the Empire of Sveran Djur, I wrote:

I can find it in myself to agree with the main points, that kings ought not to be sorcerers, and that the two kinds of power are better left in the charge of different persons. But I must confess that trouble in Sveran Djur and Senna Lirwan seems a minor issue right now. The problems of wicked mage-kings are as distant as those two king-doms, and what occupy my attention now are problems closer to home. Everyone seems to whisper about the strange delay concerning our own empty throne, but as yet no one seems willing to speak aloud. Have you any insights on why the Renselaeus family has not made any definite plans?

That sent, I changed into my riding clothes, summoned a rain canopy, and set out for sword practice, wondering about the silence from Azmus.

The long room now used as a gymnasium had formerly been some kind of drill hall for Galdran's private army, and before that it had obviously served mostly military purposes, for flags, ancient and modern, hung high on the walls, celebrating past ridings and regiments that had been deemed worthy of fame. These were not as spectacular as the House banners that were displayed on angled poles in the Throne Room, testament to Remalna's unity, but they carried their own prestige; now that I was better read about our past I recognized some of them, and there was a kind of thrill in seeing the physical evidence of past glory.

At one end of the room was a group of young teens busy with swordplay, and at the other a swarm of children circled round on ancient carved horses mounted on cart wheels or played at stick-and-ball.

I wandered toward my friends and was soon hailed by Renna, who offered me a bout. Time passed swiftly and agreeably. I finished my last engagement with one of Nee's cousins and was just beginning to feel the result of sustained effort in my arm and back

183

when a practice blade thwacked my shoulder. I spun around, and gaped.

Shevraeth stood there smiling. At his elbow my brother grinned, and next to him, Savona watched with appreciation apparent in his dark eyes.

"Come, Lady Meliara," the Marquis said. "Let's see how much you've learned since you took on Galdran."

"I *didn't* take on Galdran," I protested, feeling hot and cold at once.

"I don't know what you'd call it, then, Mel." Bran leaned on his sword, still grinning. "Looked like you went have-at-'im to me."

"I was just trying to defend *you*," I said, and the others all laughed. "And a fat lot of good it did, too," I added when they stopped. "He knocked me right out of the saddle!"

"Hit you from behind," Shevraeth said. "Apparently he was afraid to confront so formidable a foe face-to-face."

They laughed again, but I knew it was not at me so much as at the hated King Galdran.

Before I could speak again, Shevraeth raised his point and said, "Come now. Blade up."

I sighed. "I've already been made into cheese by Derec, there, and Renna, and Lornav, but if you think I merit another defeat..."

Again they laughed, and Savona and my brother squared off as Shevraeth and I saluted. My bout with the Marquis was much like the others. Even more than usual I was hopelessly outclassed, but I stuck grimly to my place, refusing to back up, and took hit after hit, though my parrying was steadily improving. Of course I lost, but at least it wasn't so easy a loss as I'd had when I first began to attend practice—and he didn't insult me with obvious handicaps, such as never allowing his point to hit me.

Bran and Savona finished a moment later, and Bran was just suggesting we exchange partners when the bells for third-gold rang, causing a general outcry. Some would stay, but most, I realized, were retreating to their various domiciles to bathe and dress for open Court.

I turned away—and found Shevraeth beside me. "You've never sampled the delights of Petitioners' Court," he said.

I thought of the Throne Room again, this time with Galdran there on the goldenwood throne, and the long lines of witnesses. I repressed a shiver.

Some of my sudden tension must have exhibited itself in my countenance because he said, "It is no longer an opportunity for a single individual to practice summary justice such as you experienced on your single visit."

"I'm certain you don't just sit around happily and play cards," I muttered, looking down at the toes of my boots as we walked.

"Sometimes we do, when there are no petitioners. Or we listen to music. But when there is business, we listen to the petitioners, accept whatever they offer in the way of proof, and promise a decision at a later date. That's for the first two greens. The last is spent in discussing impressions of the evidence at hand; sometimes agreement is reached, and sometimes we decide that further investigation is required before a decision can be made."

This surprised me so much I looked up at him. There was no amusement, no mockery, no threat in the gray eyes. Just a slight question.

I said, "You listen to the opinions of whoever comes to Court?"

"Of course," he said. "It means they want to be a part of government, even if their part is to be merely ornamental."

I remembered that dinner when Nee first brought up Elenet's name, and how Shevraeth had lamented how most of those who wished to give him advice had the least amount worth hearing.

"Why should I be there?" I asked. "I remember what you said about worthless advisers."

"Do you think any opinion you would have to offer would be worthless?" he countered.

185

"It doesn't matter what *I* think of my opinion," I retorted, and then caught myself. "I mean to say, it is not me making the decisions."

"So what you seem to be implying is that I think your opinion worthless."

"Well, don't you?"

He sighed. "When have I said so?"

"At the inn in Lumm, last year. And before that. About our letter to Galdran, and my opinion of courtiers."

"It wasn't your opinion I pointed up, it was your ignorance," he said. "You seem to have made truly admirable efforts to overcome that handicap. Why not share what you've learned?"

I shrugged, then said, "Why don't you have Elenet there?"— and hated myself for about as stupid a bit of pettiness as I'd ever uttered.

But he took the words at face value. "An excellent suggestion, and one I acted on immediately after she arrived at Athanarel. She's contributed some very fine insights. She's another, by the way, who took her own education in hand. Three years ago about all she knew was how to paint fans."

I had talked myself into a corner, I realized—all through my own efforts. So I said, "All right, then. I'll go get Mora to dig out that Court dress I ordered and be there to blister you all with my brilliance."

He bowed, lifted his gray-gloved hand in a casual salute, and walked off toward the Royal Wing.

I retreated in quick order to get ready for the ordeal ahead.

As the bells for first-green echoed sweetly up the stone walls of the great hall built round the Throne Room, I passed through the arched entrance into the room itself. I felt very self-conscious in my never-worn pale rose satin gown and gloves. I glanced down at the gemstones winking in the light, and the cunning silver and maroon embroidery, then I raised my head carefully so as not to dislodge the formal headdress.

People seemed to be milling about in an orderly fashion, the rare sunlight from the high window sparking rich highlights from brightly colored velvets and satins and jewels.

Elenet and Savona appeared, arm in arm, she dressed in forest green and he in a very dark violet that was almost black. They came directly to me, smiling welcome, and with a pretty fan-flourish of Friends' Recognition, Elenet said, "You look lovely, Meliara. Do come stand with us; we have found a good place."

And it was a good place, from which we could see all three Renselaeuses plus the petitioners. We could hear them all without too much distortion from the echoes in the huge room, for there were only twenty or thirty of us at most; not the hundreds that Galdran had required to augment his greatness.

The throne was empty, and above it hung only the ancient flag of Remalna, tattered in places from age. Galdran's banners were, of course, gone. No one was on the dais. Just below it, side by side in fine chairs, sat the Prince and Princess.

At their feet Shevraeth knelt formally on white cushions before a long carved table. He now wore white and silver with blue gemstones on his tunic and in his braided hair. *He looks like a king*, I thought, though he was nowhere near the throne.

Each petitioner came forward, assisted by stewards in the gold-and-green of Remalna. They did not have to stand before the Renselaeuses, but were bade to take a cushion at that long table, which each did, first bowing and then kneeling in the formal manner.

It really was a civilized way of conducting the business, I realized as time wore on. The Prince and Princess remained silent, except when they had a question. Their son did all the speaking, not that he spoke much. Mostly he listened, then promised a decision on this or that day; as the number of petitioners increased, I realized he'd been doing it long enough to gauge about how long each piece of business was likely to take. Then he thanked them for coming forward, and they bowed and rose, and were escorted away to the side table, where refreshments awaited any who wanted them.

I noticed some of the courtiers with cups in their hands, or tiny plates of delicately made foods. The room was chill, and the rain had come back, drumming against the high windows. The Renselaeuses did not eat or drink, and I realized I was so fascinated with the process that I did not want to steal away to get food for myself.

The last petitioner left well before the second-green, which meant that there would be no Court the following day. I suspected they'd need to use the time to go over the petitions; one change was not going to do for all that I had heard that day.

Nor did it. When the great doors at the other end were closed, we repaired into a beautiful antechamber of pink marble, where more food and drink were spread, hot and fresh.

This time everyone partook liberally and seated themselves on narrow stools along a long, high table. When I realized that these were to accommodate the women, I wanted to laugh. Court gowns, having wide skirts and delicate, costly decoration, are not made to be sat in, but one could manage with a stool. I wondered when the stools had been made, and with whom in mind, as I harkened back to elder days of fashion when it was the men whose tight, constraining clothing made sitting difficult, while the ladies knelt at their ease in their flimsy gowns.

The Prince and Princess sat at either end of the table. Both had foreign diplomats at their right and left hands. Prince Alaerec caught my eye and smiled a welcome, then he said, "So who has thoughts about Guild Mistress Pelhiam's request?"

"Seems straightforward," Baron Orbanith said, sounding, as usual, slightly pompous. "Cloth makers want glowglobes for their street for night work, citing the sail makers and the scribes as having glowglobes on theirs. They'll contact the magicians, order them, pay for them."

188

Savona lowered his wineglass. "It is straightforward. The question is, is this the time to be raising prices? Because we all know that the Guild will duly raise prices in order to meet the extra expense."

"It is not the time to be raising prices." The Princess's fluting voice was pleasant but firm. "The people who will be most affected by the price rise will need another year or more to recover from the recent hardships."

Several more people spoke then, some of them merely repeating what had already been said, and one person, Lord Olervec Elbanek, declaring that if the poor simply worked harder they could afford to buy more.

Others spoke more sensibly, and then finally Elenet said, "Perhaps the request should be granted, contingent on the Guild using some of its own funds and not raising prices. If that's summarily refused, the subject could be brought forward again in a year's time."

Shevraeth nodded. "If they want light at night badly enough, they'll unpocket the funds. If not, then they can wait."

General agreement murmured round the table, and Shevraeth leaned over to speak to the quiet scribe who sat at his elbow. He then wrote swiftly on the petition and laid it aside.

The second petition caused longer debate, which led to calls for more investigation. It seemed that one of the fortresses on the southern border—I wondered if it was one to which the troublesome army officers had been sent—was charging increasing amounts of tax money to the people they protected. The petitioners, from a nearby town, begged for a royal decree placing a ceiling on the taxes. "They claim they have more new recruits than ever before, which accounts for all the supplies and equipment and horses they are ordering. But we're no longer at war. So if they really are ordering all this, against what?" one man had said.

The debate went on, listened to but not commented on by the three Renselaeuses. Then when all seemed to have had their say, the petition was set aside pending investigation.

The third petition caused more general talk, led by the Prince; and so time sped on, the bells for blue ringing before the pile was half done. There was general agreement to meet the next day at green in the Exchequer First Chamber and then all rose and departed.

I left, having not spoken during the entire proceeding. I realized I was glad that I had gone and that I was fascinated by what I'd seen. As I walked down the long halls, listening to the *swish-swish* of my skirts on the fine mosaic tiles, I wondered how they'd investigate, who they'd hire—and just how one went about building the unseen part of a government.

When I reached my rooms, I saw a letter lying on my table.

Hastily stripping off my gloves, I sank down onto my pillows, heedless of the costly fabric of my court gown crinkling and billowing about me, and broke the seal with my finger.

The Unknown had written:

You ask why there has been no formal announcement concerning a coronation. I think this question is better addressed to the person most concerned, but I do know this: Nothing will be announced until the sculptors have finished refashioning a goldenwood throne for a queen.

NINETEEN

WELL, I HAD NO ANSWER TO MAKE TO THAT; THINK-
ing about Elenet, or Shevraeth, or that carved throne, caused a cold
ache inside, as if I had lost something I had not hitherto valued.

So I didn't write back that day. Or the next. The following
morning I received a letter that did not refer to thrones, queens,
or coronations, to my intense relief. And so, for a handful of days
anyway, things went right back to normal.

Except, what is normal at any given time? We change just as
the seasons change, and each spring brings new growth. So nothing
is ever quite the same. I realize now that what I wanted was comfort,
but that, too, does not often come with growth and change.

I did not go back to Petitioners' Court the next day, or the
next; and the morning after that, when Nee had arranged a
breakfast for Elenet and me, I moved so reluctantly that I arrived
outside Nee's tapestry somewhat late. From inside came the
sound of Elenet's laughing, and then her voice, talking swiftly.
Either she was happy over something specific, or else she felt constrained while in my company. Either way, I did not know how to
react, so I backed away from the tapestry and retreated to my
rooms.

"Mora, I think the time has come for me to remain here to

oversee the last of the preparations for the party," I said as soon as I slipped inside. And there was no mistaking the relief in her face.

One could, of course, issue orders through servants for this or that group of performers to appear, promising a sizable purse. There were many of these groups earning their living in and around Remalna-city: players, dancers, singers, musicians whose livelihood depended on their knowing the latest trends and tastes.

My idea was to transport everyone five hundred years into the past as soon as they entered the portals. The building, of course, was appropriate; I hired a ballroom near the Residence that had not been renovated for generations, knowing that the marble therein was more than five hundred years old.

As for the rest, I did not want to issue orders through servants. I wanted to see the project through myself. What I discovered was that in discussing my vision with each artist I encountered, these artists altered from hirelings into individuals—and conversely for them, I altered from a faceless courtier with money into an individual with an interest and appreciation for their expertise.

This, in turn, led to offers of cousins, friends, relations—some so distant they were beyond our borders—who were experts at this or that art. Over the month in which I prepared for that ball, my own vision slowly transformed into a much greater reality, one conceived in willing collaboration with many minds.

I'd thought to have someone scout out enough five-hundred-year-old tapestries from houses around town to borrow for suitable wall hangings. When I mentioned this to one of the palace servants Mora introduced to me, I was brought an uncle who specialized in re-creating ancient arts.

"No, no," said this wizened little old man, his eyes bird-bright. "Never tapestries for a ball, not then. Always a chimerical garden, so arranged that the air always smells sweet and fresh." His hands whirled around his head, reminding me of wings, then he darted back and forth, showing me where this or that herb would hang, and describing streams of water that one heard but did not see, which would somehow help the air to move.

One day, near the end of my planning, I traveled into the city to hear the music of the time, and to help choose the songs. In a low-roofed inn room I sat on the cushions set for me, and the group picked up the old instruments they had assembled and began to play.

At first the sounds were strange to my ear, and I marveled at how music could change so greatly over the years. There were no strumming instruments, such as the harp or tiranthe, which formed the essential portion of any ensemble nowadays. Instead the instruments were drums and air and sweet metallic bells and cymbals, combining complicated rhythms with a light-edged, curiously physical kind of sound that made one's feet itch to be moving. The drums also, I realized as I listened on, caused an echo in memory of those heard on the mountains from the unseen folk there.

Recognizing that, I laughed. "I like it! That will be perfect."

"Of course we'll have our own instruments laid by," the group mistress told me. "So we can play any of the modern dances your guests ask for. But for the arrivals, the start of the event—"

"—we will make them feel they have stepped into the past," I said.

And so it went, even with the mimery. It turned out that the Court during that period had been fond of entertaining itself, and more frequently than not had performed for one another. Thus I bade my hired players to guise themselves as figures of the period, that some of my guests might be surprised to see themselves mirrored in art.

My greatest coup was when Mora brought to me her brother, who with a few quiet words and a low bow, offered to take charge of the food, from preparation to serving. I'd been at Court long enough by then to know that he was—justly—famous. "You're the chief steward for the Renselaeuses," I said. "Surely you haven't left them?"

"I came to offer my services," he said, as blank-faced as his sister. "With the full permission of the Princess."

I accepted gratefully, knowing now that the food and drink would be the very best and perfectly served.

The morning of the ball dawned.

When I reached the ballroom for my last inspection and saw the faces awaiting me, I realized I had fully as many people working for me as there would be guests. I could feel the excitement running high among performers and servers alike, showing me this or that detail, all rehearsing their arts. As I moved about admiringly, it seemed to me that my event served as a symbolic representation of the kingdom: These artists, like the aristocrats, came to be seen as well as to see; and the servants, who worked to make all smooth, were unseen but saw everything. Everyone would have a tale to take home, a memory of performance, whether a countess or a scarf dancer or a server of pastries.

But my preparations were nearly done. I went back to my rooms to get ready.

As the bells for second-blue echoed from wall to pillar to gloriously painted ceiling, then died away, I stood alone at the midpoint of the ballroom to welcome the guests of honor. Everyone was there, or nearly everyone. Only Flauvic was missing, which did not particularly bother me.

Nee and Bran came down the stairs, arm in arm, both dressed in the violet-and-white of the royal Calahanras family.

My own gown was mostly white and dove gray, with knots of violet ribbon as acknowledgment of my role as Bran's sister. But there the reference to the royal family ended, for my colors in the ballroom were Remalna's green and gold—the green of the plant leaves, and all shades of gold, from ocher to palest yellow, picked out in the blooms. The focus, therefore, was quite properly on Nee and Bran, who grinned like children as they came to me.

I glanced up at the balcony, and a ruffle of drums brought the quiet tide of murmurings to a cease. Then an extravagant cascade of sound from all the instruments of the air, flutes to greathorns, announced the ancient promenade, and all took their places to perform the dance that their ancestors had toed-and-heeled through hundreds of years before.

Backs straight, heads high, fingertips meeting in an archway under which the honored two proceeded, followed by everyone else in order of rank.

So it began. By the end of the promenade I knew my ball was a triumph. I breathed the heady wine of success and understood why famous hosts of the past had secreted knowledge of their artists, sometimes hiring them exclusively so that no one could reproduce the particular magic that so much skill had wrought.

For a time the focus was equally on me as I made my way round the perimeter and accepted the compliments of the guests. But gradually they turned to one another, or to the entertainment, and I remained on the perimeter and thus faded into the background.

Or attempted to, anyway. For as I moved away from a group of young ladies bent on dancing, I suddenly found myself face-to-face with Flauvic. Could I possibly have overlooked him?

Not likely. He was magnificent in black, white, and gold, the candlelight making a blaze of his hair. His eyes were brilliant, their expression hard to read, but I sensed a kind of intensity in him when he bowed over my hand. "Beautifully done," he said with an elegant lift of his hand.

"It was your suggestion," I reminded him—knowing full well he didn't need to be reminded.

"You do great credit to my poor idea," he returned, bowing slightly.

And because he did not move away, I invited him to stroll with me.

He agreed, and as we walked around the perimeter, he commented appreciatively—and knowledgeably—on the fine details of my evocation of our shared past, until he was seen and claimed by friends.

As I watched him walk away, I contemplated just how skillfully he had contrived his entrance. He had managed, while saluting me as hostess, to avoid paying honor to Bran and Nee. One always arrives at a ball before the guests of honor, unless one wishes to insult them. Great dramas had been enacted in the past just this way, but he'd slipped in so quietly, no one—except me, it seemed—knew that he had not been there all along.

I watched him for a time, sipping at my wine. He moved deftly from group to group, managing to speak to just about every person. When I finished the wine, I set the glass down, deciding that Flauvic would always constitute an enigma.

Realizing I ought to be circulating as well, I turned—and found myself confronted by the Marquis of Shevraeth.

"My dear Countess," he said with a grand bow. "Please bolster my declining prestige by joining me in this dance."

Declining prestige? I thought, then out loud I said, "It's a tartelande. From back then."

"Which I studied up on all last week," he said, offering his arm.

I took it and flushed right up to my pearl-lined headdress. Though we had spoken often, of late, at various parties, this was the first time we had danced together since Savona's ball, my second night at Athanarel. As we joined the circle I sneaked a glance at Elenet. She was dancing with one of the ambassadors.

A snap of drums and a lilting tweet caused everyone to take position, hands high, right foot pointed. The musicians reeled out a merry tune to which we dipped and turned and stepped in patterns round one another and those behind and beside us.

In between measures I stole looks at my partner, bracing

for some annihilating comment about my red face, but he seemed preoccupied as we paced our way through the dance. The Renselaeuses, completely separate from Remalna five hundred years before, had dressed differently, just as they had spoken a different language. In keeping, Shevraeth wore a long tunic that was more like a robe, colored a sky blue, with black and white embroidery down the front and along the wide sleeves. It was flattering to his tall, slender form. His hair was tied back with a diamond-and-nightstar clasp, and a bluefire gem glittered in his ear.

We turned and touched hands, and I realized he had broken his reverie and was looking at me somewhat quizzically. I had been caught staring.

I said with as careless a smile as I could muster, "I'll wager you're the most comfortable of the men here tonight."

"Those tight waistcoats do look uncomfortable, but I rather like the baldrics," he said, surveying my brother, whom the movement of the dance had placed just across from us.

At that moment Bran made a wrong turn in the dance, paused to laugh at himself, then hopped back into position and went on. Perhaps emboldened by his heedless example, or inspired by the unusual yet pleasing music, more of the people on the periphery who had obviously not had the time, or the money, or the notion of learning the dances that went along with the personas and the clothes, were moving out to join. At first tentative, with nervously gripped fans and tense shoulders here and there betraying how little accustomed to making public mistakes they were, the courtiers slowly relaxed.

After six or seven dances, when faces were flushed and fans plied in earnest, the first of my mime groups came out to enact an old folktale. The guests willingly became an audience, dropping onto waiting cushions.

And so the evening went. There was an atmosphere of expectation, of pleasure, of relaxed rules as the past joined the present, rendering both slightly unreal.

I did not dance again but once, and that with Savona, who insisted that I join Shevraeth and Elenet in a set. Despite his joking remarks from time to time, the Marquis seemed more absent than merry, and Elenet moved, as always, with impervious serenity and reserve. Afterward the four of us went our ways, for Shevraeth did not dance again with Elenet.

I know, because I watched.

The two tones of white-change had rung when the scarf dances began.

To the muted thunder of drums the dancers ran out, clad in hose and diaphanous tunics of light gray, each connected to the dancer behind him or her by ropes of intertwined gold and green. Glints of silver threads woven into the floating, swirling tunics flashed like starlight, as well-muscled limbs moved with deliberate, graceful rhythm in a difficult counterpoint to the drums.

Then, without warning, notes from a single flute floated as if down on a breeze, and with a quick snap of wrists the dancers twitched the ropes into soaring, billowing squares of gauze.

A gasp from the watchers greeted the sudden change, as the gauzy material rippled and arched and curled through the air, expertly manipulated by the dancers until it seemed the scarves were alive and another kind of dance altogether took place above the humans.

Then the dancers added finger cymbals, clinking and clashing in a syncopated beat that caused, I noted as I looked about me, responsive swayings and nods and taps of feet.

Why this gift, o pilgrim, my pilgrim,
Why this cup of water for me?

I give thee the ocean, stormy or tranquil,
Endless and boundless as my love for thee . . .

Now it was time for the love songs, and first was the ancient Four Questions, sung in antiphony by the women and the men, and then reversed. High voices and deep echoed down from the unseen gallery, as the dancers below handed out smaller versions of the scarves and drew the guests into the dance.

...why this firebrand for me?

Dancers, lovers, all turned and stepped and circled, connected only by the scarves which hid them, then revealed them, then bound them together as they stepped in, his corner held high by the shoulder, hers low at her waist.

...just so my love burneth for thee

The music, flawlessly performed, the elusive perfume on the scarves—all made the atmosphere feel charged with physical awareness. In the very center of all the dancers were Branaric and Nimiar, circling round one another, their faces flushed and glowing, eyes ardent.

I scarcely recognized my own brother, who moved now with the unconscious ease that makes its own kind of grace, and in a dainty but provocatively deliberate counterpoint danced Nee. It was she, and not Bran, who—when the gauze was overhead, making a kind of canopy that turned their profiles to silhouettes—leaned up to steal a kiss. Then they separated, she casting a look over her shoulder at him that was laughing and not laughing, and which caused him to spin suddenly and crush her in both arms, just for a moment, as around them the others swirled and dipped and the gauzes rose and fell with languorous grace.

As I watched, images flitted through my mind of little Ara, the girl I'd met last year who talked so cheerily of twoing. And of Oria, and of the summer dances on our hills; and I realized, at last, how emotion-parched I was and how ignorant of the mysteries of love.

I had seen ardency in men's eyes, but I had never felt it myself. As I watched, isolated but unable to turn away, I suddenly wished that I could feel it. No, I *did* feel it, I realized. I did have the same feeling, only I had masked it before as restlessness, or as the exhortation to action, or as anger. And I thought how wonderful it would be to see that spark now, in the right pair of eyes.

Looking away from the dancers, I glanced around the room—straight into Flauvic's coin-glinting gaze. He continued to stare straight at me across the width of the ballroom, those large eyes half closed, and a pensive smile on his perfect lips.

After a moment he started toward me at a deliberate pace.

And my first reaction was to panic.

I suppressed the urge to retreat, bolstering myself with the observation that he would never be so obvious as to touch me in public.

As if he read my mind his smile widened, just slightly, and when he was near enough to speak he bowed, hand on heart, and said, "I make you my compliments, Meliara. A remarkable achievement."

I did not ask what he meant.

For a time we stood there, watching the others, as the dancers wound about the floor in intersecting circles that drew imperceptibly tighter.

"Do you think your dances will become a fad again?" he asked, still watching.

"Depends who asks for them to be played—if anyone does," I said with a shrug. "You always could," I added. "Guaranteed, the latest rage."

He laughed, one thin, well-made hand rising in the fencer's salute for a hit. Then he stepped close, still without touching me, but I could smell the clean, astringent scent he used in his hair. "I wish," he murmured, "that you had been granted the right tutor."

Tutor in what? I was not about to ask.

And then he was on his way, bowing here, smiling there, a careless flick of the hand to a third. Moments later he was gone.

Though few had seen him go, his leaving seemed to constitute a kind of subtle signal, for slowly, as white wore on, my guests slipped away, many of them in pairs. Elenet left with the Orbanith family, all but her laughing.

The Renselaeuses came all three to thank me formally for a splendid—memorable—evening, and then departed in a group.

After they left, I felt tiredness pressing on my shoulders and eyelids; and though I stood there, back straight and smile steady on my aching face, I longed for my bed.

The lake blue light of morning was just paling the eastern windows when the last guests departed and I stepped wearily up to my rooms.

They were lit, and steaming listerblossom tea awaited. A surge of gratitude rose in me as I wondered how many times Mora had summoned fresh tea that I might come back to this.

I sank down onto my cushions, wondering if I'd be able to get up again to undress and climb into my bed. My hand clattered the cup and saucer as I poured—and then froze when I heard a slight noise come from my bedroom.

I froze, not breathing.

The tapestry stirred, and then, looking two steps from death, Azmus came forward and sank down onto his knees a pace away from me.

"They're going to war," he wheezed. "The Merindars. They're going to march on Remalna-city as soon as the last of their hirelings arrive."

TWENTY

I HEARD AZMUS'S WORDS, BUT AS YET THEY MADE NO sense.

So I held out my cup of tea. He took it carefully into his trembling fingers and downed it almost at one gulp. Then he gasped and blinked, and his eyes were noticeably clearer, though nothing could banish the bruiselike smudges under them.

"Now," I prompted, pouring more tea for him. "Tell me again."

"The Merindars," he said. "Forgive me, my lady. I have not left the saddle for nearly two days. Six horses—" He paused to drink. "I dared not entrust a message to anyone. Six horses I ran near to death, but I am here. After days and days of incremental progress and extrapolation by inference, I had luck at last and chanced to position myself to overhear a conversation between the Duke of Grumareth's valet and a scout from Denlieff. The Marquise of Merindar, the Duke, and three of their supporters are all ranged at the border. Over the last several months, 'volunteers' have poured into two of the southern garrisons. Those volunteers are mercenaries—at least the Marquise thinks they are mercenaries. They are soldiers from Denlieff."

"And they're going to march on us here?"

He nodded. "Taking each town as they come. But that is not all."

"Wait. Do the Renselaeuses know? I can't believe they haven't been investigating any of this."

"I don't know how much they know," he said. "I did see some of their equerries, the ones I recognized, but of course I never spoke to them, as you desired my investigations to remain secret."

He paused to drink again. His voice was a little stronger now. "You must realize the Renselaeus equerries are constrained by the past. In the countryside, there are those who are slow to trust them because of the ambivalent role that Shevraeth was forced to play under Galdran. I might therefore have access to better information." He smiled faintly, despite cracked lips, then he slurped down more tea. "So, to conclude, they probably know about the pending attack. That kind of thing is hard to hide if you know what you are looking for. But there is a further threat that no one knows, I'm sure, because I happened upon it only by accident."

"Speak," I said, gripping my hands together.

"Wagons of supplies," he said, fighting back a huge yawn that suddenly assailed him. "Had to hide in one. Supposed to be paving stone for road-building, and there was some, but only a thin layer. Under it—I know the smell—cut and stacked kinthus."

"*Kinthus?*" I repeated. "They're harvesting kinthus as, what, pay for the mercenaries?"

He shook his head, smiling bleakly. "You have never traveled beyond our borders, my lady. You have no idea how precious our rare woods are, for they *are* rare. Nowhere on this world is there anything like our colorwoods, especially the golden. What I overheard is that the Merindars and their allies have granted permission for the hired forces to take a given amount of colorwoods from Orbanith, Dharcarad—and Tlanth—in trade for military aid."

"But—the kinthus. Are they going to plant it?" I tried to get my tired mind to comprehend what I was hearing.

He shook his head, his face blanching again. "No. They will burn it."

Shock rang through my head as though someone had struck it. "Burn," I repeated stupidly. "Burn kinthus? In the woods? Then they must want to *kill* the Hill Folk! Is that it?"

"Easiest way to get the wood unmolested," he said.

I glanced up, to find Mora standing, still as a statue, just inside the servants' door. "My riding gear," I said to her. "And send someone to have the fastest and freshest mount saddled and ready. Please." To Azmus I said, "You've got to go over to the Royal Wing and tell Shevraeth. Tell him everything. Either him or the Prince and Princess. Only they can get an army raised here to meet those mercenaries."

"What are you going to do?" Azmus murmured, rising slowly to his feet.

I was already tearing at my laces, beyond considering the proprieties. "To warn the Hill Folk, of course," I said. "There is no one who knows how to find them as quickly as I do."

I dressed with reckless speed, tearing costly cloth and flinging jewels to the floor of my room like so many seed husks. As I dressed, Mora and a palace runner—who had suddenly appeared—discussed the best route I ought to take. No pretense of secrecy. We all had to work for the good of Remalna—of the Hill Folk. We all agreed that Orbanith was where I ought to go, for that was where the mountains jutted east. They both felt that the dangers of riding the river road were not as pressing as the need for speed. Also I'd be able to hire fresh horses at inns known to both; they told me their names, repeating them so I would remember.

Then I threw together a saddlebag of money and clothing, and departed, to find the horse I'd ordered waiting on the steps of the Residence Wing, held by a worried-looking stablehand. I knew without speaking that somehow the word was spreading through the palace—at least among the servants.

The bells of first-gold began ringing just as my horse dashed past the last houses of Remalna-city. Soft rain cooled my face, and the bracing wind helped revive me. I bent my head low and urged my mount to stretch into a canter so fast it seemed we flew over the road.

As we splashed westward, I scanned ahead. If I saw any more than two riders, or anyone the least suspicious looking, I'd ride alongside the road, much as it slowed me. Though I had asked for a short saddle-sword, it was almost mere decoration. I knew how little I could defend myself against trained soldiers.

Occasionally the rain lifted briefly, enough to enable me to see ahead when I topped the gentle rises that undulated along the road. And after a time I realized that though no suspicious riders were approaching, for I had passed nothing but farmers and artisans going into the city, I was matching the pace of a single rider some distance before me. Twice, three times, I spotted the lone figure, cresting a hill just as I did. No bright colors of livery, only an anonymous dark cloak.

A messenger from Flauvic? Who else could it be? For Azmus would have reached the Royal Wing to speak his story just as I set out. No one sent by the Renselaeuses could possibly be ahead of me.

Of course the rider could be on some perfectly honest business affair that had nothing to do with the terrible threat of warfare looming like thunderclouds over the land. This thought comforted me for a hill or two, until a brief ray of light slanting down from between some clouds bathed the rider in light, striking a cold gleam off a steel helm.

Merchants' runners did not wear helms. A messenger, then.

I rode on, squinting ahead despite a sudden downpour that severely limited visibility. It also slowed my horse. Despite the paved road, the deep puddles interfered with speed and made the ride more of an effort. When bells rang over the hills, indicating the change from gold to green, both my horse and I were weary.

The plan had been for me to halt at the Farjoon Anchor. My

drooping horse could stop, I decided, though whether or not I did would depend on what the rider ahead did.

Presently I crested a hill. Spread below me in a little valley was the village I'd been told to look for. I scanned the road ahead and saw the mysterious rider splash up the narrow lane into the village, disappearing among the small cluster of houses.

My mount trotted slowly down the hill and into the village. The inn was a long, low building in the center, with an anchor painted on its swinging sign. I hunched into my wet cloak, though no one could possibly recognize me, and slid off my steaming mount as stablehands ran to the bridle. "Fresh horse," I said, surprised at how husky my voice came out—and when my feet hit the mud, the world seemed to spin for a moment.

Before I ate or drank I had to find out who that rider was.

I stepped into the common room, scanning the few people seated on cushions at the low, rough tables. They all had gray, brown, or blue cloaks hung behind them, or hats. No dark cloaks or helms. So I wandered farther inside and encountered a young woman about my age.

"Hot punch? Stew?" she offered, wiping her hands on her apron.

"My companion came in just ahead of me. Wearing a helm. Where—"

"Oh! The other runner? Wanted a private room. Third down, that hall," she said cheerily. "What'll I bring you?"

"I'll order in a moment." The savory aroma of stew had woken my insides fiercely, and I realized that I had not eaten a bite the entire day before.

As I trod down the hall, I made and discarded plausible excuses. When I reached the tapestry I decided against speaking at all. I'd just take a quick peek, and if the livery was Merindar, then I'd have to hire someone to ride back and warn the Renselaeuses.

I pulled my soggy cloak up around my eyes, stuck out my gloved finger, and poked gently at the edge of the tapestry.

Remember the surmise I recorded on my arrival at the Residence that day in early spring—that if anyone were to know everyone's business, it would be the servants?

I glanced inside in time to see a pale, familiar face jerk up.

And for a long, amazing moment, there we were, Meliara and Shevraeth, mud-spattered and wet, just like last year, looking at one another in silence. Then I snatched my hand back, now thoroughly embarrassed, and spun around intending retreat. But I moved too fast for my tired head and fell against the wall, as once again the world lurched around me.

I heard the faint metallic *ching* of chain mail, and suddenly he was there, his hand gripping my arm. Without speaking, he drew me inside the bare little parlor and pointed silently at a straw-stuffed cushion. My legs folded abruptly, and I plopped down.

"Azmus—" I croaked. "How could you—I sent him—"

"Drink." Shevraeth put a mug into my hands. "Then we can talk."

Obediently I took a sip, felt sweet coffee burn its way pleasantly down my throat and push back the fog threatening to enfold my brain. I took a longer draught, then sighed.

The Marquis looked back at me, his face tense and tired, his eyes dark with an intensity that sent a complexity of emotions chasing through me like darting starlings.

"How did you get ahead of me so fast?" I said. "I don't understand."

His eyes widened in surprise, as if he'd expected to hear anything but that. "How," he asked slowly, "did you know I was here? We told no one when I was leaving, or my route, outside of two servants."

"I *didn't* know you were here," I said. "I sent Azmus to you. With the news. About the Merindars. You mean you already *knew*?"

"Let us backtrack a little," he said, "if you will bear with my lamentable slowness. I take it, then, that you were not riding thus speedily to join me?" With his old sardonic tone he added,

"Because if you were, your retreat just now is somewhat puzzling, you'll have to admit."

I said indignantly, "I peeked in because I thought you might be one of the Merindars, and if so, I'd send a warning back to you. I mean, you if you were there. Does that make sense?" I frowned, shook my head, then gulped down the rest of the coffee.

He smiled just slightly, but the intensity had not left his eyes.

The serving maid came in, carrying a bowl of food and some fresh bread. "Will you have some as well?" she said to me.

"Please," Shevraeth said before I could speak. "And more coffee." He waited until she went out, then said, "Now, begin again, please. What is it you're trying to tell me, and where are you going?"

"I'm going to Orbanith," I said, and forced myself to look away from the steam curling up from the stew at his elbow. My mouth watered. I swallowed and turned my attention to pulling off my sodden gloves. "I guess I am trying to tell you what you already seem to know—that the Merindars are going on the attack, with hired mercenaries from Denlieff. But—why do you want me to tell you when you *do* already know all this?" I looked up from wringing out my gloves.

"I am trying," he said with great care, "to ascertain what your place is in the events about to transpire, and to act accordingly. From whom did you get your information?"

The world seemed to lurch again, but this time it was not my vision. A terrible sense of certainty pulled at my heart and mind as I realized what he was striving so heroically not to say—nevertheless, what he meant.

He thought I was on the other side.

Seen from an objective perspective, it was entirely possible that *I* was the phantom messenger from the Merindars. After all, last year I'd made a try for the crown. Since then, on the surface I'd been an implacable enemy to Shevraeth—and even though that had changed, I had not given any sign of those changes. Meanwhile I seemed to have suddenly acquired information that no one else in Athanarel had. Except for him.

And, probably, Flauvic.

I saw it now, the real reason why Flauvic had made the public gestures of friendship with me. What an easy way to foster Shevraeth's distrust, to force him to divide his attentions! The most recent gesture having been just measures ago at my ball.

The maid came in with another bowl and bread, then, and set them at my elbow, but I scarcely heeded the food. Now I couldn't eat. I couldn't even explain, because anything I gabbled out would seem mere contrivance. The fact was, I had refused all along any kind of straightforward communication with the man now sitting across from me, and too many lives were at stake for him to risk being wrong.

The real tragedy was that there were too many lives at stake in both races. And so even though I could comprehend why I might end up as a prisoner, just like last year, I also knew that I would fight, as hard as I was capable, to remain free.

I looked at him, sick and miserable.

"Tell me where you got your information," he said.

"Azmus. Our old spy." My lips were numb, and I started to shiver. Hugging my arms against my stomach, I said, "My reasons were partly stupid and partly well-meaning, but I sent him to find out what the Marquise was after. She wrote me during winter—but you knew about that."

He nodded.

"And you even tried to warn me, though at the time I saw it as a threat, because—well, because." I felt too sick inside to go on about that. Drawing a shaky breath, I said, "And again. At her party, when she took me into the conservatory. She tried again to get me to join her. Said I hadn't kept my vows to Papa. So I summoned Azmus to help me find out what to do. The right thing. I know I can't prove it," I finished lamely.

He pulled absently at the fingers of one glove, then looked

down at it, and straightened it again. Unnecessary movements from him were so rare, I wondered if he too was fighting for clear thought.

He lifted his gaze to me. "And now? You were riding to the border?"

"No," I said. "To Orbanith."

Again he showed surprise.

"It's the other thing that Azmus found out," I said quickly. "I sent him to tell you as soon as I learned—but there's no way for you to know that's true. I realize it. Still, I *did*. I have to go because I know how to reach the Hill Folk."

"The Hill Folk?"

"Yes," I said, leaning forward. "The kinthus. The Merindars have it stowed in wagons, and they're going to burn it up-slope. Carried on the winds, it can kill Hill Folk over a full day's ride, all at once. That's how they're paying Denlieff, with our woods, not with money at all. They're breaking our Covenant! I *have* to warn the Hill Folk!"

"Orbanith. Why there, why this road?"

"Mora and the servants told me this was the fastest way to Orbanith."

"Why did you not go north to Tlanth where you know the Hill Folk?"

I shook my head impatiently. "You don't *know* them. You can't know them. They don't have names, or if they do, they don't tell them to us. They seem to be aware of each other's concerns, for if you see one, then suddenly others will appear, all silent. And if they act, it's at once. Some of the old songs say that they walk in one another's dreams, which I think is a poetic way of saying they can speak mind to mind. I don't know. I *must* get to the mountains to warn them, and the mountains that source the Piaum River are the closest to Remalna-city."

"And no one else knows of this?" he asked gently.

I shook my head slowly, unable to remove my gaze from his

face. "Azmus discovered it by accident. Rode two days to reach me. I did send him . . ."

There was no point in saying it again. Either he believed me, and—I swallowed painfully—I'd given him no particular reason to, or he didn't. Begging, pleading, arguing, ranting—none of them would make any difference, except to make a horrible situation worse.

I should have made amends from the beginning, and now it was too late.

He took a deep breath. I couldn't breathe, I just stared at him, waiting, feeling sweat trickle beneath my already soggy clothing.

Then he smiled a little. "Brace up. We're not about to embark on a duel to the death over the dishes." He paused, then said lightly, "Though most of our encounters until very recently have been unenviable exchanges, you have never lied to me. Eat. We'll leave before the next time-change, and part ways at the crossroads."

No "You've never lied *before*." No "*If* I can trust you.'" No warnings or hedgings. He took all the responsibility—and the risk—himself. I didn't know why, and to thank him for believing me would just embarrass us both. So I said nothing, but my eyes prickled. I looked down at my lap and busied myself with smoothing out my mud-gritty, wet gloves.

"Why don't you set aside that cloak and eat something?"

His voice was flat. I realized he probably felt even nastier about the situation than I did. I heard the scrape of a bowl on the table and the clink of a spoon. The ordinary sounds restored me some-how, and I untied my cloak and shrugged it off. At once a weight that seemed greater than my own left me. I made a surreptitious swipe at my eyes, straightened my shoulders, and did my best to assume nonchalance as I picked up my spoon.

After a short time, he said, "Don't you have any questions for me?"

I glanced up, my spoon poised midway between my bowl and my mouth. "Of course," I said. "But I thought—" I started to wave my hand, realizing too late it still held the spoon, and winced as stew spattered down the table. Somehow the ridiculousness of it released some of the tension. As I mopped at the mess with a corner of my cloak, I said, "Well, it doesn't matter what I thought. So you knew about the plot all along?"

"Pretty much from the beginning, though the timing is new. I surmised they would make their move in the fall, but something seems to have precipitated action. My first warning was from Elenet, who had found out a great deal from the Duke's servants. That was her real reason for coming to Court, to tell me herself."

"What about Flauvic?"

"It would appear," he said carefully, "that he disassociated with this plan of his mother's."

"Was that the argument he alluded to?"

He did not ask when. "Perhaps. Though that might have been for effect. I can believe it only because it is uncharacteristic for him to lend himself to so stupid and clumsy a plan."

"Finesse," I drawled in a parody of a courtier's voice. "He'd want finesse, and to make everyone else look foolish."

Shevraeth smiled slightly. "Am I to understand you were not favorably impressed with Lord Flauvic?"

"As far as I'm concerned, he and Fialma are both thorns," I said, "though admittedly he is very pretty to look at. More so than his sour pickle of a sister. Anyway, I hope you aren't trusting him as far as you can lift a mountain, because I wouldn't."

"His house is being watched. He can't stir a step outside without half a riding being within earshot."

"And he probably knows it," I said, grinning. "Last question, why are you riding alone? Wouldn't things be more effective with your army?"

"I move fastest alone," he said. "And my own people are in place, and have been for some time."

I thought of Nessaren—and the fact that I hadn't seen her around Athanarel for weeks.

212

"When I want them," he said, reaching into the pouch at his belt, "I will summon them with this." And he held up something that glowed blue briefly: the summons-stone I had seen so long ago. "Each riding has one. At the appropriate moment, we will converge and, ah, *convince* the Marquise and her allies to accompany us back to Athanarel. It is the best way of avoiding bloodshed."

In the distance the time-change rang. "What about those Denlieff warriors?" I asked.

"If their leaders are unable to give them orders, they will have to take orders from me."

I thought about the implied threat, then shook my head. "I'm glad I have the easy job," I said. "Speaking of which..."

He smiled. "There's a room adjacent. I suggest you change your clothes and ride dry for a time." Before I could say anything, he rose, stepped to the tapestry, and summoned the maid.

Very soon I was in the little bedroom, struggling out of my soggy clothing. It felt good to get into dry things, though I knew I wouldn't be dry long. There was no hope for my cloak, except to wring it out and put it back on. But when I left the room, I found my cloak gone, and in its place a long, black, waterproof one that I recognized at once.

With very mixed feelings I pulled it on, gathering it up in my arms so it wouldn't drag on the ground behind me. Then I settled my hat on my head, and very soon I was on the road to the west.

TWENTY-ONE

I WAS VERY GRATEFUL FOR THAT CLOAK BEFORE MY journey's end.

The weather steadily turned worse. I forbore hiring horses in favor of sturdy mountain ponies, on whose broad backs I could doze a little.

For I did not dare to stop. The driving rain and the deep mud made a swift pace impossible. Halting only to change mounts and stuff some hasty bites of food into my mouth, I kept going, even in the dark, and hired a glowglobe to carry with me as I neared the mountains.

The third morning I reached the foothills below Mount Toar. My road rounded a high cliff from which I could see the road to the south. On this road I descried a long line of wagons trundling their way inexorably toward the mountains. They were probably half a day's journey behind me—and I knew that they wouldn't have to go as high.

This sight was enough to kindle my tired body into renewed effort.

At the next inn, I mentioned the wagons to a friendly stable-hand as I waited for my new mount. "Do you know anything about them?"

The stablegirl gave me a quick grin. "Sure do," she said cheerily. "Orders came straight from the Duke of Grumareth himself, I'm told. Those wagons are full of paving stones for the castle up-mountain. Halt 'em, get in the way, and you're dead. Too bad! We wouldn't mind pinching a few. Maybe next time they'll think of us. Ever seen such a wet summer? Roads are like soup."

I thanked her and left, my spirits dampening again. So much for rousing the locals to stop those wagons. Of course they might be willing to fight for the Covenant despite the orders given the Duke's forces—but what if these were not the right wagons? And even if they were, sending unarmed villagers against warriors would be a slaughter. All I could think was that I had to solve this myself.

I bought some bread and cheese, and was soon on my way, eating as I rode. Very soon the rain returned, splashing down at a slant. I pulled the edge of Shevraeth's cloak up onto my head and my hat over it, then arranged the rest as a kind of tent around me, peering through the thin opening to see the road ahead. Not that I had to look, except for the occasional low branch, for the pony seemed to know its way.

As we climbed, the air got colder. But when the woods closed around me at last, I forgot about the discomfort. I was breathing the scents of home again, the indefinable combination of loam and moss and wood and fern that I had loved all my life.

And I sensed presence.

The woods were quiet, except for the tapping of raindrops on leaves and, once or twice, the sudden crash and scamper of hidden animals breaking cover and retreating. No birds, no great beasts. Yet I felt watchers.

And so, tired as I was, I tipped back my head and began to sing.

At the best of times I don't have the kind of voice anyone would want to hear mangling their favorite songs. Now my throat was dry and scratchy, but I did what I could, singing wordlessly some of the old, strange patterns, not quite melodies, that I'd heard in my childhood. I sang my loudest, and at first echoes rang off stones and trees and down into hollows. After a time my voice dropped to a husky squeak, but as the light bent west and turned golden, I heard a rustle, and suddenly I was surrounded by Hill Folk, more of them than I had ever seen at once before.

They did not speak. Somewhere in the distance I heard the breathy, slightly sinister cry of a reed pipe.

I began to talk, not knowing if they understood words, such as "Marquise" and "mercenary," or if they somehow took the images from my thoughts. I told them about the Merindars, and Flauvic, and the Renselaeuses, ending with what Azmus had told me. I described the wagons on the road behind me. I finally exhorted them to go north and hide, and that we—Shevraeth and his people and I—would first get rid of the kinthus, then find a way to keep the Covenant.

When I ran out of words, for a long moment there was that eerie stillness, so soundless yet full of presence. Then they moved, their barky hides dappling with shadows, until they disappeared with a rustling sound like wind through the trees.

I was alone again, but I felt no sense of danger. My pony lifted her head and blinked at me. She hadn't reacted at all to being surrounded by Hill Folk.

"All right," I said to her. "First thing, water. And then we have some wagons to try to halt. Or I do. I suppose your part will be to reappear at the inn as mute testimony to the fallen heroine."

We stopped at a stream. I drank deeply of the sweet, cold water and splashed my face until it was numb. Then we started on the long ride down. From time to time quick flutings of reed pipes echoed from peak to peak, and from very far away, the rich chordal hum of the distant windharps answered. Somehow these sounds lifted my spirits.

I remained cheery, too, as if the universe had slipped into a kind of dream existence. I was by now far beyond mere tiredness, so that nothing seemed real. In fact, until I topped a rise and saw the twenty wagons stretched out in a formidable line directly below me, the worst reaction I had to rain, to stumbles, to my burning eyes, was a tendency to snicker.

The wagons sobered me.

I stayed where I was, squarely in the center of the muddy road, and waited for them to ascend my hill. I had plenty of time to count them, all twenty, as they rumbled slowly toward me, pulled by teams of draught horses. When I caught the quick gleam of metal on the hill beyond them—the glint of an errant ray of sun on helms and shields—my heart started a rapid tattoo inside my chest.

But I stayed where I was. Twenty wagons. If the unknown riders were reinforcements to the enemy, I couldn't be in worse trouble than I already was. *But if they weren't . . .*

"Halt," I said, when the first wagon driver was in earshot.

He'd already begun to pull up the horses, but I felt it sounded good to begin on an aggressive note.

"Out of the way," the man sitting next to the driver bawled. Despite their both being clad in the rough clothing of wagoneers, their bearing betrayed the fact that they were warriors.

That and the long swords lying between them on the bench.

"But your way lies back to the south." I pointed.

The second driver in line, a female, even bigger and tougher looking than the leader, had dismounted. She stood next to the first wagon, squinting up at me in a decidedly unfriendly manner. She and the leader exchanged looks, then she said, "We have a delivery to make in yon town."

"The road to the town lies that way," I said, pointing behind me. "You're heading straight for the mountains. There's nothing up here."

They both grinned. "That's a matter for us and not for you. Be about your business, citizen, or we'll have to send you on your way."

"And you won't like the way we do the sending," the woman added.

They both laughed nastily.

I crossed my arms. "You can drop the paving stones here if you wish, but you'll have to take the kinthus back to Denlieff."

Their smiles disappeared.

I glanced up—to see that the road behind the last wagon was empty. The mysterious helmed riders had disappeared. What did that mean?

No time to find out.

"Now, how did you know about that?" the man said, and this time there was no mistaking the threat in his voice. He laid his hand significantly on his sword hilt.

"It's my business, as you said." I tried my best to sound assured, waving my sodden arm airily in my best Court mode.

The woman bowed with exaggerated politeness. "And who might you be, Your Royal Highness?" she asked loudly.

The leader, and the third and fourth drivers who had just joined the merry group, guffawed.

"I am Meliara Astiar, Countess of Tlanth," I said.

Again the smiles diminished, but not all the way. The leader eyed me speculatively for a long breath. "Well, then, you seem to have had mighty good luck in the past, if half the stories be true, but even if they are, what good's your luck against forty of us?"

"How do you know I don't have eighty-one armed soldiers waiting behind that rise over there?" I waved my other hand vaguely mountainward.

They thought that was richly funny.

"Because if you did," the female said, "they'd be out here and we wouldn't be jawin'. Come on, Kess, we've wasted enough time here. Let's shift her majesty off our road and be on our way."

The man picked up his sword and vaulted down from his wagon. I yanked my short sword free and climbed down from my pony. When I reached the ground, the world swayed, and I staggered back against the animal, then righted myself with an effort.

The man and woman stood before me, both with long swords

gripped in big hands. They eyed me with an odd mixture of threat and puzzlement that made that weird, almost hysterical laughter bubble up inside my shaky innards. But I kept my lips shut and hefted my sword.

"Well?" the woman said to her leader.

They both looked at me again. I barely came up to the middle of the shortest one's chest, and my blade was about half the length and heft of theirs.

The man took a slow swing at me, which I easily parried. His brows went up slightly; he swung again, faster, and when I parried that he feinted toward my shoulder. Desperately, my heart now pounding in my ears, I blocked the next strike and the next, but just barely. His blade whirled faster, harder, and that block shook me right down to my heels. The man dropped his point and said, "*You're* the one that whupped Galdran Merindar?"

Unbidden, Shevraeth's voice spoke inside my head: "You have never lied to me..." I thought desperately, *Better late than never!* And for a brief moment I envisioned myself snarling *Yes, ha ha! And I minced fifty more like him, so you'd better run!* Except it wasn't going to stop them; I could see it in their eyes and in the way the woman gripped her sword.

"No," I said. "He knocked me off my horse. But I'd taken an oath, so I had to do my best." I drew in a shaky breath. "I know I can't fight forty of you, but I'm going to stand here and block you until you either go away or my arms fall off, because this, too, is an oath I took."

The woman muttered something in their home language. Her stance, her tone, made it almost clear it was "I don't like this."

And he said something in a hard voice, his eyes narrowed. It had to mean "We have no choice. Better her than us." And he took up a guard position again, his muscles tightening.

My sweaty hand gripped my sword, and I raised it, gritting my teeth—

And there came the beat of hooves on the ground. All three of us went still. Either this was reinforcements for them, in which case I was about to become a prisoner—or a ghost—or . . .

Blue and black and white tunicked riders thundered down through the trees toward the wagons. On the other side of the road, another group rounded the rise, and within the space of ten heartbeats, the wagons were surrounded by nine ridings of warriors, a full wing, all with lances pointed and swords at the ready.

One of them flashed a grin my way—Nessaren! Then my attention was claimed when the wing commander trotted up, stopped, and bowed low over his horse's withers. "Your orders, my lady?"

He was utterly serious, but the impulse to dissolve into helpless laughter was shaking my already watery insides. "These gentle people may unload their stones, and pile them neatly for the locals to collect," I said. "And then the drivers and their companions are yours. I think local villagers might be hired to drive the cargo of the wagons to the sea. Brine-soaked kinthus won't hurt anyone and becomes mere wood. The wagons then might be offered to said villagers as partial payment."

The wing commander bowed again, turned, and issued orders. I noted from the salutes that Nessaren had risen in rank—she now appeared to have three ridings under her.

Within a very short time, the prisoners were marched off in one direction and the wagons trundled slowly in another, driven by warriors whose fellows had taken their horses' reins.

All except for one riding. Nessaren presented herself to me and said, "My lady, if it pleases you, I have specific orders."

"And they are?"

"You're to come with us to the nearest inn, where you are to sleep for at least two candles. And then—"

I didn't even hear the "and then." Suddenly, very suddenly, it was all I could do to climb back onto my pony. Nessaren saw this and, with a gesture, got her group to surround me. In tight formation we rode slowly back down the mountain. . . .

And I dismounted . . .

220

And walked inside the inn...

I don't even remember falling onto the bed.

The next morning I awoke to find a tray of hot food and drink awaiting me, and, even better, my wet clothes from my saddlebag, now dry and fresh.

When I emerged from the room, I found the riding all waiting, their gear on and horses ready.

I turned to Nessaren. Until that moment I hadn't considered what it meant to have them with me. Was it possible I was a prisoner?

She bowed. "We're ready to ride, my lady, whenever you like."

"Ride?" I repeated.

She grinned—all of them grinned. "We thought you'd want to get caught up on events as quick as could be." Her eyes went curiously blank as she added, "If you wish, we can ride to the city. We're yours to command."

An honor guard, then.

I rubbed my hands together. "And be left out of the action?"

They laughed, obviously well pleased with my decision. In very short order we were flying eastward on fast horses, scarcely slowed by a light rain. The roads down-mountain were good, and so we made excellent progress. At the end of the day's ride, we halted on a hill, and Nessaren produced from her saddlebag a summons-stone. She looked down at it, turning slowly in a circle until it gleamed a bright blue, and then she pointed to the north. We rode in that direction until we reached an inn, and next morning she did the same thing.

That afternoon we rode into an armed camp. I glanced about at the orderly tents, the soldiers in battle tunics of green and gold mixing freely with those in the blue with the three white stars above the black coronet. As we rode into the camp, sending mud flying everywhere, people stopped what they were doing to watch. The closest ones bowed. I found this odd, for I hadn't even been bowed to by our own warriors during our putative revolt. Attempting a Court curtsy from the back of a horse while clad in grubby, wet clothes and someone else's cloak didn't seem right, so I just smiled, and was glad when we came to a halt before a large tent.

Stablehands ran to the bridles and led the horses to a picket as Nessaren and I walked into the tent. Inside was a kind of controlled pandemonium. Scribes and runners were everywhere that low tables and cushions weren't. Atop the tables lay maps and piles of papers, plus a number of bags of coinage. In a corner was stacked a small but deadly arsenal of very fine swords.

Seated in the midst of the chaos was Shevraeth, dressed in the green and gold of Remalna, with a commander's plumed and cor-oneted helm on the table beside him. He appeared to be listening to five people, all of whom were talking at once. One by one they received from him quick orders, and they vanished in different di-rections. Then he saw us, and his face relaxed slightly. Until that moment, I hadn't realized he was tense.

Meanwhile the rest of his people had taken note of our arrival, and all were silent as he rose and came around the table to stand before us. "*Twenty* wagons, Lady Meliara?" he said, one brow lifting.

I shrugged, fighting against acute embarrassment.

"We've a wager going." His neatly gloved hand indicated the others in the tent. "How many, do you think, would have been too many for you to take on single-handed?"

"My thinking was this," I said, trying to sound casual, though by then my face felt as red as a glowing Fire Stick. "Two of them could trounce me as easy as twenty wagons' worth. The idea was to talk them out of trying. Luckily Nessaren and the rest of the wing arrived when they did, or I suspect I soon would have been part of the road."

Shevraeth's mouth was perfectly controlled, but his eyes gleamed with repressed laughter as he said, "That won't do, my lady. I am very much afraid if you're going to continue to attempt heroic measures you will have to make suitably heroic statements afterward—"

"If there is an afterward," I muttered, and someone in the avidly watching group choked on a laugh.

"—such as are written in the finest of our histories."

"Huh," I said. "I guess I'll just have to memorize a few proper heroic bombasts, rhymed in three places, for next time. And I'll also remember to take a scribe to get it all down right."

He laughed—they all did. They laughed much harder than the weak joke warranted, and I realized that events had not been so easy here.

I unclasped his cloak and handed it over. "I'm sorry about the hem," I said, feeling suddenly shy. "Got a bit muddy."

He slung the cloak over one arm and gestured to a waiting cushion. "Something hot to drink?"

A young cadet came forward with a tray and steaming coffee. I busied myself choosing a cup, sitting down, and striving to reestablish within myself a semblance of normalcy. While I sipped at my coffee, one by one the staff finished their chores and vanished through the tent flaps, until at last Shevraeth and I were alone.

He turned to face me. "Questions?"

"Of course! What happened?"

He sat down across from me. "Took 'em by surprise," he said. "That part was easy enough. The worst of it has been the aftermath."

"You captured the commanders, then. The Marquise and—"

"Her daughter, the two mercenary captains, the two sellout garrison commanders, the Denlieff wing commander, Barons Chaskar and Hurnaev, and Baroness Orgaliun, to be precise. Grumareth's nowhere to be found; my guess is that he got cold feet and scampered for home. If so, he'll find some of my people waiting for him."

"So the Marquise is a prisoner somewhere?" I asked, enjoying the idea.

He grimaced. "No. She took poison. A constitutional inability to suffer reverses, apparently. We didn't find out until too late. Fialma," he added drily, "tried to give her share to me."

"That must have been a charming scene."

"It took place at approximately the same time you were conversing with your forty wagoneers." He smiled a little. "Since then I have dispatched the real mercenaries homeward, unpaid, and sent some people to make certain they get over the border. What they do in Denlieff is their ruler's problem. Fialma is on her way back—under guard—to Erev-li-Erval, where I expect she'll become a permanent Imperial Court leech. The Denlieff soldiers I'm keeping in garrison until the ambassador can squeeze an appropriate trade agreement from his soon-to-be apologetic king and queen. The two sellouts we executed, and I have trusted people combing through the rest to find out who was coerced and who not."

"Half will be lying, of course."

"More. It's a bad business, and complete justice is probably a dream. But the word will get out, and I hope it won't be so easy to raise such a number again."

I sighed. "Then the Merindar threat is over."

"I sincerely hope so."

"You do not sound convinced."

He said, "I confess I'll feel more convinced when the courier from Athanarel gets here."

"Courier?"

"Arranged with my parents. Once a day, even if the word was 'no change.' Only she's late."

"How late?" I asked, thinking of a couple of measures, or maybe a candle, or even two. "The rain was bad yesterday—"

"A day."

Warning prickled at the back of my neck. "Oh, but surely if there was a problem, someone would either send a runner or come in person."

"That's the most rational way to consider it," he agreed.

"And of course you sent someone to see if something happened to the expected courier? I mean something ordinary, like the horse threw a shoe, or the courier fell and sprained her leg?"

He nodded. "I'll wait until the end of blue, and make a decision then." He looked up. "In the meantime, do you have any more questions for me?" His voice was uninflected, but the drawl was gone.

I knew that the time for the political discussion was past, for now, and that here at last were the personal issues that had lain between us for so long. I took a deep breath. "No questions. But I have apologies to make. I think, well, I *know* that I owe you some explanations. For things I said. And did. Stupid things."

He lifted a hand. "Before you proceed any further..." He gave me a rueful half smile as he started pulling off his gloves, one finger at a time. When the left one was off he said, "This might be one of the more spectacular of *my* mistakes—" With a last tug, he pulled off the right, and I saw the glint of gold on his hand.

As he laid aside the gloves and turned back to face me, I saw the ring on his littlest finger, a gold ring carved round with laurel leaves in a particular pattern. And set in the middle was an ekirth that glittered like a nightstar.

"That's my ring," I said, numb with shock.

"You had it made," he replied. "But now it's mine."

I can't say that everything suddenly became clear to me, because it didn't. I realized only that he was the Unknown, and that I was both horrified and relieved. Suddenly there was too much to say, but nothing I *could* say.

As it turned out, I didn't have to try. I looked up to see him smiling, and I realized that, as usual, he'd been able to read my face easily.

By then my blood was drumming in my ears like distant thunder.

"It is time," he said, "to collect on my wager."

He moved slowly. First, his hands sliding round me and cool light-colored hair drifting against my cheek, and then softly, so softly, the brush of lips against my brow, my eyes, and then my lips. Once, twice, thrice, but no closer. The sensations—like starfire—that glowed through me chased away from my head all thoughts save one, to close that last distance between us.

I locked my fingers round his neck and pulled his face again down to mine.

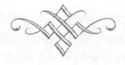

TWENTY-TWO

I DIDN'T WANT THAT KISS TO EVER STOP. HE DIDN'T
seem to, either.

But after a time, I realized the drumming sound I heard was
not my heart, it was hoofbeats, and they were getting louder.

We broke apart, and his breathing was as ragged as mine. We
heard through the tent the guard stop the courier, and the courier's
response, "But I have to report right away!"

A moment later the courier was in the tent, muddy to the chin,
and weaving as he tried to stand at attention. "You said to return
if I found Keira, or if I saw anything amiss," he gasped out.

"And?" Shevraeth prompted.

"Streets are empty," the courier said, knuckling his eyes. I
winced in sympathy. "Arrived ... second-gold. Ought to have been
full. No one out. Not a dog or a cat. No sign of Keira, either.
Didn't try to speak to anyone. Turned around, rode back as fast as
I could."

"Good. You did the right thing. Go to the cook tent and get
something to eat. You're off duty."

The courier bowed and withdrew, staggering once.

Shevraeth looked grimly across the tent at me. "Ready for a
ride?"

It was well past sunset before we got away. All the details that couldn't be settled had to be delegated, which meant explanations and alternative orders. But at last we were on the road, riding flat out for the capital. The wind and our speed made conversation under a shout impossible, so for a long time we rode in silence.

It was just as well, leastwise for me. I really needed time to think, and—so I figured—if my life was destined to continue at such a headlong pace, I was going to have to learn to perform my cerebrations while dashing back and forth cross-country at the gallop.

Of course my initial thoughts went right back to that kiss, and for a short time I thought wistfully about how much I'd been missing. But I realized that, though it was splendid in a way nothing had been hitherto and I hoped there'd be plenty more—and soon—it didn't solve any of the puzzles whose pieces I'd only recently begun to comprehend. If anything, it made things suddenly more difficult.

I wished that I had Nee to talk to, or better, Oria. Except what would be the use? Neither of them had ever caused someone to initiate a courtship by letter.

I sighed, glad for the gentle rain, and for the darkness, as I made myself reconsider all of my encounters with Shevraeth—this time from, as much as I was able, his perspective.

This was not a pleasant exercise. By the time we stopped, sometime after white-change, to get fresh horses and food and drink, I was feeling contrite and thoroughly miserable.

We stepped into the very inn in which we'd had our initial conversation; we passed the little room I had stood outside of, and I shuddered. Now we had a bigger one, but I was too tired to notice much beyond comfortable cushions and warmth. As I sank down, I saw glowing rings around the candles and rubbed my eyes.

When I looked up at Shevraeth, it was in time to catch the end of one of those assessing glances. Then he smiled, a real smile of humor and tenderness.

"I knew it," he said. "I knew that by now you would have managed to see everything as your fault, and you'd be drooping under the weight."

"Why did you do it?" I answered, too tired to even try to keep my balance. Someone set down a tray of hot chocolate, and I hiccuped, snorted in a deep breath, and with an attempt at the steadying influence of laughter, added, "Near as I can see I've been about as pleasant to be around as an angry bee swarm."

"At times," he agreed. "But I take our wretched beginning as my own fault. I merely wanted to intimidate you—and through you, your brother—into withdrawing from the field. What a mess you made of my plans! Every single day I had to re-form them. I'd get everyone and everything set on a new course, and you'd manage to hare off and smash it to shards again, all with the best of motives, and actions as gallant as ever I've seen, from man or woman." He smiled, but I just groaned into my chocolate. "By the time I realized I was going to have to figure you into the plans, you were having none of me, or them. At the same time, you managed to win everyone you encountered—save the Merindars—to your side."

"I understand about the war. And I even understand why you had to come to Tlanth." I sighed. "But that doesn't explain the letters."

"I think I fell in love with you the day you stood before Galdran in the Throne Room, surrounded by what you thought were enemies, and glared at him without a trace of fear. I knew it when you sat across from me at your table in Tlanth and argued so passionately about the fairest way to disperse an army, with no other motive besides testing your theories. It also became clear to me on that visit that you showed one face to all the rest of the world, and another to me. But after you had been at Athanarel a week, Russav insisted that my cause was not hopeless."

"Savona? How did he know?"

The Marquis shook his head. "You'd have to address that question to him."

I rubbed my eyes again. "So his flirtation *was* false."

"I asked him to make you popular," Shevraeth admitted. "Though he will assure you that he found the task thoroughly enjoyable. I wanted your experience of Court to be as easy as possible. Your brother just shrugged off the initial barbs and affronts, but I knew they'd slay you. We did our best to protect you from them, though your handling of the situation with Tamara showed us that you were very capable of directing your own affairs."

"What about Elenet?" I asked, and winced, hating to sound like the kind of jealous person I admired least. But the image of that goldenwood throne had entered my mind and would not be banished.

He looked slightly surprised. "What about her?"

"People—some people—put your names together. And," I added firmly, "she'd make a good queen. Better than I."

He lifted his cup, and I saw my ring gleaming on his finger. He'd worn that since he left Bran and Nee's ball. He'd been wearing it, I thought, when we sat in this very inn and he went through that terrible inner debate on whether or not I was a traitor.

I dropped my head and stared into my cup.

"Elenet," he said, "is an old friend. We grew up together and regard one another as brother and sister, a comfortable arrangement since neither of us had siblings."

I thought of that glance she'd given him when I spied on them in the Royal Wing courtyard. She had betrayed feelings that were not sisterly. But he hadn't seen that look because his heart lay otherwhere.

I pressed my lips together. She was worthy, but her love was not returned. Suddenly I understood why she had been so guarded around me. The honorable course for me would be to keep to myself what I had seen.

Shevraeth continued, "She spent her time with me as a mute

warning to the Merindars, who had to know that she came to report on Grumareth's activities, and I didn't want them trying any kind of retaliation. She realized that our social proximity would cause gossip. That was inevitable. But she heeded it not; she just wants to return to Grumareth and resume guiding her lands to prosperity again." He paused, then said, "As for her quality, it is undeniable. But I think the time has come for a different perspective, one that is innate in you. It is a problem, I have come to realize, with our Court upbringing. No one, including Elenet, has the gift you have of looking every person you encounter in the face and accepting the person behind the status. We all were raised to see servants and merchants as faceless as we pursued the high strategy. I'm half convinced this is part of the reason why the kingdom ended up in the grip of the likes of the Merindars."

I nodded, and for the first time comprehended what a relationship with him really meant for the rest of my life. "The goldenwood throne," I said. "In the letter. I thought you had it ordered for, well, someone else."

His smile was gone. "It doesn't yet exist. How could it? Though I intend for there to be one, for the duties of ruling have to begin as a partnership. Until the other night, I had no idea if I would win you or not."

"Win me," I repeated. "What a contest!"

He smiled, but continued. "I was beginning to know you through the letters, but in person you showed me that same resentful face. Life! That day you came into the alcove looking for histories, I was sitting there writing to you. What a coil!"

For the first time I laughed, though it was somewhat painful.

"But I took the risk of mentioning the throne as a somewhat desperate attempt to bridge the two. When you stopped writing and walked around for two days looking lost, it was the very first sign that I had any hope."

"Meanwhile you had all this to deal with." I waved westward, indicating the Marquise's plots.

231

"It was a distraction," he said with some of his old irony.

I thought about myself showing up on his trail, put there by servants who were—I realized now—doing their very best to throw us together, but with almost disastrous results. It was only his own faith that saved that situation, a faith I hadn't shared.

I looked at him, and again saw that assessing glance. "The throne won't be ordered until you give the word. You need time to decide if this is the life you want," he said. "Of all the women I know you've the least interest in rank for the sake of rank."

"The direct result of growing up a barefoot countess," I said, trying for lightness.

He smiled back, then took both my hands. "Which brings us to a piece of unpleasant news that I have not known how to broach."

"Unpleasant—oh, can't it wait?" I exclaimed.

"If you wish."

At once I scolded myself for cowardice. "And leave you with the burden? Tell me, if the telling eases it."

He made a faint grimace. "I don't know that anything can ease it, but it is something you wanted to know and could not find out."

I felt coldness turn my bones to water. "My mother?"

"Your mother," he said slowly, still holding my hands, "apparently was learning sorcery. For the best of motives—to help the kingdom, and to prevent war. She was selected by the Council of Mages to study magic. Her books came from Erev-li-Erval. Apparently the Marquise found out when she was there to establish Flauvic at the Court of the Empress. She sent a courier to apprise her brother."

"And he had her killed." Now I could not stop the tears from burning my eyes, and they ran unheeded down my cheeks. "And Papa knew about the magic. Which must be why he burned the books."

"And why he neglected your education, for he must have feared that you would inherit her potential for magic-learning. Anyway, I found the Marquise's letter among Galdran's things last year. I just did not know how to tell you—how to find the right time, or place."

"And I could have found out last year, if I'd not run away." I took a deep, unsteady breath. "Well. Now I know. Shall we get on with our task?"

"Are you ready for another ride?"

"Of course."

He kissed my hands, first one, then the other. I felt that thrill run through me, chasing away for now the pain of grief, of regret.

"Then let's address the business before us. I hope and trust we'll have the remainder of our lives to talk all this over and compare misguided reactions, but for now..." He rose and pulled me to my feet. Still holding on to my hands, he continued, "...shall we agree to a fresh beginning?"

I squeezed his hands back. "Agreed."

"Then let me hear my name from you, just once, before we proceed further. My name, not any of the titles."

"Vidanric," I said, and he kissed me again, then laughed.

Soon we were racing side by side cross-country again, on the last leg of the journey to Remalna-city.

I now had fresh subjects to think about, of course, but it is always easier to contemplate how lucky one is than about past betrayal and murder—and I knew my mother would want my happiness above anything.

Who can ever know what turns the spark into flame? Vidanric's initial interest in me might well have been kindled by the fact that he saw my actions as courageous, but the subsequent discovery of passion, and the companionship of mind that would sustain it, seemed as full of mystery as it was of felicity. As for me, I really believe the spark had been there all along, but I had been too ignorant—and too afraid—to recognize it.

I was still thinking it all over as dawn gradually dissolved the shadows around us and the light strengthened from blue to the peach of a perfect morning. There was no wind, yet the grasses and shrubs in the distance rustled gently. Never near us, always in the distance either before or behind, as if a steady succession of breezes rippled just ahead of us, converging on the capital. Again I sensed presence, though there was nothing visible, so I convinced myself it was just my imagination.

We clattered into the streets of Remalna under a brilliant sky. The cobblestones were washed clean, the roofs of the houses steamed gently. A glorious day, which should have brought everyone out not just for market but to talk and walk and enjoy the clear air and sunshine.

But every window was shuttered, and we rode alone along the main streets. I sensed eyes on us from behind the barriers of curtain, shutter, and door, and my hand drifted near the saddle-sword that I still carried, poor as that might serve as a weapon against whatever awaited us.

And yet nothing halted our progress, not even when we reached the gates of Athanarel.

It was Vidanric who spotted the reason why. I blinked, suddenly aware of a weird singing in my ears, and shook my head, wishing I'd had more sleep. Vidanric edged his mount near mine. He lifted his chin and glanced up at the wall. My gaze followed his, and a pang of shock went through me when I saw the white statues of guards standing as stiff as stone in the place where living beings ought to be.

We rode through the gates and the singing in my ears intensified, a high, weird note. The edges of my vision scintillated with rainbow sparks and glitters, and I kept trying—unsuccessfully—to blink it away.

Athanarel was utterly still. It was like a winter's day, only there was no snow, just the bright glitter overlaying the quiet greenery and water, for even the fountains had stopped. Here and there more of the sinister white statues dotted the scene, people frozen mid-stride, or seated, or reaching to touch a door. A danger sense, more profound than any I had yet felt, gripped me. Beside me Vidanric rode with wary tension in his countenance, his gaze everywhere, watching, assessing.

We progressed into the great courtyard before the Royal Hall. The huge carved doors stood wide open, the liveried servants who tended them frozen and white.

We slowed our mounts and stopped at the terraced steps. Vidanric's face was grim as he dismounted. In silence we walked up the steps. I glanced at the door attendant, at her frozen white gaze focused beyond me, and shuddered.

Inside, the Throne Room was empty save for three or four white statues.

No, not empty.

As we walked further inside, the sun-dazzle diminished, and in the slanting rays of the west windows we saw the throne, its high-lights firelined in gold and crimson.

Seated on it, dressed entirely in black, golden hair lit like a halo round his head, was Flauvic.

He smiled gently. "What took you so long, my dear cousin Vidanric?" he said.

TWENTY-THREE

COUSIN? I THOUGHT.

Vidanric said, "Administrative details."

Flauvic made an ironic half bow from his seat on the throne. "For which I thank you. Tiresome details." The metallic golden eyes swept indifferently over me, then he frowned slightly and looked again. "Meliara. This is a surprise; I took you for a servant." His voice was meant to sting.

So I grinned. "You have an objection to honest work?"

As a zinger it wasn't much, but Flauvic gave me an appreciative smile. "This," he waved lazily at Vidanric, "I hadn't foreseen. And it's a shame. I'd intended to waken you for some diversion, when things were settled."

That silenced me.

"You included sorcery among your studies at Court?" Vidanric asked.

Personal insults vanished as I realized what it was my inner senses had been fighting against: magic, lots of it, and not a good kind.

"I did," Flauvic said, stretching out his hands. "So much easier and neater than troubling oneself with tiresome allies and brainless lackeys."

I sighed, realizing how again he'd played his game by his own rules. He'd showed me that magic, and though he had called it illusion, I ought to have let someone else know.

"I take it you wish to forgo the exchange of niceties and proceed right to business," he went on. "Very well." He rose in a fluid, elegant movement and stepped down from the dais to the nearest white statue. "Athanarel serves as a convenient boundary. I have everyone in it under this stone-spell. I spent my time at Meliara's charming entertainment the other night ascertaining where everyone of remotest value to you would be the next day, and I have my people with each right now. You have a choice before you. Cooperate with me—obviating the need for tedious efforts that can be better employed elsewhere—or else, one by one, they will suffer the same fate as our erstwhile friend here."

He nodded at the statue, who, I realized then, was the Duke of Grumareth. The man had been frozen in the act of groveling or begging, if his stance was any indication. An unappealing sight, yet so very characteristic.

Flauvic suddenly produced a knife from his clothing and jabbed the point against the statue, which tipped and shattered into rubble on the marble floor.

"That will be a nasty mess when I do lift the spell," Flauvic went on, still smiling gently. "But then we won't have to see it, will we?" He stopped, and let the horrifying implications sink in.

The Prince and Princess. Savona. Tamara. Bran and Nee. Elenet. Good people and bad, silly and smart, they would all be helpless victims.

I'd left my sword in the saddle sheath, but I could still try. My heart crashed like a three-wheeled cart on a stone road. *I must try,* I thought, as I stepped forward.

"Meliara," Vidanric said quickly. He didn't look at me, but kept his narrowed gaze on Flauvic. "Don't. He knows how to use that knife."

Flauvic's smile widened. "Observant of you," he murmured,

saluting with the blade. "I worked so hard to foster the image of the scholarly recluse. When did you figure out that my mother's plans served as my diversion?"

"As I was walking in here," Vidanric replied just as politely. "Recent events having precluded the luxury of time for reflection."

Flauvic looked pleased; any lesser villain would have smirked. He turned to me and, with a mockingly courteous gesture, said, "I fault no one for ambition. If you wish, you may gracefully exit now and save yourself some regrettably painful experience. I like you. Your ignorance is refreshing, and your passions amusing. For a time we could keep each other company."

I opened my mouth, trying to find an insult cosmic enough to express my rejection, but I realized just in time that resistance would only encourage him. He would enjoy my being angry and helpless, and I knew then what he would not enjoy. "Unfortunately," I said, striving to mimic Vidanric's most annoying Court drawl, "I find you boring."

His face didn't change, but I swear I saw just a little color on those flawless cheeks. Then he dismissed me from his attention and faced Vidanric again. "Well? There is much to be done, and very soon your militia leaders will be here clamoring for orders. We'll need to begin as we mean to go on, which means *you* must be the one to convince them of the exchange of kings." He smiled—a cruel, cold, gloating smile.

Flauvic was thoroughly enjoying it all. He obviously liked playing with his victims—which gave me a nasty little hint of what being his companion would be like.

My eyes burned with hot tears. Not for my own defeat, for that merely concerned myself. Not even for the unfairness. I wept in anger and grief for the terrible decision that Vidanric faced alone, with which I could not help. Either he consigned all the Court to death and tried to fight against a sorcerer, or he consigned the remainder of the kingdom to what would surely be a governance more dreadful than even Galdran's had been.

Vidanric stood silently next to me, his head bowed a little, his forehead creased with the intensity of his thought. There was nothing I could do, either for him or against his adversary. I had from all appearances been dismissed, though I knew if I moved I'd either get the knife or the spell. So I remained where I was, free at least to think.

And to listen.

Which was how I became aware of the soughing of the wind. No, it was not wind, for it was too steady for that. But what else could it be? A faint sound as yet, like a low moan, not from any human voice. The moan of the wind, or of—

I sucked in a deep breath. Time. I sensed that a diversion was needed, and luckily there was Flauvic's penchant for play. So I snuffled back my tears and said in a quavering voice, "What'll happen to us?"

"Well, my dear Meliara, that depends," Flauvic said, with that hateful smile.

Was the sound louder?

"Maybe I'll change my mind," I mumbled, and I felt Vidanric's quick glance. But I didn't dare to look at him. "Will you save Branaric and Nimiar from being smashed if I—" I couldn't say it, even to pretend.

Flauvic's gold-lit eyes narrowed. "Why the sudden affect of cowardice?"

The sound was now like muted drums, though it could be the rushing of my own blood in my ears. But the scintillation had intensified, and I felt a tingle in my feet, the faintest vibration.

Flauvic looked up sharply, and the diversion, brief as it was, was lost. But it had been enough.

"For time," I said. "Look outside."

Flauvic shoved past us and ran in a few quick strides to the doors. Vidanric and I were a step behind. Meeting our eyes was the strangest sight I believe ever witnessed at Athanarel: Standing in a ring, reaching both ways as far as we could see, was what appeared at first glance to be trees. The scintillation in the air had increased so much that the air had taken on the qualities of light in water, wavering and gleaming. It was hard to see with any clarity, but even so it was obvious what had happened—what the mysterious breezes just before dawn had been.

By the hundreds, from all directions, the Hill Folk had come to Athanarel.

Flauvic's mouth tightened to a line of white as he stared at me. "This is *your* work!" And before I could answer, his hand moved swiftly, grasping my wrist. I tried to pull free—I heard Vidranric rip his blade out of its sheath—then Flauvic yanked me to him with a vicious twist so that my arm bent up behind me, and my other was pinioned between our bodies. A hot line of pain pricked me just under the ear: the knife.

With me squirming and struggling, Flauvic backed into the Throne Room again. "Tell them to vanish," he said to Vidanric. "Or she dies."

"Don't do it—" I yelled, but the arm around me tightened and my breath whooshed out.

Flauvic backed steadily, right to the edge of the dais. Vidanric paced forward, sword in hand.

The moaning sound increased and became more distinct. The rubbing of wood against hollow wood drums had slowly altered into a rhythmic tapping, the deliberate thunder of Hill Folk magic, a sound deep with menace.

For a moment no one moved, or spoke. The thunder intensified.

"Tell them *now!*" Flauvic yelled, his voice cracking.

And the pain in the side of my neck sent red shards across my vision; warmth trickled down my neck. I gasped for breath, then suddenly I was free, and I fell onto my hands and knees on the dais. The knife clattered on the marble next to me.

I heard the sound of boot heels on stone, once, twice, and arms scooped me up as the ground trembled.

I flung my head back against Vidanric's chest in time to see Flauvic raise his arms and cry a series of strange words. A greenish glow appeared between his hands, then shot out toward us—but it diminished before reaching us and evaporated like fog before the sun. The air between Flauvic and us now wavered, and through it we saw Flauvic twist, his arms still raised, his head thrown back and his golden hair streaming down.

Loud cracks and booms shook the building, and with a flourish of bright light, Flauvic's limbs grew and hardened, reaching and branching. Down through the marble of the dais, roots ramified from his feet. His legs and body twisted and grew, magnificent with red and gold highlights. And with a resounding smash, the branches above breached the high ceiling and sent mortar and stone and glass raining harmlessly down around us.

Abruptly the sound disappeared. Movement ceased. We remained where we were, looking up at a great goldenwood tree where once the throne had been.

Behind us we heard a cough, and we both turned, me dizzily, to see one of the liveried door attendants fall to her knees, sobbing for breath. A moment later she fell full length into what appeared to be sleep. Her companion slumped down and snored. On the floor near the great tree, the remains of the Duke of Grumareth had turned into clear stones.

Beyond the doors, the street and the gates were empty. The Hill Folk had vanished as mysteriously as they had come.

A shuddering sigh of relief, not my own, brought my attention home and heartward. I shut my eyes, smiling, and clung with all my strength to Vidanric as kisses rained on my hair, my eyes, and finally—lingeringly—on my lips.

The duel was over, and we had won.

AFTERWORD

It has taken me very nearly a year to write down this record. In fact, today is my Name Day. As my adventures began on that day two years ago, it seems appropriate to end the story of my life thus far on its anniversary.

Will there be more adventures to write down? I don't know. Vidanric thinks I am the kind of person who is destined to be in the midst of great events despite herself. Flauvic's mighty tree in the Throne Room is silent testimony to how great events can overtake even the provincial denizens of a small, unknown kingdom like Remalna. Word of the tree, and how it got there, certainly spread beyond our borders, because visitors from far beyond the empire have traveled here just to see it.

Who is to say if any among these observers have been the ones who trained Flauvic in his magic? The Hill Folk do not easily take lives. Flauvic might well continue to grow there, silent witness to all that is good and bad in government, for centuries. I suspect that the Hill Folk somehow know how to commune with him, and it is my fancy, anyway, that someday, should he suffer a change of heart, they will release him.

Unless, of course, those mysterious sorcerers from whom he learned appear first, and we awaken one morning to find the tree gone.

But that's for the future—generations ahead, I trust.

What I need to finish up is the past.

By the time everyone in Athanarel, from the highest to the lowest status, had woken from the groggy slumber they'd fallen into when released from that spell, Vidanric and I had had a chance to comb through Merindar House. We found very little of interest. The Marquise had taken her papers with her, and Flauvic apparently kept all his plotting in his head. What we did find were his magic books, which we took away and locked safely in an archive.

After that, events progressed swiftly. On midsummer Branaric and Nimiar were married amid great celebration. They withdrew to Tlanth soon after, leaving me behind to lay down the stones, one by one, for a new life-path—one I wanted, one that gave me new things to learn every day. But from time to time, usually when the wind rose, I would stop and look westward and think about roaming freely over my beloved mountains, hearing the distant windharps and reed pipes. I've promised myself that when I have children, they will spend more than one summer up there, running barefoot through the ancient mosses and dancing through soft summer nights to the never-ending music of the Hill Folk.

But here I am again, looking ahead.

Except there is little enough left to tell. At least, no events of great import, save one, which I will come to anon. The days passed swiftly in a series of little happinesses, each forging a bright link in the living chain with which Vidanric and I bound ourselves into a partnership. One can imagine how many nights were needed to talk through, until dawn, to lay to rest all the shadows of past misunderstanding. And of course the business of government had to be carried on, for no longer were our lives our own.

There were no more thrones in the Royal Hall, not with that awe-inspiring monument to what can happen when ambition goes astray. We sit on cushions, as do our petitioners—and the Court, which in turn caused an alteration in Court fashions. In fact, there is less constraint of formality—a loosening of masks, and a corresponding increase in laughter—which Vidanric insists has been like a fresh breeze blowing through the ancient buildings, and which he attributes directly to my influence.

Perhaps. I still wander sometimes from room to room in the Royal Wing here and think back on the days when I slept in the kitchen of our crumbling old castle at Erkan-Astiar, wearing my single suit of clothes, and I marvel at how far my life has come— and wonder where it might yet lead.

There is left to tell only that on New Year's Day was Vidanric's and my wedding, and the coronation. I don't need to describe those because the heralds and scribes wrote them up exhaustively, right down to the numbers and quality of jewels on each guest's clothing. The rituals are long, and old, and I felt like an effigy most of that day. I still can't remember most of it. The resulting celebrations— a much more pleasant business!—went on for a month, after which the Prince and Princess withdrew to Renselaeus, to take up once again the quiet threads of their own lives.

And so I come to the end of my tale. I look through my window at the early buds of spring and think of placing this little book on the shelf here with all the other memoirs of queens and kings past. Who is reading my words now? Are you a great-granddaughter many years ahead of me? Ought I to offer you advice? Somehow it doesn't seem appropriate to detail for you how to properly go about organizing a revolt—and likewise it seems kind of silly to exhort you to look, if you should suddenly start receiving mysterious letters of courtship, for possible inkstains on the fingers of the fellow you quarrel with the most.

So let me end with the wish that you find the same kind of happiness, and laughter, and love, that I have found, and that you have the wisdom to make them last.